It was like running into a fire without any protection...

McQueen's hands spread wide on either side of Tamara's face, and in the instant before she closed her eyes she saw those dark lashes come down like inky spikes over his. His mouth more than covering hers, his tongue licked the wetness of her inner lips and then went deeper.

She wanted to see him in shadowy half-light, that big body over hers, those corded arms braced on either side of her, that wet hair falling into his eyes.

He'd said a woman had struck the match. He'd said that he'd been burning so long he'd grown to like it. But whoever that woman had been she'd walked away years ago, leaving him smoldering.

And that was dangerous. A damped-down flame needed only the slightest breath of air to bring it into a full-blown blaze.

Lightly she blew against his ear.

Dear Harlequin Intrigue Reader,

Yeah, it's cold outside, but we have just the remedy to heat you up—another fantastic lineup of breathtaking romantic suspense!

Getting things started with even more excitement than usual is Debra Webb with a super spin-off of her popular COLBY AGENCY series. THE SPECIALISTS is a trilogy of ultradaring operatives the likes of which are rarely—if ever—seen. And man, are they sexy! Look for *Undercover Wife* this month and two more thrillers to follow in February and March. Hang on to your seats.

A triple pack of TOP SECRET BABIES also kicks off the New Year. First out: *The Secret She Keeps* by Cassie Miles. Can you imagine how you'd feel if you learned the father of your child was back…as were all the old emotions? This one, by a veteran Harlequin Intrigue author, is surely a keeper. Promotional titles by Mallory Kane and Ann Voss Peterson respectively follow in the months to come.

And since Cupid is once again a blip on the radar screen, we thought we'd highlight some special Valentine picks for the holiday. Harper Allen singes the sheets so to speak with *McQueen's Heat* and Adrianne Lee is *Sentenced To Wed* this month. Next month, Amanda Stevens fans the flames with *Confessions of the Heart*. **WARNING:** You may need sunblock to read these scorchers.

Enjoy!

Sincerely,

Denise O'Sullivan
Associate Senior Editor
Harlequin Intrigue

McQUEEN'S HEAT

HARPER ALLEN

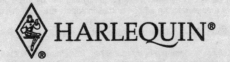

TORONTO • NEW YORK • LONDON
AMSTERDAM • PARIS • SYDNEY • HAMBURG
STOCKHOLM • ATHENS • TOKYO • MILAN • MADRID
PRAGUE • WARSAW • BUDAPEST • AUCKLAND

ISBN 0-373-22695-0

McQUEEN'S HEAT

Visit us at www.eHarlequin.com

Printed in U.S.A.

ABOUT THE AUTHOR

Harper Allen lives in the country in the middle of a hundred acres of maple trees with her husband, Wayne, six cats, four dogs—and a very nervous cockatiel at the bottom of the food chain. For excitement she and Wayne drive to the nearest village and buy jumbo bags of pet food. She believes in love at first sight because it happened to her.

Books by Harper Allen

HARLEQUIN INTRIGUE
468—THE MAN THAT GOT AWAY
547—TWICE TEMPTED
599—WOMAN MOST WANTED
628—GUARDING JANE DOE*
632—SULLIVAN'S LAST STAND*
663—THE BRIDE AND THE MERCENARY*
680—THE NIGHT IN QUESTION
695—McQUEEN'S HEAT

*The Avengers

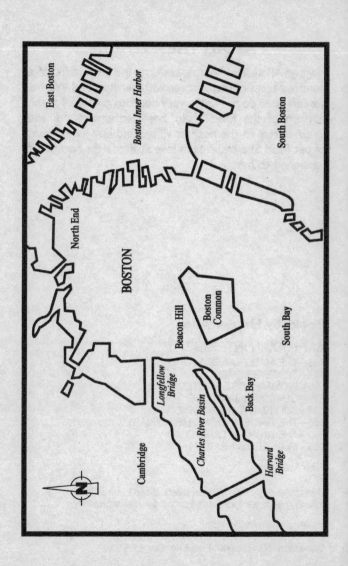

CAST OF CHARACTERS

Tamara King—As a firefighter, she thought she knew what danger was—until she walked into a burning building and met the smoke-gray gaze of Stone McQueen.

Stone McQueen—The ex-arson investigator is a man who's reached rock bottom. And he doesn't want Tamara King to save him.

Petra Anderson—The little girl adores McQueen, despite his hard-edged manner.

Robert Pascoe—He's a man who never existed. But McQueen thinks he's returned to finish what he started seven years ago.

Claudia Anderson—Once Tamara's best friend, Claudia betrayed her by running off with her fiancé on her wedding day. Now it's too late to make amends.

Jack Foley—The gruff ex-firefighter and his late wife adopted Tamara when her family was killed in a fire, and he'd do anything to keep his adored Tammy safe.

Bill Trainor—The arson investigator once had a thing for Claudia. Now he and his partner are looking into her death—and trying to pin it on McQueen.

To the real heroes

Chapter One

The beast had devoured her world. At five years old she'd looked into its face and had barely escaped from its jaws. Now she was twenty-six—okay, twenty-seven in a couple of weeks, Tamara King thought grimly. She was still battling the beast.

She was a firefighter. She *hated* fire.

"Anybody in there?" She saw Joey Silva spare her a glance from a few yards down the corridor, but already she was kicking the door open. She entered, moving quickly through the tiny rooms before racing back into the corridor.

"These freakin' rooming houses." Under his helmet, her partner's expression was disgruntled. "Freakin' fire-traps. Come on, I found another freakin' hallway."

"Gosh darn it all anyway." Tamara looked at the stairway behind them. "You know, Joey, you're going to have to get a couple new cuss words one of these days."

He followed her glance. "We can't wait for the hose. Let's go rouse the rest of the rubbies and the junkies."

She fell into step behind him, not taken in by his seeming callousness. It and his profanity were part of the protective shell that all of them had to grow, in their own individual ways.

The yellow bands on Joey's coat were bobbing smears of color in the smoke, and she reached with her leather-gloved hand for the air-pack at her chest. Following him into the secondary corridor Tamara realized that although a few tendrils of smoke were eddying in from the hallway they'd just left, this one was clear.

Bad sign, she thought, instantly alert. *It's trying to trick us.*

"The bitch is around here somewhere."

Joey's gaze had narrowed in identical suspicion, and despite the situation she hid a smile as she scanned the hallway. She called it the beast. For reasons known only to himself, he saw fire as a heartless female who—

Her thoughts screeched to a halt. Running along the top of the walls in front of them was a tracery of glowing red.

"Hell, Joey—it's in the ceiling," she whispered hoarsely.

"And the freakin' ceiling could go any minute." He wiped his mouth. "Come on, Red, the faster we check this hall the faster we can get out of here."

He'd bestowed the roughly affectionate nickname on her the first day she'd walked into the stationhouse six years ago, her auburn hair scraped back into a braid that kept unraveling. His use of it now didn't mask his apprehension. Her gaze sharpened.

"Where's your air-pack?"

He shrugged, avoiding her frown. "Guess I'll just have to eat the smoke. You take this room, I'll check out the one at the end of the hall."

With a father and grandfather who'd both been Boston firefighters, Joey knew better. But too often he arrived at a fire without his air-pack and ended up having to eat the smoke, as the old-timers called it. Tamara thudded her gloved palm on the door before pushing it open with more force than she needed.

Even as her gaze took in the man standing at the window with his back to her, she knew he was going to be trouble.

He was big—six foot two or three at least, to her five-six. As she entered he spoke without bothering to turn around.

"Don't worry about me, buddy, I can take care of myself." His tone was flat. "Up until yesterday the room down the hall was unoccupied but you might want to check it out anyway. The fire's in the ceiling, so there's not much time."

She tamped down the spark of anger that flared in her at his offhand attitude. Except for his height and the breadth of his shoulders, it was obvious he was no different from the rest of the lost souls she'd glimpsed as she'd run into the building. His hair, dark brown and too long, brushed the collar of his sweatshirt and his khaki pants had seen better days. The leather of his military-style shoes was cracked.

He wasn't a junkie. His build was too solid for a drug-user, so the addiction that had brought him to a room in this rundown building had to have been alcohol. Still, he'd travelled so far down the road to self-destruction he couldn't even recognize how much danger he was in.

But he'd known the fire was in the ceiling, and he'd known what that meant. She didn't have time to wonder how or when he'd gained that kind of knowledge.

"My partner's checking it out." From another part of the building came a muffled crash as something fell. "You're my responsibility, mister. Let's move."

He'd obviously assumed she was a man, because at her first words he'd turned to face her, his eyes widening as they met hers. Now he gave her a hard smile. She blinked, feeling as if a tiny shock had just gone through her.

"You passed the department physical so you're probably pretty strong, honey, but I've got almost a foot on you and I'm a whole lot heavier. I don't see you getting me through that door if I don't want to go." His shrug was dismissive. "Find your partner and the two of you get out while you can."

His eyes were the color of smoke—so pale in the tan of his face that it seemed as though they were looking through her. The tan she could understand, even in an unseasonably wet Boston May. Men like him picked up odd jobs, usually outdoor work, to pay for their habit.

His age was impossible to pinpoint. From the hard planes and blunt angles of his face he looked to be in his mid-thirties, but though his smile had held little humor and no warmth, for the briefest of instants it had transformed his whole expression. Not so long ago the man in front of her had been a very different person, Tamara thought with sudden certainty. If even now there was a destructively dangerous aura about him, what impact had that smile had on women before his life had spiralled out of control?

Who cares, King? Abruptly she shoved her speculations aside. The man's past didn't concern her. How and why he'd arrived at this dead end wasn't her business. Her job was to get him out of here, whether he wanted to go or not.

But that wasn't going to be easy. The sleeves of his sweatshirt were pushed up to his elbows, and the corded muscles of his forearms and the strength of those hands looked formidable. Squaring her shoulders, she clamped a gloved hand on his arm.

"That's not the way it works," she said, some of the anger she'd tried to suppress seeping through into her voice. "I'm a firefighter. If you understood anything at all about what that means you'd know I can't walk away and leave you here."

"Yeah, you can. You're going to." Under her hand his arm felt like a slab of rock maple. His tone was even harder. "Let me put in words you'll understand, honey. I don't want you risking your life for someone like me."

"Then both of us just ran out of luck, *honey*," Tamara grated, her grip on him tightening. "Because risking my life is part of the job, and I'm not about to make an exception in your case."

For the space of a heartbeat their gazes locked, hers coldly stubborn, his opaquely unreadable. Then he exhaled sharply, his posture rigid.

"My conscience seems to have taken everything else I've thrown at it over the years, but even I've got my limits," he said, his tone tight. "You win. Let's find your partner and get the hell out of here."

The whole encounter had taken only seconds, but somehow she felt as if she'd just gone ten rounds with Holyfield and had only squeaked by on a technicality, she thought as she stepped out into the hall, acutely aware of the man behind her. What the hell was his problem?

Or maybe she should be asking herself what her problem was, Tamara conceded. His wasn't that hard to figure out. In a city like Boston men like him came to the same decision every day: that they'd reached the end of the line, and it wasn't worth the pain and effort of going on. So why had she been so sure that if she hadn't gotten him out she would never be able to forgive herself, never be able to forget a distant gray gaze that for only a moment had held hers?

Because this is my watch, she told herself sharply. *If the man decides to jump off a bridge next week, fine. But he doesn't get to do it on my watch, for crying out loud.*

"Where's your partner?"

Coming out of the room and carefully closing the door behind him—he knows that about fire, too, Tamara thought in faint surprise—the big man frowned at her. She felt her eyes tearing up, and realized that the smoke had thickened noticeably. Through the haze she could see Joey appear in the open doorway at the end of the hall.

"He's coming," she said curtly. "It looks like you were right. There couldn't have been anyone in—"

Beside her he tensed, his glance swinging quickly upwards. Following his gaze, her own widened in instant dread.

"Move!" Even as she opened her own mouth to scream out a warning to Joey the stranger's sharply shouted command overrode her. "Goddammit, man, *move!* The damned ceiling's giving way!"

Joey jerked his attention to the pulsating red above him, and through the intervening smoke she saw sudden fear on his face. He looked down again, his expression strained. "There's some—"

He never got to finish the rest of his sentence. Since she'd stepped into the hall, Tamara had been increasingly aware of a dull rumbling sound coming from above. She'd known it was the beast, feeding off the rapidly depleting air supply of the building's attic in order to gain enough strength to break through into another rich vein of oxygen.

As if a door had suddenly opened into a forgotten anteroom of hell, suddenly she saw the decades-old lathe framework standing out in stark black relief against the billowing crimson just above it, like a lattice holding back some nightmarish burden of roses in a poisoned garden. She heard Joey's boots striking the carpet of the floor as he ran toward them with desperate speed. She saw the lathe seemingly vanish into nothingness and knew with terrible certainty he wasn't going to make it.

"Get back!"

The hoarse shout in her ear was obliterated by the roar of the fire as it poured triumphantly downward. A powerful arm slammed across her upper body, and she felt herself being jerked almost off her feet even as her horrified gaze saw Joey's anguished face disappear behind the wall of flame that came down between them.

She fumbled with the air-pack at her chest but her hand was struck away, her wrist grabbed in a steel grip.

"No time for that. *Run!*"

"He's my *partner!*"

Furiously she turned to confront him, but already he'd pulled her into motion, his hold on her wrist unbreakable. She darted a look over her shoulder and saw the air waver, as if some unimaginably strong force was tearing at the atmosphere.

That was *exactly* what was happening, Tamara thought in sharp terror. Wrenching her gaze forward, she put on a burst of speed, saw the man at her side gather himself and leap the last few yards to the main corridor, felt her shoulder joint scream in protest as she was yanked along with him.

And then they were flying through the air, the drag

created by her heavy turnout coat more than counter-balanced by the strength of the arms now wrapped tightly around her. There was a deafening whoosh behind them, and her helmet was knocked from her head as her face was pressed into a sweatshirt-clad chest. A moment later the ground crashed up to meet them.

The beast had needed oxygen. At the instant it had broken through and found it, it had opened its jaws and sucked in the whole hallway-full of air, replacing it with a heat searing enough to burn anything it came in contact with.

Guess I'll just have to eat the smoke. Joey had been caught in that maelstrom, Tamara thought sickly—as she would have been, if not for the reaction of the man holding her. She felt the blast of boiling air pass over them and ebb back again like a spent wave. Only then did she raise her head.

His face was so close to hers that his lashes, dark and thick, brushed against her cheekbones as he blinked. Raggedly he exhaled.

"You all right?" His words came out in a gasp, and she nodded, unable for the moment to speak. His jaw tightened.

"We've got to get out of here." Unsteadily he stood, hauling her up with him as her boots scrambled for purchase on the carpeting. "The rest of the roof's going to fall in on us any minute now."

He was right, she thought, glancing up at the spreading inferno above them and at the wall of flame devouring the hall. But he was wrong, too. She shook her head.

"My partner's in there. I have to get him out."

"Your partner's probably dead." His tone was as brutal as his statement. "I didn't want you to throw your life away on me, and I won't stand by and watch you do it for him. He was a firefighter. He knew the risks involved.''

''And if it was me instead of him trapped there, Joey would *take* the risk,'' she rasped unsteadily. ''I'm a firefighter, too. We don't let each other *down,* dammit!''

As she raced back toward the flames she heard his footsteps pounding behind her. She felt him grab at her once more and she spun around, fury and fear spilling through her, but as she turned she saw something out of the corner of her eye.

She whirled back to face the fire in disbelief. Then she broke free, and this time he didn't attempt to stop her but instead ran with her to the figure emerging from the flames just as it took one last staggering step and crashed face forward onto the floor.

''Joey!''

Falling to her knees, Tamara turned him over. In the instant before she shut her mind to what she was looking at, she felt stark horror sweep through her. The bitch had gotten him, she thought frantically. His face was badly burned, and as she clapped her air-mask over his mouth she saw his eyes open dazedly to meet hers. He pushed the mask away and she saw with shock that he was trying to speak.

''Don't talk, Joey. Don't try to talk, for heaven's sake,'' she gabbled, fighting to get the mask back on him. ''The hose crew's on their way.''

His hand in its still-smoking glove swatted the mask away with a strength she hadn't anticipated, and his eyes glared up at her. His seared lips stretched open.

''For God's sake, Joey, don't—''

''What the hell is it, buddy?'' The big man shot her

a look. "He's trying to tell us something. What is it, pal?"

Joey's eyes bulged with strain. He drew in a shallow, rattling breath and raised his head a few inches from the floor, clutching urgently at Tamara's coat. *"Child,"* he wheezed. "Mother...dead. The child ran. Too much smoke to see her...flashlight broke." He fell back, his desperate gaze holding hers a moment longer before his eyes lost focus.

What she'd told him hadn't been a comforting lie, Tamara thought, tearing the air-pack from around her neck and affixing the mask over his face. From the main corridor she could hear shouts and the splintering sound of axes sinking into wood. But if there was a child trapped behind that wall of fire she couldn't stand around waiting for help to arrive. As she got to her feet, she glanced over her shoulder.

"You stay here with him. I'm going—"

She blinked. The stranger wasn't there anymore. Her head jerked up and her disbelieving gaze flew to the encroaching fire just in time to see a broad-shouldered, sweatshirt-clad figure run into the devouring flames.

"King, thank God! Where's—"

Crew chief Chandra Boyleston turned to bark out an urgent command. "Man down here! There's a man *down* here, dammit!" She switched her attention back to Tamara. "Silva wasn't wearing his air-pack?"

"There's a civilian in there, plus at least one 10-45 already." Her own voice edged as she used the code that veiled the harshness of the word body, Tamara ignored her superior's question. "Joey said he also saw a child, but the kid ran away from him. He was coming to get my flashlight when he...when it..."

She flicked a glance at the wall of fire dividing the

hall. Bending down, she picked up her helmet from where it had fallen and crammed it onto her head.

"The civilian went in for the child. I've got to go after him."

Without waiting for Boyleston's reply she took off down the hallway, covering the lower half of her face with her glove as she got nearer to the roiling mass of crimson and orange. Beside her a wall burst into flame, but instead of increasing her fear, she felt an eerie calm settle over her.

"You want me. You want me, the man and the child," she ground out. "You might get one of us. You might even get me and the man. But if there's a child in there, either he or I will make sure you don't take a life that hasn't even had a chance to *begin* yet."

Just ahead of her was solid fire. She took a last desperate breath, put on a final burst of speed and nearly stumbled in shock.

He came toward her from out of the flames. The sweatshirt had caught on fire and his face was a grease-smeared mask, but his stride didn't falter. In his arms he carried a bundle tightly wrapped in sheeting, and from the steam that rose from it she guessed that the sheet, along with its precious cargo, had been doused with water only seconds before.

Red-rimmed gray eyes met hers as she ran to him, holding out her arms for the child. A corner of his mouth lifted, and right then and there the full force of his basic and overpowering maleness struck her like a blow.

Something sliced through her, as bright and as piercing as pain. Unable to tear her gaze from his Tamara simply stood, drinking in the sight of him.

Her first impression had been right, she thought shakily. He was a man who'd been to hell and back sometime in his past. He'd returned unhesitatingly to the inferno to save the life of a child or die trying.

"Smart little girl," he rasped. "She was in the bathtub. She was holding this in her hand—wouldn't leave until I promised to keep it safe. Then she fainted."

Dragging the smoldering shirt over his head and dropping it to the floor, he peeled a piece of paper from his sweat-drenched chest and held it out to her.

"Bet you didn't figure you'd end up right next to my heart when we met a few minutes ago, did you, honey?" he asked, his voice cracking with hoarseness. "Where the hell's the hose crew, anyway?"

Taking one more step forward, he crumpled heavily to the ground, the photograph of a much younger Tamara King fluttering from his fingers.

Chapter Two

"Joey's going to pull through."

Tamara reached for a tissue from a box on the nursing station counter. Blowing her nose furiously, she turned away and dabbed surreptitiously at her eyes. "That—that's great, Lieut. I—I was afraid he—" She cleared her throat. "When do we get to see him?"

"Not today. Not tomorrow, either, from what his doctor tells me." The other woman's features softened. "Hey…you don't have to keep up the tough act with me, King. You and Joey are more than just partners, aren't you?"

"What?" Tamara's head jerked up. "Where'd you get that idea, Lieutenant?"

"It's just us girls here right now, so make it Chandra," Boyleston said dryly. She placed a hand on Tamara's back, steering her away from the nursing station toward a group of potted plants by the waiting area. "That photo of you. It had to have fallen out of his helmet."

"Out of Joey's helmet?" Tamara stared at her. "You're joking, right?"

"What's tucked into the liner of yours?" Chandra wasn't smiling. "You showed me once, so I know—a

St. Florian medal pinned to the sweatband, a photo of your family taken before they died and a laminated four-leaf clover.''

"Half the jakeys in the country must have a St. Florian medal somewhere on their person." Tamara's tone took on an edge. "He's the patron saint of our profession."

"Yeah, the patron saint of jakeys, like you say." The strong features relaxed momentarily at the slang term firefighters used to describe themselves. "And the shamrock's for luck. But the photo keeps the people you love close when you're on the job—most of the crew tuck a picture of a husband or a wife or a girlfriend in their helmet. Who knows why the child picked it up, but it must have fallen from Joey's gear." She frowned. "Unless there's some connection between you and that little girl you haven't told me about."

"How would I know who she is?" Tamara shrugged before she remembered her sprained shoulder. It had been examined when she'd arrived here at Mass General three hours ago, but she'd refused any medication. "Until she gives us her name we don't even know who her mother was, and like you told me earlier, she hasn't said one word yet."

"That's not surprising." Chandra's expression was closed. "The doctor pegged her at about seven or eight, poor tyke—it has to be pretty rough on a little girl like that, seeing her mom dead and nearly dying herself. You sure you never saw her before, King?"

Tamara's lips tightened impatiently. "She looks like a girl I went to school with a long time ago, for God's sake. Except this kid's got green eyes, and Claudia Anderson had blue."

"That could be it. Maybe the child's mother was this

girlhood friend of yours, fallen on hard times and hoping to get in touch with you to see if you could help.''

''Your theory's all wrong, Lieut.'' Tamara pushed her hair back from her forehead. ''Claudia was my best friend all through school and even after, but I haven't seen her for years. The last I heard she'd gotten married.'' She went on reluctantly. ''Besides, I'd be the last person she'd want to see. The man she married was my fiancé. He literally left me standing at the altar and ran off with her.''

Boyleston's eyes widened. ''That must have been a blow,'' she said softly. ''Sorry I stirred up old memories, Tamara.''

Tamara saw the sympathy in the other woman's eyes. ''Hey, Lieut—I'm over it, okay? It happened a long time ago, and though I'll admit it was pretty devastating to be jilted in front of a whole churchful of people, I went on to make a new life for myself. I even went through with the reception, *sans* groom, of course.''

Chandra grinned in startled amusement. ''Jeez, girl, talk about ballsy. You threw the party without the wedding?''

''Threw the party, danced up a storm, drank too much and awoke the next morning with the first and only hangover I've ever had in my life.'' Tamara nodded. ''The whole evening was a blur, but I remember some of Rick's friends were there. I didn't want him hearing I'd had to be escorted from the altar sobbing broken-heartedly or anything like that.'' A corner of her mouth lifted ruefully. ''I saved the messy breakdown for the next day, when no one could see me.''

Not true, King, a small voice in her head said with annoying precision. *You fell apart that night, and in front of a total stranger. A stranger you'd just—*

She shut the voice off with an effort. "Anyway, that's why I know Claudia wouldn't come looking for me."

"Which leaves us with Joey. He obviously realized you only saw him as a friend, so he kept his feelings under wraps." As an orderly wheeled an empty gurney past them, Chandra went on. "I'd still like to know who the civilian was. In all the excitement I never even got a good look at him. The crew told me if he hadn't passed out again while they were trying to get him into the ambulance, he probably would have taken off on us. He didn't give you his name?"

Tamara frowned as she heard the clatter of something metal in one of the nearby rooms. A male nurse at the station looked up in annoyance and then headed down the corridor.

"No, but it wasn't hard to figure out his story, Lieutenant. Like the child's mother, he was down and out enough to be staying in that dump. I—I got the feeling life didn't mean much to him anymore," she added.

"His life, maybe." The brown eyes watching her sharpened. "But he went to the wall to bring that little girl—"

"It's against the rules to just walk out!" The curt remonstration came from one of the rooms. "Dr. Jasper left specific instructions—"

"Tell him I discharged myself. And since I'd prefer not to waltz down Charles Street bare-assed, how about handing over my pants before I leave?"

The smoky growl was almost drowned out by another crash, and Tamara heard the no-nonsense tones of the male nurse who'd just left the station.

"You're in no shape, mister. They pumped you full of drugs when you arrived, so why don't you—"

His placating words ended abruptly. The next moment

a tall figure strode into the corridor, shirtless and still zipping up the fly of the soot-smeared khaki pants he was wearing. Beside Tamara, Chandra stiffened.

"Don't tell me. Our Mr. X?"

"I was going to find out what floor he'd been taken to and see how he was," Tamara answered, her attention focused on the tableau being enacted only yards away from them. "I guess that's not necessary now."

The male nurse had been joined by an orderly, and even as she watched he stepped in front of their patient. In the doorway of the room they'd left a ward nurse appeared.

"At least let us call someone to take you home—a family member or a friend." Taking advantage of the momentary standoff in the corridor, the female nurse advanced to the big man's side, her posture rigidly disapproving. "If we could release you into someone's care—"

"I don't have any family. I don't have a home anymore, for that matter." The husky voice held a note of impatience. "So why don't you call off the guarddogs here, sweetie, and I'll just be on my way?"

"You've got friends, McQueen." Boyleston's tone was arid. "God knows why, with a personality like yours, but you've got a few. Or at least you used to, before you dumped us all and dropped out of sight." Her voice lost a little of its edge. "How've you been, Stone?" she asked quietly.

Tamara looked at her in astonishment and then back at the man again. With a second small start she realized that those dark gray eyes were fixed on her, not her companion.

It all made sense now, she thought—the heroism he'd shown, the way he'd known too much about fire. He'd been a firefighter. He'd gone up against the beast. She met his eyes. He blinked, and looked at the woman beside her.

"I see you made rank, Chandra," he replied flatly. "How about using your pull to remind Florence Nightingale here that it's still a free country? Buddy, you've got exactly three seconds to get that hypo away from me," he added to the male nurse.

"I'll take responsibility for him," Boyleston sighed. One slim brown hand went to her forehead to massage her temples. "Still a charmer, McQueen. But after what you did today I guess I owe you." She glanced sideways at Tamara. "Stone McQueen. Tamara King. I hear you guys didn't introduce yourselves earlier."

"So what happened to your partner?" As the lieutenant followed the still-glowering nurse to the station and began putting her signature on what seemed to be endless forms, Stone McQueen gave his attention to buckling his belt. His question was perfunctory. Tamara was taken aback by his attitude, but she kept her voice even.

"Joey's going to make it," she began, but he cut her off, his head still bent to his task.

"He nearly got you killed, honey. What was he playing at, arriving at a fire without a respirator?"

"He made a mistake. He's going to be paying for it for a long time, according to the doctors." She took a deep breath. "I nearly made a mistake, too. Thanks for getting me out of that hallway in time."

He raised his head abruptly. "A mistake? Is that how you explain it to yourself?" He shrugged, the muscles shifting under that broad expanse of tanned chest. "Okay, honey. Then thanks for not letting me make the same mistake when you barged into my room and wouldn't take no for an answer. I guess we're even."

He frowned, looking down at the gauze dressing that

covered most of his left forearm. "God, I hate hospitals," he said under his breath. "I hate every damn thing about them." His jaw rigid, he ripped the bandage off with a muttered oath.

"But you didn't want to get out of that room, McQueen," Tamara said sharply. "Your being there wasn't a mistake, and both of us know it. I don't see the connection between that and me almost getting caught in that hallway."

"You don't?" Carelessly he tossed the crumpled square over his shoulder into the wastebasket by the pay phone behind him. "Joey was just the excuse. You wanted to look into its face, honey. You wanted to know who it was." He spared her a smile. "You thought you might see yourself looking back," he said softly.

"You're going to have to run that one by me again." She heard the tightness in her own voice. "Whose face? What am I supposed to have seen myself looking back from?"

As he stood just inches away from her, Tamara suddenly realized that the destructive aura she'd only sensed before was all around her.

If she let herself, she thought, she could reach out and touch that solidly muscled torso, trace the coarse scattering of hair leading from those tanned pectorals, veeing down to his exposed navel, vanishing under the worn leather of the belt at his hips. The garish hospital lighting revealed every flaw in his skin—the grainy weariness, the small scar by his full bottom lip, the angry-looking scrape high up on one hard cheekbone. It was obvious he'd never been a pretty man. It was obvious he'd never needed to be. He practically *smelled* like sex.

"The *fire,* honey. You think if you look close enough, you might see your face staring back at you from the fire.'' He was near enough to her that the warmth of his breath touched her lips. ''You're afraid you brought the beast to life. You think maybe there's only one way to stop it for good.''

How did he know? The shocked thought tore through her mind. How did he know what she called it, how did he know how she felt when it was raging all around her?

''You're out of your mind,'' she said, trying to match the evenness of his tone, and almost succeeding. ''I *hate* fire, McQueen. It's the enemy. It's the thing I go up against. I don't start fires, for God's sake—I spend most of my life running around putting them out.''

''You can't put them all out.'' A corner of his mouth lifted humorlessly. ''You'd better learn that fact before it's too late.''

''You sound like you're talking from experience.'' Her voice was ice. ''You were a jakey once, too, weren't you?''

He didn't answer, but she took the slight flicker in his gaze for affirmation and went on, her tone edged. ''Maybe *you're* the one with an unresolved conflict about fire, McQueen. Except you just gave up the fight— gave it up so totally that today you were only minutes away from surrendering completely.''

She brought her face to within inches of his. ''You're the one who's burning up,'' she ground out. ''What I'd like to know is who or what struck the match with you. Was it a woman? Is that how you were destroyed, Stone?''

With a slight sense of shock she saw her random arrow had found a mark. At her last words he froze.

''You got it a little wrong, honey,'' he said woodenly.

Without making a move he seemed somehow to be looming over her. But his size wasn't the most overwhelming thing about him, Tamara thought. What would strike even the most casual observer was the impression of power held just barely in check that appeared to be an integral part of him. Coupled with the aura of self-destructiveness she'd already noticed, the combination of the two seemed perilously volatile.

"The job destroyed me." That velvet voice wrapped itself around her like an invisible snare. "But yeah, a woman struck the match, and I've been burning ever since. Maybe I could have done something about it once…but after all these years I think I like it."

His smile was crooked. "You might find yourself liking it, too. Why don't you try it and see?"

"You're officially discharged, McQueen." Lieutenant Boyleston was standing beside them, her expression quizzical. "Now all we have to do is find you somewhere to sleep tonight. Here, put this on before you get a candystriper all hot and bothered."

She was holding out an orderly's jacket to him, but as she spoke her eyes narrowed on Tamara's set features. "I'd offer you a bed at my place, but for some reason Hank's not real crazy about you."

Without glancing at it, Stone took the jacket. His eyes were still locked on Tamara's, and for one illogical moment she thought she saw the hard light in that smoky gaze replaced by a flash of regret. He looked away.

"Your husband?" Impatiently he wrestled into the jacket. "I don't remember meeting him. Hell, Chandra, I can't wear this thing." Glaring at the white sleeves ending inches above his own wrists, he tried half-heartedly to pull the front edges across his chest.

"It was in a bar downtown last year. You were a little the worse for wear," Chandra said tiredly. "The jacket's a loaner, Stone, so don't rip it. King, while I was at the desk—"

"Tell Hank I'm sorry."

Boyleston's lips tightened at the interruption. "What?"

Stone started to shrug, and stopped as a seam gave way. "Whatever I said, whatever I did—apologize for me, would you? You're one of the few who stuck by me." His voice dropped. "Hell, Chand, I wouldn't want to think I'd lost your friendship, too."

"You've come close a couple of times, Stone." Boyleston held his gaze steadily. "But we go back a long way, you and me...back to before everything fell apart for you. I told Hank you were a jerk, but that deep down you were still one of the good guys."

Her smile wavered. Sighing, she turned back to Tamara. "Like I was saying, King, your uncle Jack called. Apparently he dropped round to the stationhouse to chew the fat with some of his old buddies and some fool told him you'd been taken to the hospital. I told him it was nothing serious but that I was giving you a few days off to let that shoulder mend."

"You're putting me on sick leave?" Tamara shot the other woman a glance. "Come on, Lieut, it's just a pulled muscle."

"Until you can swing an axe or carry a hose you're off the roster, and that's not negotiable." Boyleston frowned. "Count your blessings, King. Joey might never return to work. When will we get the message through to the public, dammit—smoking in bed is like drinking and driving. You just don't *do* it."

"What's your point?" McQueen's thumb was on the call button of the elevator. He looked impatiently over his shoulder.

"My point is that if the dead woman had exercised some common sense, her little girl would still have a mom, Stone. She was smoking in bed. The only reason her room didn't go up in flames first was because a previous tenant had punched a hole in the drywall, and it acted as a kind of crude chimney."

Boyleston raked a hand through her cropped hair. "That's a preliminary assessment, of course, but I doubt the official investigation's going to find different. The bed smoldered just enough so that the woman died from asphyxiation, but the fire itself went into the walls and the attic."

"Nice theory."

As the elevator doors slid open Stone planted one hand solidly against them. Lieutenant Boyleston stepped in, but Tamara paused, alerted by something in the big man's tone.

"Nice theory but what?"

He shrugged. "Nice theory but it's crap."

The elevator doors started to close and he slammed them back into place. This time Tamara heard the seam in the borrowed jacket give way completely, but his next words drove everything else from her mind.

"That fire today was arson—and whoever set it was targeting your friend and her child."

Chapter Three

"I thought you knew who the kid was! I didn't know I was the only one she'd talked to."

Stone swung his gaze from the woman sitting beside him in the waiting room. He was handling this all wrong and he knew it, he thought. It would have helped if Chandra had come with them but the child's attending physician had stood firm on that, so it was just him and the woman.

And already it wasn't working.

Tamara was sitting as stiffly as a statue, her face white, the strands of auburn hair escaping her braid like tiny flames flickering around her. He began again, aware that beyond the swinging doors was a ward full of sick children.

"Like I said, she was in the bathtub when I got to her. She already knew her mother was dead."

And when I tried to lie about that, I just about lost her trust right then and there, he added silently, remembering the almost adult note of scorn in the childish voice.

"If Mom's only sleeping, why isn't she breathing?" He'd had an arm around the small shoulders while he'd been hastily dipping a torn sheet into the water, and he'd felt a tremor run through them. "She's dead. She was dying of cancer anyway, so I'm glad. This way it didn't hurt. It—it *didn't* hurt, did it?"

That question he'd been able to answer truthfully. "She wouldn't have known anything, Tiger," he'd told her.

He blinked, torn from his thoughts by the quiet approach of the nurse entering the room. She was young and pretty, he saw. He was relieved. The kids behind those swinging doors deserved to hear a soft voice, see a kind face.

"Dr. Pranam says if you'd like, we can phone you when she wakes up."

"I'd rather wait." Tamara's lips barely moved. "Tell Dr. Pranam I appreciate him bending the rules for us. I know visiting hours are over."

"We bend a lot of rules." The nurse smiled, but there was sadness in her voice. "Some of these little ones won't be leaving, so we do what we can to make them happy. And like Dr. Pranam told you, the only way we could calm her when she arrived was to tell her that we'd find Mr. Stone and bring him to see her."

"Stone." He looked away uncomfortably. "It's my first name. Stonewall."

"Like the general?" The nurse laughed softly as she pushed open the swinging doors. "That explains a lot. I hear you laid waste to the fifth floor."

"Stonewall Jackson was shot by his own troops." As the nurse exited Tamara spoke, her face still white but the blank look in her eyes replaced with a glitter of anger. "So unless you want the similarities between yourself and your namesake to go further, I'd suggest you tell me everything you found out from Claudia's daughter—starting with why you're so certain she *is* her daughter. Why would Claudia come back to Boston to see *me?*''

"Petra said she was dying of cancer." Stone saw her lashes fall over the angry blue of her eyes. He continued, wanting to get it over with. "Petra's the kid," he added. "I told her to call me Stone, and she told me what her name was. I was trying to keep her mind off what was happening."

Tamara nodded tightly. "Go on."

He didn't want to go on. In fact, he didn't want to be here at all, Stone thought savagely. The whole damn thing was bringing back too many memories—memories of other vigils in other hospitals—and the urge to just walk out was overpowering. *Walk out and find a bar, you mean,* an amused voice in his head said. *So why don't you, McQueen?*

"She wanted you to take care of her daughter when she was gone," he said shortly. "That's why the photo was so important to Petra. She knew that with her mom gone she'd have to find you all by herself."

"She didn't mention her father?" Tamara was rubbing her thumb against a smudge of soot on her jeans. "She has to have a father, for heaven's sake. Where's he?"

"He died in a car accident before she was born, if I understood her right." The smudge was now a smear, he saw. "I wasn't listening to everything she said. I was too busy wondering what our chances were of getting out of there alive."

He paused. "You don't want her to be Claudia's daughter, do you? You don't want to believe any of this."

"And I don't believe it."

Abruptly she stood. She walked over to a bulletin

board and stood there studying flyers for a hospital fund-raiser, her back to him. Stone rose, too, his movements more controlled than hers.

"What's not to believe? If nothing else, she had that photo of you. How the hell do you explain that away?"

She lifted stiff shoulders in a shrug. "Chandra thought it might have fallen from Joey's helmet. It seems like the most logical explanation."

"For the love of Mike—logical? Isn't it more *logical* to accept that the kid's telling the truth?" He had the sudden impulse to take her by the shoulders and force her to listen to reason. With an effort he turned away.

He was getting too involved in this, he told himself tightly. He'd spent the past seven years making sure any involvement he had with the rest of the world was as minimal as possible, and lately he'd come to realize even that was becoming too much to take—although her accusation that he'd been ready to detach completely in that rooming house today was far from being a given, he thought, frowning.

He'd wanted to look into its face. He'd been pretty sure he would see his own staring back at him. Instead he'd looked around and seen her, and that had been the biggest shock of all. He closed his eyes.

Beyond those swinging doors was a little girl whose world had been smashed to pieces—a little girl who was asking for him. He knew why she wanted to see him. He hadn't told the woman who'd been her mother's best friend everything that had passed between him and the child, he thought heavily.

He'd crashed through the doorway of the rented room. It had been years since he'd run through a burning building but all at once he'd been back in the past, knowing that there had to be clues if only he could see them, knowing that in seconds those clues could disappear forever.

The woman had been lying on a smoldering cot by the wall. Even before he'd fallen to his knees beside her and placed his thumb firmly on what should have been the pulse-point of her neck he'd known instinctively that Joey had been right. She was gone. An even earlier habit had come back to him, and without conscious volition he'd swiftly crossed himself.

"Rest easy, sister." For some reason it had been important to put it into words, just in case any shadow of her had lingered and could hear him. "I'll take care of her for you. I'll get her out of here."

As he'd started to rise the information he'd automatically noted even while he'd been concentrating on the woman clicked into place and his heart sank. Between the fingers of the outflung hand was the burned-down butt of a cigarette, the sheet the hand had been resting on now only charred fragments. The cot itself had caught and smoldered, he'd realized, and whatever outdated material it had been filled with had thrown off the toxic fumes that had proven so fatal for its occupant. But at some point the smoldering should have become a full-fledged blaze. Why hadn't it? And how had the fire skipped to the rest of the building, leaving this room untouched?

He'd gotten swiftly to his feet. Finding the child and getting her to safety was his main concern. Giving the woman on the cot one final glance, he'd seen a remnant of the sheet leading from the cigarette to the emptiness of the hole knocked into the wall, and had realized he was looking at the answer to the questions he'd just dismissed.

But as he'd lifted Petra into his arms only moments

later, he'd known that the most deadly question hadn't been answered at all.

"You're going to find out who killed my mom, aren't you, Stone?" In the shadows her eyes had been wide with anguish and fixed stubbornly on his. "You'll put him in jail, right?"

He hadn't answered her right away. He hadn't known what to say, since the truth was too brutal. *Gee, Tiger, your mom started it herself. She was smoking in bed, see, and the cigarette just rolled from her fingers when she fell asleep.* Maybe one day the kid would find out, but he wasn't going to be the one to—

Except the cigarette hadn't rolled from her fingers. It had burned right down to her hand. The pain would have woken her immediately.

But by then she was already dead, McQueen. In fact, I'd lay odds she was dead before that damned cigarette was lit. The voice in his head had been coldly professional. His voice when he'd answered the child staring so trustingly up at him had been hoarse with sudden anger, but she'd seemed to know his anger wasn't directed at her.

"Yeah, Tiger, we're gonna find the person who killed your mom." Striding toward the open door, he'd tightened his hold on her. "We're gonna find him and put him away. That's a promise."

Only then had he felt the stiff little body in his arms suddenly go limp, as if upon his words she'd finally been able to hand over a burden too heavy for her to bear...

He'd gotten her out safely, as he'd vowed he would, Stone thought now. He'd told Boyleston what he'd seen before the fire had roared through the room, obliterating the telltale signals that made it arson, not an accident. With that information, the investigative team's initial hasty evaluation would have to be reversed. He'd passed on the burden to the people who were paid to shoulder it.

So he could just walk away. He'd gotten good at walking away from things these past few years.

But this time he wasn't going to be able to. Petra had asked for him. He'd made her a promise. And whether Tamara knew it or not, she was a part of it.

"She told you her name was Petra?" Tamara's voice was barely audible. "You're sure?"

"I'm sure," he said steadily, taking in the rigidity of her posture, the bleakness in those blue eyes now holding his gaze. "Does it make a difference?"

"Claudia's father died when she was a baby so she never knew him, but she used to say she would name her own child after him when she became a mother," she rasped. "Peter if she had a son. Petra if her child was a daughter."

"Then that clinches—" he began, but she cut him off, her voice still low.

"Let me tell you a story, McQueen. It's about two little girls who'd both lost family and who were both lonely. Except then they met each other, and it was like getting a part of their families back again."

She smiled crookedly at him. "When they were ten years old, one of them snuck an embroidery needle out of her mom's sewing box and they gathered up enough nerve to prick their palms with it. It was something they'd read about." She shrugged. "They clasped their hands together and took a blood oath, promising to be sisters until death. Dumb, huh?"

She was a world away from the tough, helmeted figure who'd bulldozed him out of that room today, Stone thought, watching her. Who was the real Tamara King—

the firefighter who put her life on the line everyday without thinking twice about it, or the woman standing only inches away from him, her eyes haunted, her whole body so tense that it seemed as if she was in danger of breaking apart right in front of his eyes?

Maybe she was both. She went on, her tone devoid of emotion.

"Even after we grew up, I knew that no matter what else happened in our lives we would always be able to count on each other. I was wrong. She betrayed me with the man I loved, and I never saw or heard from either of them again."

Her voice was a fraying thread. "So tell me, McQueen—if she was dying, if she was out of her mind with worry for the child she was going to be leaving behind—why would she come back to me?"

She shook her head decisively. "She wouldn't. Don't you *see*? It wasn't Claudia. Claudia didn't come to Boston looking for my help. She didn't die in that rooming house today, worried and frightened and hoping for my forgiveness."

Her eyes, blue and glittering, were fixed on his. Stone took a step toward her, feeling all at once too big and too clumsy. "I wish I could tell you different, but I can't."

Awkwardly he reached out for her, but even as his hands clasped her shoulders she stiffened and struck them away.

"You *have* to tell me different!" The harsh whisper seemed torn from her throat. "No matter what happened between us, I don't think I could bear it if I thought that was how it ended for her!"

"She died in her sleep, overcome by the smoke. She would have died hoping the bond between the two of

you still held. She would have been right," he added
huskily.

This time when his hands went to her shoulders she
did nothing. The brilliance overlaying her gaze wavered
and became a shimmer, but he knew with sudden certainty that she wasn't going to allow herself to cry.

"I think I knew it was her as soon as I saw the child,
but I wouldn't let myself believe it." Her voice cracked.
"Do you want to hear why, McQueen?"

I think I already know, honey, he thought, sudden self-
loathing sweeping over him. What was it he'd so recklessly accused her of only half an hour ago—that she
wanted to look into the destruction? That she thought
she might see her own face staring back?

Tamara King had already stared into the heart of darkness. She'd already recognized it in herself. The knowledge was tearing her apart.

"Why couldn't you let yourself believe it?" he asked
tonelessly.

"Because I hadn't *forgiven* her," she whispered, her
eyes wide with pain. "And if there hadn't been a fire
and she'd phoned today asking to see me, I would have
turned her down. What kind of a monster does that make
me?"

"It doesn't make you a monster." He tightened his
grip on her. "It makes you a human being, dammit. And
you wouldn't have turned her down...not if you'd
known you were her last hope."

"It would be nice to think that." She shrugged. "I'll
never know for sure, will I?"

Her eyes held his for a final moment. Then she
squared her shoulders, stepping out of his embrace as
she did.

And that's the end of show and tell, boys and girls,

Stone thought disconcertedly, feeling as if she'd placed a firm palm on his chest and physically pushed him away. *Pack up your feelings and lock them away real tight, so no one gets a chance to see them again.* She was already regretting that she'd revealed herself. She was already a little angry he hadn't stopped her.

"Sorry. I had no right to dump all my emotional baggage on you like that," she said flatly. "What we should get straight is how we're going to answer any questions Petra has about her mom's death. I'm with Lieutenant Boyleston on this one, McQueen. I can't see how you came to the conclusion it was arson, and I don't want Petra to start believing that. I think it's best to tell her it was just a terrible accident, without bringing in your theories or mine."

"Your theory being what?" Funny, Stone thought. He'd been taken aback when he'd seen the flash of dubiousness in Chandra's glance as she'd promised to pass on his suspicions to the investigative team. But Tamara's offhand dismissal of his assessment touched a fuse inside him. "She fell asleep with a cigarette in her hand?"

"It happens, tragically." She shot him a glance. "Claudia did smoke, McQueen—only occasionally, and only when she was stressed, but judging from what was going on in her life lately I'd say stress had to be present. It all fits."

"Yeah, it fits." He bit off the words. "And that worries me even more. That means the torch watched her long enough to know her habits."

She arched her brows. "Let's face it, McQueen, it doesn't really matter what you or I think. I'm just a jakey, like you used to be, and neither one of us is qualified to give an opinion. We'll leave it up to the experts." Her gaze clouded. "Whatever their final verdict, it won't bring her back."

"Nothing can do that," he agreed tersely. "You don't know who I am, do you? Who I was," he corrected, watching her. At her blankly inquiring look he shook his head. "Of course you don't. I must have been just before your time. I started out as a firefighter, honey, but I didn't end up as one—and that's why I'll back my assessment of that fire against a dozen of your so-called experts."

"You were an arson investigator?" There was enough disbelief in her tone that despite himself he winced.

Okay, so maybe he couldn't blame her for taking him at face value. And at face value, he guessed he looked pretty much like what he'd become—a man who'd washed his hands of the world, a man the world had forgotten, too. When she'd come across him in that rooming house it must have seemed to her that he'd fit right in.

Because he *had* fit in. The revelation was unpalatable but true. He'd been sinking for seven years, Stone thought bleakly, and if today she'd seen him as a man who'd gone just about as far down as he could go, it was only because he had. He was surprised to find he still had enough pride left for her incredulity to wound.

But apparently he did.

"No, honey, I wasn't just an arson investigator," he growled, closing the gap between them. "I was a damn legend. I was the best there was. And I say you're *wrong*—the fire that killed Claudia wasn't a result of her smoking in bed."

Too late he heard the sighing of the doors as they swung fully open behind him. The tense expression on Tamara's face disappeared instantly, to be replaced by immediate concern, and as he turned and saw the stiff little figure standing there in a hospital gown, Stone's heart sunk.

"You're trying to make it look like that fire today was all Mom's fault, aren't you?" Petra's gaze, green and accusing, was leveled at Tamara. "I don't think you were her friend at *all*."

The cold little voice shook. "I—I think you *hated* her!"

Chapter Four

"You were right, Lieut," Tamara said under her breath, furiously pulling on the clean pair of sweatpants she'd laid out on her bed. "He *is* a jerk. Thanks to Stone McQueen that little girl thinks I'm the bad guy. What's worse, as far as she's concerned the sun rises and sets on *him*."

From the bathroom down the hall came the sound of running water. She narrowed her eyes.

"So how did he end up crashing at my place for the night?" she said loudly. "I must have been out of my mind."

The cat that had just strolled into the bedroom halted as it saw her, turned around again and walked out, insolently graceful despite the fact that it only had three legs. Securing her wet hair in a covered elastic, Tamara followed the animal down the hall to the kitchen.

"You don't get to sleep on the guest bed tonight, fleabag. But the good news is you can ignore another human being besides me for a change."

Except the way things were going the damn cat would probably end up fawning all over McQueen, she thought, depositing a couple of teabags in the flowered china pot that had been one of Aunt Kate's favorite possessions.

Briefly she wondered if the man drank tea or not, and then dismissed the question. If he didn't like it, tough.

I think you hated her.

Dropping suddenly into the nearest chair, Tamara squeezed her eyes shut. She couldn't even remember her own response, but whatever it had been the child's glare hadn't wavered. Only when McQueen had scooped her up in his arms had the pinched features lost their tight look.

"That's crazy talk, Tiger," he'd rasped, scowling at Petra. She hadn't seemed fazed by his manner.

"It's not." She'd scowled back at him, but her arms had crept around his neck. "She's trying to blame the fire on Mom, Stone." She'd twisted around in his grip to face Tamara. "You *know* she quit smoking last year. She told you in her letters."

Petra hadn't even looked back as McQueen had carried her down the hall. The sound of his husky rumble mixing with the little girl's chatter had wafted through the swinging doors, getting gradually fainter. Unhappily Tamara had wondered how she was going to heal the breach that had opened up between her and Claudia's daughter.

"You never wrote me, Claudie," she murmured now as she poured her tea. "I think that's what hurt the most in the end—knowing that the two of you had completely erased me from your lives."

Although from what Stone had gathered from Petra, Rick had been killed in a car accident before his daughter had been born, she reflected somberly. About to lift her mug to her lips, she paused.

"She's got to be almost seven," she whispered. "Oh, Claudie—you were pregnant with her *then*, weren't you?"

Trembling, she set the mug down on the table. The wedding that hadn't happened—the wedding where her groom had run off with her chief bridesmaid—had been just over seven years ago. A vision flashed into her mind of Claudia, dressed in a baggy sweatshirt and leggings, tossing her bridesmaid's dress onto the floor of her bedroom.

"I tried it on at the store, Tam. It fits, all right? Can we talk about something other than the darn wedding for once?"

The peevishness hadn't been like her, but it had flared up again after that. At the time Tamara had put it down to Claudia's worry over her mother's health.

"And maybe if your mom hadn't been going through chemo just then you might have confided in her. You'd always told me everything, but this was the one thing you couldn't share, wasn't it, Claudie?" Tamara wrapped her hands around the hot mug. "I wish you had. Everything might have been so different," she said softly.

The thing was, she thought painfully, she'd gotten over Rick in a matter of months—although at the time she couldn't admit to herself that losing the man she'd thought of as the love of her life hadn't devastated her. She'd put her name in for the fire department and had written the preliminary exam, more from a desire to discard the routine of her old life than from any real urge to begin a new one, and to her shock she'd been accepted. She'd taken the medical at Quincy and passed the physical, with a little coaching from Uncle Jack, and finally had begun the intensive thirteen-week training process on Moon Island, across the harbor from Boston.

It had been gruelling. It had been exhausting. She'd never felt more alive, more fulfilled.

And a few weeks later when she'd tried to remember exactly what shade of green Rick's eyes had been she'd found she couldn't.

But losing Claudia had been a wound that hadn't healed. McQueen had been right, she thought. Maybe the bond between them had been stretched, but it had never really broken.

She took a sip of her tea, her throat aching with unshed tears. "She reminds me of you, Claudie. But she's her own person already, isn't she?" she whispered. "I don't know how qualified I am to take on your role in her life, but I'll give it my best shot."

Except they'd already gotten off to a rocky start, thanks to McQueen. She set her mug down on the table with a sharp click.

Lieutenant Boyleston had driven them home from the hospital, Tamara's vehicle being still in the stationhouse parking lot, and upon Stone's request—*demand, more like,* Tamara thought—Chandra had made a stop at a small mall on the way. Without a word, McQueen had gotten out of the car and headed for a army surplus store that had a quelling display of gas masks and bayonet-style knives in its window. Chandra had shrugged.

"Best not to ask, with Stone." She'd given Tamara a lopsided smile. "If you're having second thoughts, he can stay the night at my place. Hank knows I've always had a soft spot for McQueen."

"Second thoughts?" Tamara had snorted. "Try third or fourth thoughts. But I've got to have this out with him, Lieut, the sooner the better. Petra wants to see him again, and Dr. Pranam seems to think we should let her, since for some reason she's opened up to him. I want him to understand he can't encourage her in this arson thing." She'd shot Boyleston a searching glance. "He's wrong, isn't he?"

Chandra had sighed. "He *was* a legend, like he says. Eight years ago, he was the only one who wouldn't accept the Dazzlers nightclub blaze was due to faulty electricals—he insisted it had been deliberately set, and he made it a personal mission to hunt down the person responsible for those twenty-two deaths. In the end he was proven right. Jimmy Malone's still behind bars."

She'd closed her eyes tiredly. When she'd opened them again, her gaze had been bleak. "But everytime I've run into him over the past few years it's been obvious he's been hitting the bottle pretty hard. His last case destroyed him." She'd taken a deep breath. "He seems sober enough today, but do I think his information about what he saw in that room is reliable enough that anyone's going to take him seriously? No."

Tamara had been about to ask her about the case she'd referred to, but at that moment the man himself had returned, a paper sack under one arm and a closed look on his face, and she hadn't had the opportunity.

Which was probably just as well, she thought, getting up from the table. Chandra might have a soft spot for Stone McQueen, but she didn't. Any interest she had in him began and ended with his influence on Petra, despite what she'd thought she'd felt in that room today when he'd turned from the window and his eyes had met hers.

For God's sake, King—a flophouse bum who pushed the self-destruct button a long time ago, she thought impatiently. *If you're trying to tell yourself you had the hots for a man like that, even for a second, then you're in need of some serious therapy.*

"How'd your cat lose his leg?"

The abrupt question, delivered in that smoke-and-gravel voice, came from the hall. She turned, and was immediately grateful that she had the solidity of the counter behind her.

An olive-drab T-shirt, obviously new, stretched across that massive chest. Tanned biceps strained the seams of the sleeves. The shirt was tight enough to mold itself to the washboard abs it covered, and past them it was tucked into a securely belted pair of chinos. But that wasn't all.

The stubble that had shadowed his jawline earlier was gone, evidence that another of his on-the-fly purchases had been a razor. The dark brown hair, damp at the moment, still brushed the collar of the tee and a renegade strand looked ready to fall into those gray eyes, but now it only added a carelessly sexy edge to the rest of his spit-and-polish appearance.

Stone McQueen cleaned up good, Tamara thought weakly. Damn the man anyway.

The only incongruous note was the three-legged tortoiseshell tom draped languidly around his neck.

"I rescued him as a kitten from an apartment fire. One leg was too badly burned for the vet to save," she croaked. She cleared her throat too loudly. "He hates me. Tea?"

"I don't know why, but cats go crazy over me. Kids, too." Complacently Stone detached a purring Pangor from his neck and deposited him onto the floor. "I'm not a friggin' Limey. Got any coffee?"

She'd already lifted the teapot. With infinite care she set it on the counter again, just as a dull throbbing shot through the back of her jaw. She was gritting her teeth, Tamara realized.

So the man cleaned up good. So what? He still had

all the charm and personality of a wolf with its paw in a trap. She turned to him.

"Yes, Stone, I have coffee. I even have a coffee-maker." She smiled tightly at him. "That cats and kids thing. Why doesn't it hold true for women, do you think?"

"You'll never get a decent cup of coffee from a machine." He opened the refrigerator door. "Got any eggs? You bring the coffee almost to a boil, with a couple of eggshells thrown in at the last minute for shine."

He closed the refrigerator door and turned to her, the two eggs he was holding looking more like they'd been laid by hummingbirds than hens in the oversized cradle of his palm. "It works on the occasional woman, honey. You look beat. I'll get a couple more of these out and make us an omelet while I'm at it."

Tamara stared at him. Then she shrugged. "Fine, you go right ahead and make us something to eat, McQueen. Just let me get my mug of friggin' Limey tea here out of your way before you get started." She picked up her mug. "By the way, when Chandra introduced us I distinctly recall her telling you my name was Tamara, not honey."

He'd been rummaging around in the drawer under the stove. He straightened, a frying pan in his hand and a frown on his face. "That bugs you?" There was a note of honest surprise in his voice, and she frowned back at him.

"Yeah, it bugs me, McQueen. For one thing it sounds sexist, and for another I get the impression you can't be bothered to remember my name. How would you like it if I called you babe or sweetheart all the time?"

He set the pan on a burner and nodded. "I see what you mean." He turned to the refrigerator. "Go with babe, honey. It sounds kind of tough-girl, and I like it when you talk tough.''

His back was to her. She unclenched her grip on the mug, set it safely on the table, and took a deep, furious breath. Just as she opened her mouth to speak he glanced guilelessly over his shoulder at her.

She hesitated, disconcerted. A corner of his mouth lifted, and he turned back to the refrigerator.

She watched as he juggled a brick of cheddar, a slightly wilted bunch of scallions she hadn't remembered she'd had and a bottle of hot sauce that had been hidden behind a box of baking soda for as long as she could remember. He slammed the refrigerator door closed with his foot.

She gave him a quelling look. ''That was a joke, right?''

He deposited the food on the counter, grabbing an egg just as it was about to roll off, and turned to face her.

To her surprise there was uncertainty on the hard features. ''Sure it was a joke. It's been a grim day, you're saddled with a stranger in your house and it suddenly occurred to me I'd never heard you laugh.'' He paused. ''Honey,'' he added under his breath.

She gave him a incredulous look. The next moment she felt her lips curving into a reluctant smile, and the tension that had been building inside her all evening dissipated into a small bubble of laughter. She shook her head at him.

''You're pushing it, McQueen. That better be the best damn omelet I've ever eaten, or you're outta here.'' She narrowed her eyes at him. ''Babe.''

She hadn't expected to end up bantering with the man, she thought, watching as he deftly cracked the eggs into a bowl, setting aside a couple of shells. And she wasn't foolish enough to think this temporary truce between them would last, especially since she still needed to talk to him about Petra. But it *had* been a grim day, and her job had taught her to seize the lighter moments when they came along or risk losing her sanity.

Stone McQueen was still a jerk, she thought. But maybe not a *total* jerk.

"Best damn omelet, best damn coffee. Count on it." He was grating cheese now and he went on, his back to her. "The thing is, my social encounters these past few years have been pretty limited. The women working the bars I frequented didn't want the lowlifes they served to know their names, so honey and sweetheart got to be a habit." He shrugged. "They called me big guy. At the end of the evening the bouncers called me pal. Hell, I had a whole circle of friends who didn't exchange names with me."

She'd just been given an apology, Tamara realized— an apology or an explanation. Whichever, she had the feeling it hadn't been easy for the usually closed-off man in front of her to reveal even that fleeting glimpse of himself.

"I wondered today when I saw you in that rooming house," she said steadily. "You've got a drinking problem, haven't you, McQueen?"

He was chopping scallions. He stopped, and she saw his grip tighten on the knife in his hand.

"Not anymore." His words were clipped. He brought the knife down once more on the scallions, and then halted again, setting the utensil on the chopping board and turning to her.

"That was the wrong answer." Beside him, the pan on the stove began to sizzle, and he moved it from the burner without taking his gaze from her. "If I haven't learned anything else over the last eight months, I've learned that. Yeah, the drinking became a problem. I used it as a crutch, and one day I found I couldn't function without the crutch. Then I realized I was in danger of not being able to function at all. I took the longest walk of my life that night—right past my usual watering hole to the basement of St. Mary's Church a couple of blocks away, where there was an AA meeting going on. I've been clean and sober since that first meeting, but kidding myself I've got the problem licked for good would be the worst mistake I could make. I take it day by day. I still go to the meetings every couple of weeks. And sometimes I try to remember how to pray.''

He held her gaze a moment longer and then turned back to the counter, picking up the knife again. "And I drink one hell of a lot of coffee, honey, so I make sure it's not crap out of a machine,'' he growled.

Beneath his abrasiveness she thought she'd heard a hint of relief, Tamara thought slowly. Maybe he needed someone to talk to about this. Maybe since she'd opened up to him earlier this evening, he wanted to talk to her.

"Chandra said your last arson case was the reason why you gave it all up and walked away from the job, McQueen,'' she said softly. "That's when you started needing a crutch, wasn't it?''

"For crying out loud.'' He poured the beaten eggs into the pan, scattered the grated cheese over the mixture and turned to her, all in one economical movement. "This isn't a talk show, honey. I told you about the drinking because I can't afford not to be upfront about it, okay? And the next time you talk to Boyleston, tell her the whole of freakin' Boston doesn't need to hear the story of my life. Forget it—I'll tell her myself.''

Taken aback by his abrupt about-face, Tamara glared

at him, any warmth she'd been beginning to feel toward the man evaporating instantly. "Take a pill, McQueen," she snapped. "For God's sake, I was trying to be a *friend*."

"A friend?" His laugh was short. "And what comes next—you and I watch chick-flicks and talk about boys before we fall asleep? Dammit, I don't want you as a *friend*, honey." He sounded as outraged as she felt, and her temper finally gave way completely.

"That's fine by me." Without even being conscious of getting to her feet, she was standing in front of him, her furious face only inches from his. "You'd make a *lousy* friend. Hell, you make a lousy acquaintance! And the damn omelet's burned, so you're not even a competent cook. Tell me, *babe*—what's left?"

"Aw, crap, the omelet." Reaching behind him he slid the pan from the burner without looking and turned off the stove. He shrugged, his gaze holding hers. "You know what's left, honey," he muttered impatiently. "Try not to make me screw up on this, too, will you?"

"As if you need my help for that," Tamara said under her breath, as his mouth came down on hers and her arms went around his neck.

Chapter Five

It was like running into a fire without any protection. His hands spread wide on either side of her face, and in the instant before she closed her eyes she saw those dark lashes come down like inky spikes over his. He swayed slightly, immediately regaining his balance by widening his stance. Leaning back against the counter, he pulled her with him, a hard-muscled leg on either side of her thighs.

Dear God, Tamara thought dizzily. Stone McQueen had come close to *swooning.* She felt him harden against her.

He wasn't a subtle man. But though his lack of finesse in a social setting might be something he could consider working on, she thought, right here and right now it was incredibly, overwhelmingly erotic.

His mouth more than covering hers, his tongue licked the wetness of her inner lips and then went deeper. She felt her head tipping back with the force of his kiss, and her arms tightened around his neck. *Oh, no, McQueen,* she thought disjointedly. *No fair. I get to taste you, too.*

She slid her fingers upward through the coarse silk of his still-damp hair, and felt the solidity of his jaw graze her cheek. With no preliminaries, greedily the tip of her tongue lapped against his with short, flicking strokes. It was like licking sweet cream, she thought—like desperately licking up sweet, melting ice cream from a cone on a hot summer's day, before it could run down her hand.

Except she *wanted* him to melt all over her. She wanted him running down her, running into her, pouring over her. She wanted to see him in shadowy half-light, that big body over hers, those corded arms braced on either side of her, that wet hair falling into his eyes.

He'd said a woman had struck the match. He'd said he'd been burning so long he'd grown to like it. But whoever that woman had been she'd walked away years ago, leaving the fire unattended. Tamara felt his hands move to her neck, to her shoulders, down her rib cage until they were spanning her waist. Whoever she'd been, she'd walked away, leaving him smoldering.

And that was dangerous. Any firefighter knew a damped-down flame only needed the slightest breath of air to bring it to a full-blown blaze. He pushed her sweatshirt up, and she gave an involuntary little gasp. Impatiently he shoved the sweatshirt higher, his palms sliding up to the cotton bra she was wearing. She dragged her mouth from his, raised herself swayingly to her tiptoes, and nipped the lobe of his ear.

Lightly she blew against it.

An immediate shudder ran through him, and his fingertips tightened convulsively on her skin. With deliberate slowness she lowered herself from her raised toes, her exposed flesh rubbing against his taut stomach, the thin material of his T-shirt hardly a barrier. The chinos he was wearing were even less of an obstruction. Through the soft fleece of her jogging sweats she could feel every hard, rigidly outlined inch of him, pressing stiffly and immediately against her thighs.

"You *do* like to burn, don't you, McQueen?" she whispered, looking up into his face and feeling the heat of his breath on her lips. "You're liking it right now."

His eyes were still closed. With a carefully controlled movement he nodded, cautiously exhaling as he did. She saw the bulge of his jaw muscle tighten.

"Yeah, honey, I am," he rasped. "You're going to take advantage of that, aren't you?" Opening his eyes just enough so she could see the smoky gleam of his gaze through the dense lashes, he looked down at her. "But I told you I thought you'd like it, too."

His hands were still splayed open against her bra, the ball of each thumb just under the thin cotton. Smoothly he hooked them farther under the scrap of material and tugged upward. Before she had time to do more than throw him a startled glance, her vision was cut off as he unhesitatingly drew both her top and her still-secured bra up and over her head.

In the bright kitchen light she felt immediately, shockingly exposed. Her first impulse was to cover her breasts with her hands, and instinctively she started to do just that. Dropping the clothes he'd just stripped from her to the floor, he caught her wrists, trapping them lightly.

"Uh-uh, Tam. Don't cover anything up." His voice cracked on the husky plea. "They're so damn pretty, honey." She felt herself flushing at his words. His gaze flicked back up to her face, and he gave her a slow smile. "Pink and cream. Like ornaments on a Christmas tree—perfect little globes."

"Stop it, McQueen." Her laugh was breathily uneven. She tried to take her gaze from his, and found she couldn't. "You—you're embarrassing me."

"The tough girl, embarrassed? I don't believe it." He ran a finger along her collarbone to the base of her throat, and let it trail lightly downward. When he got to the hollow between her breasts, he stopped. "Call me by my first name, Tam. I want to hear you say it," he added softly.

"But I think of you as McQueen." She blinked at him.

"I know you do, honey." He brushed his palm against her nipple and instant weakness spread through her. "That's why I want to hear you say it. Just for now, I want you to think of me as Stone." His smile was one-sided. "Let's face it, as far as you're concerned Mc-Queen's a total jerk, right?"

A gurgle of shocked laughter escaped her. "Not a *total* jerk," she protested, arching her back and letting her lashes drift over her eyes as his other hand skimmed down her shoulder to her breast. "Not—not all the time, Stone," she murmured, finally giving in to the sensations that were swirling around inside her.

"Oh, stop," he muttered against the corner of her mouth. "Now you're embarrassing *me,* honey."

The blunt ends of his hair fell forward onto her skin as he bent his head to her breasts. As he took one nipple into his mouth, his tongue circling the aureole around it and his lashes brushing against the sensitive swell just above, her teeth sank into her bottom lip, but not fast enough to stifle the small moan that escaped. Through her own half-closed lashes she could see the dark tan of his hands against her creamier flesh, could see his palms cradling her breasts so that it seemed as though they were being pushed up and together by the most wanton of tightly laced bustiers. His mouth moved with excru-ciating deliberation to the shadowed tunnel he'd created between her cradled breasts and she felt his tongue stroke first one uplifted curve and then the other.

The silk of his hair, the tiny flickering movements of his closed lashes, that steady, circling wetness...did the man have any idea what he was *doing* to her?

It was like being on some sensuously adult version of a carousel. She let her head tip back on her neck, feeling suddenly as if it was too heavy to support, and behind her closed lids a spangle of colors danced crazily around and around. Liquid heat fused through her—as if, she thought ridiculously, the painted horse she was riding in her fantasy had been transformed into molten gold even as she straddled it.

This had to be what he'd meant when he had said he could make her burn, and make her like it. But he'd also said he'd been burning for years. If Stone McQueen walked around every day feeling just a little of what she was feeling right now, she told herself tremulously, no wonder the man gave the impression of being a loaded gun.

Except that doesn't explain why the safety slipped so easily off your own inhibitions a few minutes ago. You're one wet kiss away from falling into bed with a complete stranger—a stranger you don't even like, for God's sake.

The voice inside her head was as cold and jolting as water from a hose. It was nothing compared to the shock that ran through her a split second later.

"Hell."

At the muttered imprecation, Tamara's eyes flew open. His eyes dark and his jaw tight with tension, McQueen met her startled gaze. He shook his head.

"We both know it's not going to work, you and me." His tone was ground glass. "What are we friggin' *thinking?*"

The mouth that only moments ago had been driving her out of her mind was a hard line. The hands that had been touching her so intimately were now clenched at his sides. The last tattered remnants of desire fled from her and she narrowed her eyes, her shock giving way to anger.

Not *everything* about him had withdrawn, she thought icily. Whatever he was playing at, it seemed his libido hadn't totally gotten the message.

Of course, she was still standing there giving him a free show, she told herself in swift chagrin.

She snatched up her sweatshirt, dragging it over her head as she straightened. Out of the corner of her eye she saw something white protruding from the neckline, and disgustedly she pulled her bra out, tossing it onto the nearest chair.

"Tell Rover down boy." Her glance flicked south of his beltline and to his face again. "Or take him for a walk or a cold shower or something. I don't know what we were freakin' thinking a couple of minutes ago, McQueen." Sometime in the last half hour her hair had escaped from its elastic. With a frustrated gesture, she scooped it back with both hands. "I know what I'm freakin' thinking now, though."

"Good for you." He gave her a tight smile. "If you do, you're one up on me." He exhaled tensely.

"Look, Tam, this isn't me being a jerk again. This is me trying my hardest not to be one. As you so sensitively point out, it's pretty damn obvious I'd rather be throwing you over my shoulder and hauling you into the bedroom right now."

"You've been reading the romance poets again, McQueen," Tamara said flatly. "You must know what those flowery phrases do to a girl. But I'll bite—just how do you see yourself *not* being a jerk here?'' Her voice rose on the question.

Sighing, he scrubbed his palm irresolutely across his mouth, as if he was trying to come to some decision on a problem that was proving thornier than he'd expected. His lashes dropped over his eyes, and when they flickered back up again his gaze was shadowed.

"Marry me, Tam." Under the huskiness was an undefinable note. His smile was wry. "You know, the white dress, the church—hell, the whole nine yards. Petra can be your flower girl. What do you say?"

She realized she was gaping at him, and she closed her mouth with a snap. "Are you *crazy*, McQueen? Because it's either that or you managed to pick up a bottle at the mall today, and I was close enough to you a couple of minutes ago to have known if you'd been drinking." She shook her head in disbelief. "What are you trying to prove, asking me that?"

"That you would have hated me two minutes after we did the deed, Tam." His tone held an edge of the anger she'd displayed. "You don't like me that much in the first place, and we sure wouldn't have lain in bed holding hands and whispering sweet nothings to each other afterward."

He lifted his shoulders tensely. "I know you want me, though I'm damned if I know why. Maybe you just go for big and basic. Except that's all she wrote, honey, and I'm not enough of a jerk to screw and run. Not in this situation, anyway. We've got the kid to think about."

Meeting his grim gaze with a wary one of her own, Tamara suddenly felt the ballooning anger in her deflate.

He was right. He was right about everything. Even in the insanity of that fire today she'd taken one look at him and fallen, not in love, but in lust. She'd known instinctively how dangerous he could be to her, and she hadn't cared.

And as hard as it was for her to admit it, he was right about Petra, too. The child was emotionally fragile and she'd formed a bond with the stranger who'd rescued her—a closer bond than the frayed connection she had with the woman who'd once been her mother's best friend.

He was still watching her. Walking stiffly past him to the cupboard, she took down a couple of plates. With the spatula he'd used to cook with she hacked the omelet into two jagged pieces, slapped one on a plate and held it out to him.

"Omelet McQueen," she said curtly. "One of your specialities, I believe? It used to be hot. Then it got burned by you. Now it's cold. Enjoy."

Dishing out her own portion, she turned back to the table and dropped into her chair as he sat down.

"Your friend was killed," McQueen said tonelessly. "I know Chandra thinks I'm crazy and I know you think I'm crazy, but I'm not. What do you intend to do about it?"

"Nothing," she replied. "We're going to leave it to the people who get paid to look into these things. They've got the resources and the contacts. We don't."

"Says who? I might be able to dig up a few old contacts, and I'm a hell of a lot more resourceful than the two bozos Chandra told me were assigned to this case." He leaned back in his chair. "Tommy Knopf and Bill Trainor were the geniuses who pegged the Dazzlers fire as an accident, and they weren't real happy when I came up with the evidence that put Jimmy Malone behind bars."

He shrugged. "Besides, to get the Dazzlers case re-opened I may have mentioned something to the press about their incompetence. If Knopf and Trainor still hold that against me they're not going to listen too hard to anything I say about what I saw in that room today."

"Two more names on the list of people you've alienated," she said shortly. "What a surprise." She got to her feet and collected their untouched plates. "Look, McQueen, you got a split-second glimpse of the scene, and based on that you seem to assume everyone should ignore the rest of the evidence. Claudia smoked. She'd been smoking in bed. And she was dead by asphyxiation before the fire took hold in the rest of the room, which is an almost textbook example of this kind of...of this kind of tragedy."

Noisily she scraped the plates into the garbage, her back to him. This wasn't the way she wanted to be talking about Claudia's death, she thought unhappily—with brutal logic and cold reasoning. Being put in the position of blaming the victim wasn't anything she enjoyed, either, but she had to make him see how dangerous his misplaced certainty in his own theory could prove to be. She turned to find him standing only a foot or two away.

"I accept that you used to be good at your job, Stone," she said tremulously. "But that was years ago. From what you tell me of how you spent those years, they had to have taken their toll on your skills. As long as you encourage Petra in this notion that her mom's death wasn't an accident she's going to believe there's a bogeyman out there who could come back for her. I can't allow you to do that."

"I didn't put the idea into her head, Tam." His eyes darkened. "How irresponsible do you think I am? She seemed to know from the first that someone deliberately started that fire. The real harm would be in brushing aside her belief in herself—and her mother. Do you really want to do that?"

That his question only put her own fears into words didn't help, Tamara thought edgily. In fact, it made the situation even less tolerable.

"Of course I don't!" she cried, her nerves lending a rawness to her tone. "Don't you think I know how hard it's going to be to build a relationship with Petra even without a complication like this? She's just lost her mom and I'm the stranger who's suddenly appeared to take her place—she'd resent me under the best of circumstances. But Claudia left the responsibility for raising her child to me, despite the rift that kept us apart until it was too late—despite the fact that when she could have used my help, I wasn't *there* for her!" Her vision shimmered. "I won't let her down, dammit! Not this time, and not if I have to fight you every inch of the way!"

She bridged the distance between them with one swift step, her fists going to his chest to grab handfuls of the olive-drab T-shirt. "I know what she's going through, Stone," she said, her voice low. "Believe me, I *know.* Children want the world to make sense so badly they'll seize on anything that might provide an explanation. If they don't learn to accept that some things aren't anyone's fault, are just tragic, terrible accidents, they can end up blaming *themselves.* Petra's not going to go through that." She jerked sharply on the T-shirt. "I'm going to make *sure* she doesn't, understand?"

She stared up at him, her face white and set. He reached for her wrists, his own gaze shadowed.

"Maybe I do. Your parents and your brother—they died in a fire just like Claudia did, didn't they? Were you Petra's age when you lost them?"

"I was five." Her answer was automatic. She tightened her grip on his shirt. "How—how did you know? Did Chandra say something?"

He shook his head. "The photo in your helmet." A ghost of a smile touched his features. "I figured the little sweetheart with the carrot-red hair had to be you. It followed that the boy on the bike was your brother and the man and woman standing by the car were your parents. But it had obviously been taken a couple of decades ago, and I guessed if your family was still alive you'd have something more recent. Was it a fire, Tam?"

She nodded, her eyes wide. "In a motel. Mikey was in an out-of-town hockey tournament that weekend. When did you see what was in my helmet?"

He shrugged. "The medal and the cloverleaf and the photo? In that hallway. It got blown off during the flashover, remember?"

Slowly Tamara unclenched her fists. Her brows drew together in a frown.

The beast had been fast—so fast that everything had seemed to happen at once. Stone had been moving even faster, pulling her along with him, shielding her from the worst of the blast with his own body. At some point she'd lost her helmet.

In the smoke and confusion he'd caught a glimpse of it, lying overturned in the hall. Moments later Joey had appeared out of the flames and Stone had gone in after the child.

Stone McQueen had the reputation of being a jerk, and she wasn't going to argue with that. He was abrasive and overbearing.

He also had the reputation of being a legend. Now she knew why.

"You saw all that in a glance, McQueen?" she asked

quietly. "Not only the photo, but who was in it? How is that possible?"

He looked nonplussed. "For God's sake, fire burns up a lot of evidence and once it's gone, it's gone forever. If you're lucky enough to get on scene before everything's destroyed you keep your eyes open. I do, anyway," he added with a snort. "I can't vouch for those clowns Knopf and Trainor."

He shoved his hands in his pockets, his manner suddenly diffident. "But you're right. I've got no official standing anymore. Probably the best thing I can do for the kid is walk away from this." He raised his eyes to Tamara's. "She's a little scrapper, isn't she? Funny how she took to me like that."

He fell silent, his smile uncertain. Then he took a deep breath and looked restlessly around the room.

"Listen, honey, this whole setup's a little too domestic for me—the cat, the friggin' tea, the togetherness. I think I'll be shoving off." He cleared his throat. "Tomorrow I'll drop in at the hospital to see the kid and tell her I was way off base about it being arson."

Tamara turned to the counter and began gathering up the eggshells he'd left lying on the cutting board. She set a couple aside and bent to retrieve a saucepan from the cupboard. Behind her she heard him inhale.

"That's that, then," he said huskily. "I'll let myself out, honey."

Filling the pan with water, she set it on the stove. Out of the corner of her eye she saw him bend quickly to rub Pangor behind one ear. When he straightened his posture was rigid. He was almost at the door of the kitchen when she spoke.

"How much damn coffee, McQueen?"

He halted at the doorway and she looked up from the

stove. "I've never made it this way. How much coffee do I use?"

He took a step back into the room, his expression unreadable. "I thought you liked tea."

"Tea doesn't keep me awake," Tamara said shortly. "You're a crappy cook. For all I know you're a lousy lay. But you were a hell of an arson investigator once, and I think you probably still are. I believe you saw what you say you did in that room, and that means you're right—someone murdered my best friend."

Her lips tightened. "Of course, after years of pissing off just about anyone who might be able to do something about this, no one's going to listen to your theory. Which leaves just you and me." She sighed. "So make us some coffee, McQueen. I've got a feeling we're going to be up for a while."

He stared at her for a moment. Then he nodded, and brushed past her to the stove. "Three big scoops of coffee. Hell, go crazy and make it four." He took the canister she handed him. "You can tell you're a tea drinker, honey. You don't know jack about what kind of coffee to buy. There's a couple other things you're all wrong on, too."

"And what might they be, McQueen?" Tamara folded her arms.

"I didn't piss everyone off. Chandra stuck by me." He shook out what looked to be a good half pound of coffee. She handed him the eggshells.

"You said I was wrong on two things. What was the other?"

She owed him, she thought. That crack about his sexual prowess had been over the line, and if she were honest with herself, she'd only said it to salve her own piqued pride.

Going to bed with him *would* have been a bad idea. But where did he get off being the first one to come to that conclusion?

"What was the second one, McQueen?" she repeated, mentally tapping her toe. The coffee came to a rolling boil, and with the air of a maestro, he tossed the eggshells in.

"The other one?" His brow cleared. "The crappy cook remark, of course. I'm one *hell* of a cook. Now get out of the way, this is the crucial part." He gave her a bland look and turned back to the stove, but as she walked out of earshot he added one last remark under his breath.

"I can cook all night and still be up to give you breakfast in bed, honey. And one of these days I intend to do just that."

Chapter Six

"Thanks, Lieut, I appreciate it."

Tamara cradled the kitchen phone on her shoulder and drew her stockinged feet onto the chair she was sitting on. On the other end of the line Chandra's voice rose questioningly.

"What? Oh, McQueen. I don't know, probably still sleeping. We kept each other up pretty late last night." She stifled a yawn. "No, I would have called you anyway. It's good to hear that Joey's out of danger."

She should have asked for the number of the room he'd been moved to, she thought a few minutes later, padding to the refrigerator and taking out a carton of orange juice. Although it probably didn't make much difference, if he still wasn't being allowed visit—

Dear God, had she really said Stone and she had kept each other up all night? No wonder Chandra had ended the call so briskly. Tamara stared at the container of juice in her hand, and then tilted it recklessly to her mouth. One of the perks of being a single woman living alone, she told herself, closing her eyes and chugging back a much-needed dose of vitamin C. You could walk around in mismatched socks, drink from the carton and scarf down a whole tub of ice cream at a sitting if you felt like it. Not that she ever—

"That brings back memories. Make it a bottle of ripple wine and you could be me a year or so ago."

She choked and hastily set the carton down. Beside her Stone began unpacking a bag of groceries and went on talking.

"I found your spare set of keys on the hall table, so I made my first stop the stationhouse and got your car. I looked in on you to tell you, but you were out like a light." He glanced at the clock on the wall. "I've been up since five, honey, and it's nine-thirty now. You planning to stay in those godawful pajamas all day?"

Ground rules, Tamara thought tightly. They needed to lay down some ground rules here. No—*she* needed to lay down some ground rules.

She gazed narrowly at him—at his back rather, since, typically oblivious to her outrage, he was hunkered down on the floor beside Pangor's food bowl. The cat was going into ecstasies as McQueen scraped something that looked and smelled unpleasantly like kidneys out of a can and into the bowl. Giving Pangor's tail a roughly affectionate tug, he sat back on his heels to watch the animal eat.

She'd been about to ream him out. The words died in her throat.

He'd shown that same awkward affection to Petra, she reflected slowly, and the child had reacted with the same adoration that the normally aloof Pangor was bestowing on Stone. In fact, though he nearly always followed it up with some remark that had her gritting her teeth, he'd occasionally shown his tenderer side to *her,* she admitted. He'd tried to make her dinner last night. He'd retrieved her vehicle. He'd picked up extra groceries.

Stone McQueen was a diamond in the rough. Too bad most of the time *rough* was the operative word.

And too bad she'd been left with no alternative but to take a stand right here and now, she thought in resignation. She looked down at the badly pilled sleepshirt she was wearing and saw with embarrassment that she'd obviously put it on backward last night before crashing like a fallen log into bed. The shirt hung down past her knees, and from there to her socks a pair of flannel pajama pants covered her legs.

The drinking from the carton thing had weakened her position, too. But she couldn't let this go on any longer.

"Number one." She was gratified to hear a trace of his own growl in her voice. "You don't barge into my bedroom and watch me while I'm sleeping. While I'm doing anything, for that matter," she added. "Number two—"

She paused. What exactly *was* number two? she thought helplessly. Stop being such a jerk all the time? Try to lose the junkyard dog attitude? Slowly she shook her head at him.

"What's *with* you, McQueen?" She really wanted to know, she thought suddenly. "Why are you so…*abrasive* most of the time?" Her gaze searched his face. "You couldn't always have been this hard to get along with, even if we have to go back to when you were just a kid. I'll bet your mom and dad didn't let you snap their heads off everytime you talked to them."

"That would have been tough to do." His voice was expressionless. "Especially since I never knew who my old man was, and the day after she gave birth to me my mother walked out of the hospital without remembering to take me with her. I'd say sassing off to the folks would have been quite a trick under the circumstances."

Tamara stared at him, stricken. He shot her a sharp glance. "Quit it, honey. I'm thirty-four years old. I wasn't mothered when I was in diapers, and I'm damn well not looking for that kind of response from a woman now. I wasn't cute so I got fostered out, and to more families than I can remember. I grew up fast and I grew up tough—and since this is a good world to be tough in I'm glad I learned the lesson early." He shrugged. "But so did you. We're not that different, you and me."

"I wasn't bounced around from home to home," she said softly. "My parents' best friends adopted me, and Uncle Jack and Aunt Kate made sure I grew up knowing I was loved. There's a world of difference between our backgrounds, Stone."

"If you say so." He sounded unconvinced. "But if losing your family wasn't it, what did happen to make you the way you are?"

"The way I am?" She smiled at him, her tone a little less soft than it had been a moment earlier. "I don't get what you mean."

"You live alone, except for a cat that can't stand you," he said flatly. "You were hurt on the job yesterday, and from what I can tell, you don't have anyone close enough to you that you felt you had to phone them to say you were okay."

"My uncle called the hospital and talked to Chandra," she interrupted. "She told him it was no big deal."

"Okay, but he's family. Your only family, right?"

"Since Aunt Kate died last year, yes." She pressed her lips together. "I still don't get your point."

"You can't have a boyfriend, or I wouldn't have spent the night ten feet down the hall from you, honey. My point is that you keep the world at arm's length. I think you might even be worse than me in that respect, except you just hide it better. So what took away your trust?''

"Unbelievable." She lifted her eyebrows at him. "If I were a man you wouldn't think twice about my lifestyle, but because I'm a woman you assume there must be some deep, dark reason for me not having a boyfriend or a husband. For starters, I *was* engaged to be married, remember? Maybe having my fiancé take off with my best friend shook my faith in humanity for a time, but the simple truth is that when I got over it I realized I liked being single."

"Yeah, but not because you don't need someone in your life," he rasped. "You're too afraid to trust anyone enough to fall in love with them. Go ahead and tell yourself that jerk dumped you, but you were never in love with him in the first place. You know why you and I came so close to ripping each other's clothes off last night, honey? Because I'm the perfect guy for you—I'm a stranger, I'm no one you could ever imagine yourself falling in love with and I'm so damned bad tempered you're pretty sure I'd never soften up enough to fall in love with *you*. Hell, I was made for you."

A couple of minutes ago she'd been thinking of him as a diamond in the rough, Tamara thought, icy anger flooding through her. *This* was the real Stone Mc-Queen—coarse, offensive, surly to the point of rudeness and beyond. And he felt he had the right to examine *her* life?

"This is over *now*," she said in a splintered tone. "You and I aren't alike at all, McQueen. Hell, we're so different we can't even work together. But that should be nothing new to you. Tell me, did you quit investigating fires because you'd run out of people to piss off or did everyone just get so tired of you that they finally voted you off the island?''

Her eyes were on his as she spat the words out, and even before she finished speaking she saw the shuttered look that slammed down over his gaze. His features seemed to lock into immobility, and the heavy muscles under his T-shirt tensed.

She'd crossed over some invisible boundary, she realized, immediately wishing she could take back whatever it was she'd said. All of a sudden she didn't want to be the latest in the long line of people who'd wounded Stone McQueen.

But it was too late.

"You've been dying to know." The touch of velvet she'd always heard beneath the gravelled tone was completely gone. "I guess there's no reason not to tell you. If you'd asked around, sooner or later someone would have been only too happy to fill you in, honey."

"I don't want to know." Her voice shook, and she steadied it. "Whatever it is, it's something you don't want to talk about, so I don't want to know. I don't even know why I lashed out at you like that."

"Because I got too close." Like lightning briefly illuminating a blasted landscape, just for a second the dead look in his eyes seemed lit by a flash of pain. "Because you wanted to push me away. I let five firefighters die. That's why I walked away from the job."

"Five firefighters—" She stopped, her eyes widening in partial comprehension. "Four men and Donna Burke," she said hollowly. "The old Mitchell Towers office complex. They went in to fight the blaze and they never came out."

"They never came out." His tone was barren. "I saw

the building collapse on them myself. I went to the funerals, one after another, and then I quit.''

The tragedy had still been fresh when she'd been in training, Tamara recalled, and the fact that one of the five lost had been a woman had brought home to her the potential dangers of the profession she'd decided to enter. She'd gone to the library and looked up copies of the *Boston Globe* from the time of the deaths, and found the newspaper had honored the jakeys by profiling each one.

She'd learned that Donna Burke had saved a toddler from a day-care fire less than a week before she'd been killed. She'd left the library knowing that earning the opportunity to follow in the footsteps of a woman like Burke would be a privilege.

Stone's name was unusual enough that she would have remembered seeing it in the articles, she thought. He hadn't been mentioned.

"I don't understand." It was important he didn't glimpse even the slightest sheen in her eyes. He would mistake any sign of compassion for pity. "How do you see their deaths as your fault? You were an investigator, so you wouldn't have had anything to do with fighting the blaze—in fact, why were you on the scene at all? Your job would have begun *after* the fire was put out."

"That's right. And I screwed up on my job." He looked away from her. "Listen, the sharing's been swell, honey, but what say we drop the subject now, okay?''

His tone held a hard note of finality. He'd said all he was going to say, Tamara thought in frustration. He'd closed down, shut off, retreated behind the barrier of abrasiveness that was his way of keeping the demons at bay, and there was nothing she could do about it. Maybe in a month or two, his demons would become once again intolerable to him, and he would find himself standing in an empty room, looking sightlessly out of a window and wondering whether it was worth it to go on.

Not on my watch, dammit.

"How did you sneak onto the site this morning without anyone stopping you?" Her voice held detached curiosity, nothing more, she observed. Good. She bent down to pick up Pangor's water bowl, and noted the tremor in her hand as she waited to see if he would reply.

"I know you were there, Stone." She didn't look at him as she refilled the bowl at the sink. "I can smell the smoke on your clothes. Did you find anything?"

For a moment longer he remained silent. Just as she was beginning to believe he wasn't going to answer her at all, he spoke, his voice low, as if he were talking more to himself than to her.

"The whole third floor was gone. When Trainor and Knopf finally make it their business to do a walk-through, they'll have to bring in a dog if they want to do any serious investigating. I don't think they'll bother." He looked down at the front of his khakis and brushed something from them. Walking over to the table, he dropped into a chair.

"Dammit, I made her a promise." Wearily he raked a tanned hand through his hair. "I shouldn't have made it, and maybe I won't be able to carry it through. But I can't just quit on her without giving it my best shot. She's counting on me." His smile was bleak. "I can't remember the last time I used those words," he said softly.

"And Claudia was counting on me." Tamara gazed steadily back at him, her eyes bright. "God knows why. She could have reached into a hat and come up with at least a dozen others who would have made a better mom for Petra, but she chose me. You said you were up at five, Stone. Where the hell'd you get a dog at that time in the morning?''

He raised startled eyes to hers. Then the ghost of a grin passed over his features, and he looked down again at the telltale hairs on his khakis.

''I told you I still had some contacts. One of them just happens to be four-legged.'' He shrugged. ''Jerry the Wonder-Dog. He used to be a legend, too, but unlike me he was pensioned off with full honors and adopted by the widow of a retired firefighter I used to work with. Betty told me he spends his days playing with the grand-kids and napping in the sun. She wasn't even sure if he still had what it takes to sniff out a site. Frankly, neither was I.''

''He was a chemical-sniffing canine?''

She'd seen them at their work, criss-crossing every square inch of still-smoking ruins, their extraordinary sense of smell trained for one purpose only—to pick out the single part in a thousand that bore the chemical makeup of an accelerant.

''I'd used him in the past. I know of at least two dirtbags who got sent up because Jerry sniffed out the evidence that convicted them.'' Stone shook his head. ''I swear that old German shepherd knew exactly where I was taking him as soon as he got into the car, and when we arrived at the scene...'' His words trailed away.

''I had no trouble getting in, Tam. It was cordoned off, but it's not even being treated as a suspicious origin fire.''

''That doesn't make sense.'' She stared at him. ''Boy-leston would have passed on what you saw. They have to go through the motions, at least.''

"I think you were right." His smile didn't match the suddenly hard look in his eyes. "I think I got voted off the island, honey. I bet what I saw doesn't even make it into the official report. They're going to screw this one up just like they did the Dazzlers blaze."

"Dear God, he *found* something." Alerted by his tone, Tamara's gaze sharpened. "Jerry still has the magic. He *found* something, didn't he, Stone?"

He nodded once, his jaw tight. "I don't know what it was, but Jerry found something. And as near as I could tell, the piece of twisted metal he located it on came from the springs of a cot like the one Claudia was lying on when she died."

"Then that means Trainor and Knopf are going to have to listen to—" she began, but he interrupted her, his voice harsh.

"*Nobody* has to listen to me, honey! Don't you get it? I'm a has-been, an ex-drunk, a loose cannon that everyone knew would go down in flames one day. Even Chandra thinks I've gone over the edge on this. She said as much to you, didn't she?"

"She said she didn't think your information was reliable," Tamara said reluctantly. "But that was before you had anything to corroborate it with, McQueen."

"I told you the site was unsecured. What's to prove that crazy bastard McQueen didn't plant a trace of accelerant there himself in some feeble attempt to bring back his glory days, before he crashed and burned? That's what they'll say, Tam. I don't even know that I blame them, but the fact remains that I need some heavy-hitting support behind me and I don't have anyone left to ask for that kind of help."

"I do."

Why hadn't she thought of it before? she berated herself. The solution had been right in front of her all the time.

"Uncle Jack officially retired from the department a few years ago, but he stayed pretty active in public relations for them. He's still got a lot of pull with the powers that be."

She saw the doubt in his eyes. "I know what you're thinking, Stone, but for a man who started out as an ordinary jakey Uncle Jack's got some influential friends. He was cited for bravery when he nearly got killed in a factory fire, bringing out a pregnant woman. After that he was never able to go back to on-the-line firefighting, and he was offered a position as liaison between the department and city hall."

He was frowning at her. "His name's Jack King? When he and his wife adopted you, your name was changed to theirs?"

She shook her head, not understanding what he was getting at. "Jack Foley. You probably ran into him once or twice when you were on the job."

"It was the Corona shoe factory." Under the tan his face had paled. "Ladder 11 got the call and by the time they arrived the place was an inferno. Some hotshot rookie got trapped in a stairwell trying to reach that pregnant secretary, and after your uncle got her out he went back in for the stupid son of a bitch. He brought him out, too, didn't he?"

"He went back in and brought out a firefighter, yes." Tamara gave him a wry smile. "Except the secretary gave birth the next day and named her little boy after my uncle. The papers loved that angle, and that's what he got the citation for."

Her smile grew thoughtful. "But if you'd joined the department by then I guess it would be the jakey you'd remember. When it's one of our own it hits home, doesn't it?''

"It sure did with me." He got to his feet, his movements suddenly restless. "Honey, you've got exactly ten minutes to get into a pair of jeans, or I'm leaving without you."

"In my car? I don't think so, McQueen." He'd reverted, Tamara told herself resignedly. He was being a jerk again.

She was getting kind of used to it, she thought in surprise.

"And just where were you planning on going, anyway?" she demanded, crossing her arms and fixing him with a half-hearted glare. He returned it with one of his own, but she could see a gleam of humor at the back of those smoke-gray eyes.

"I'm going to renew an old acquaintance, Tam." His voice was huskier than normal. "I'm going to look up your uncle. I was the stupid son of a bitch Jack Foley pulled from the Corona fire."

Chapter Seven

"I wasn't tryin' to be a hero when I saved your sorry butt at the Corona fire, McQueen. You owed me ten bucks on a Red Sox loss. I wasn't about to let you welsh out on me."

As they entered his kitchen, Jack Foley placed a hand on the younger man's shoulder. "How've you been, laddie? I heard you hit a patch of rocky road these past few years, but no one seemed to know where to contact you."

He wasn't one to tiptoe around a subject, Tamara thought in affectionate resignation, studying the man she'd always thought of as a surrogate uncle. In his mid-fifties now, the full head of sandy hair he'd once possessed had thinned and his blue eyes were surrounded with a network of faint lines. Shorter than Stone by half a foot or so and with his once-muscular build a little stockier than it had been, he still projected an air of energetic enthusiasm. With relief she saw Stone didn't seem to be taking offence at the bluntness of the question.

"You know how it is, Jack." His answering smile was onesided. "You've seen more than a few of the boys go down that rocky road. I'm one of the lucky ones who found his way back.''

"The job can break you if you let it get to you." Jack rubbed his jaw. ''But there's days when if you're any kind of human being, you won't be able to stop it from getting to you. My Tammy here found that out pretty fast, didn't you, punkin?''

"It was only my second day on the job, Uncle Jack, and even some of the old-timers on the crew were shaken up by that fire.'' There was a touch of defensiveness in her reply. ''I'm tougher now. But yeah, I've got to admit I didn't protest when Aunt Kate made up the bed in my old room and tucked me in like I was five years old again.''

"If Katie'd had her way, you never would have moved out in the first place. But she was the one who insisted we hang on to your parents' house, instead of selling it and putting the money into trust for you.'' Jack Foley's blue eyes dimmed in remembrance. ''She said you'd want to spread your wings someday, and if we kept the house for you at least you wouldn't fly too far. God, I miss her, Tammy.''

He turned to Stone. ''My wife,'' he said simply. ''She passed away last year. But enough about me—I want to hear how the two of you ran into each other. You back on the job, McQueen?''

Tamara went to the refrigerator, talking over her shoulder as she did. ''It's a long story, Uncle Jack. I'm going to have some lemonade—what can I get for the two of you?''

"The sun's over the yardarm, so grab me a bottle of beer, will you, darlin'?'' Jack looked suddenly dismayed. ''Maybe that's not such a great idea,'' he added gruffly. ''Make it lemonade for me, too.''

"Hell, Jack, watching you drink beer isn't going to send me out on the streets looking for a bar," McQueen growled. "Go ahead, for God's sake. I'll have some of the good stuff with Tam."

There was no real heat behind his words. The firefighter's world was small and tightly knit, Tamara reflected, and she shouldn't have been surprised that the two men had crossed each other's paths in the past. But given her uncle's bluntness and Stone's impatience, it was fortunate there'd been a bond forged between them that had led to their mutual liking now.

As Jack took a long pull at his bottle and Stone, after a first suspicious sip of the lemonade, raised an eyebrow and drained the glass, she launched into an edited version of the events of the past twenty-four hours. There was no need to go into Stone's actions at the moment of their encounter, she thought, or her apprehensive reading of his state of mind at the time. When she reached the part about Joey, she faltered.

"Lieutenant Boyleston says the doctors are being pretty closemouthed about his condition. He's off the danger list, but they won't give us any details."

"He's going to need some skin grafts on his face, but they saved his esophagus. He'll be back on light duty within six months and on the roster again within eight," McQueen said briefly. "Maybe the next time he goes racing into a fire he'll remember to put on his damn respirator."

She stared at him. "How did you find out all that?"

There was a sliver of ice left in his glass and he tipped it into his mouth without looking at her. "I used to date one of the nurses who works in the burn ward," he said, crunching down on the ice. "I phoned her this morning, which probably ruined her day since the last time I saw her she said there'd be a cold snap in hell before she ever went out with me again. I told her the temperature was dropping quickly, and if she didn't want to find me on her doorstep with a bunch of roses and dinner reservations she could give me the scoop on your partner. She couldn't talk fast enough. I don't remember being that awful," he added. "But anyway, Mr. Look Ma, No Air-pack is going to be okay, no thanks to his own foolishness."

"She obviously never took the time to get to know your sensitive side," Tamara said dryly. She winced as he crunched the last of his ice, and her expression softened. "Thanks, Stone. I—I was worried about him."

"I knew you were." He fixed his attention on the glass in his hand as if he was hoping to find more ice there. "Get on with the story, Tam."

She flicked an exasperated glance at him but complied, only stopping at the point where he'd gone into the apartment for Petra. "You take it from here, McQueen. It's better if Uncle Jack hears it firsthand."

"She's right, laddie." Jack's eyes narrowed in interest. "That first glance at the scene can tell a lot. Something looked wrong to you?"

"Dead wrong," Stone said shortly. "But it didn't hit me immediately."

In a few curt sentences he outlined his suspicions and the reasons for them, ending with what he'd discovered that morning. As he fell silent, Tamara turned to her uncle, holding on to her composure with an effort.

"I haven't told you the most important part. The woman in that room was Claudia, Uncle Jack—Claudia Anderson. The little girl is her daughter Petra, and apparently Claudia came back to Boston to ask me to look after Petra when she was gone. She...she was dying,

Uncle Jack. She had some kind of cancer, just like her own mom did.''

He didn't seem to hear this last. ''Claudia? Claudia came back here to see *you?*''

He shook his head at Stone. ''Did Tammy tell you what her best friend Claudia *did* to her, for the love of Mike?'' Without waiting for the other man's response he went on, his voice uneven. ''Fifteen minutes before my little girl was supposed to walk up the aisle, her bridesmaid sent her a note saying she'd just ran off with the groom. I never thought Rick was good enough for Tammy, but *Claudia*—for God's sake, Kate and I thought of her as our second daughter.''

She'd guessed the news would be hard on him, Tamara thought with a pang. At the wedding when, stunned and disbelieving, she'd passed Claudia's note to her uncle and aunt, only his wife's shaky entreaties had prevented a wrathful Jack Foley from acting on his threats to find the man who'd jilted his adored Tammy and thrash him within an inch of his life. But when it had sunk in that Rick had run off with Claudia, his fury had turned to incomprehension.

''Your aunt never stopped caring for her.'' Jack lifted his gaze. ''Kate always used to wonder if she wanted to come back, and was too afraid to.''

He scrubbed his face wearily. ''And dammit, I always knew I couldn't bring myself to stop caring about her, either. If she'd showed up on the doorstep I would have read her the riot act, but in the end I don't think I would have been able to turn her away.'' He shook his head. ''Little Claudie, dead. That's hard to take in.''

''It was hard for me to take in, too.'' Tamara reached over and laid her fingers lightly on his hand. ''But maybe Aunt Kate was right. Maybe Claudia always wanted to come home to us. After all, in the end she did just that.''

He gave her fingers a squeeze, his expression clouded. ''Except she left it too late, punkin. She should have come to us sooner.'' His brows drew together. ''But don't ask me to forgive and forget with that bastard Rick, dammit. Why wasn't he with his wife and child, and what's all this about you looking after the little girl when it's her father who should be taking the responsibility for her?''

''The authorities are checking into Petra's story, but it seems Rick was killed in a car accident only a few weeks after he ran off with Claudia.'' Tamara bit her lip. ''I keep thinking I should feel something more than just regret at how things turned out for him.''

''He was the one who broke faith with you, punkin,'' Jack Foley said gruffly. ''It's the child you have to concentrate on now—the child, and the fact that Stone thinks someone was trying to kill her and Claudia with that fire.'' He grunted thoughtfully. ''What did the investigators assigned to the case say when you handed over what you found, McQueen?''

''I didn't,'' Stone said flatly. ''The investigators are Knopf and Trainor, and I'd get more results tossing evidence into the Charles River than I would giving it to those two. We want you to have someone run tests on it, Jack.'' He frowned. ''But maybe you wouldn't feel comfortable doing something like that. Hell, for all I know you're tight with Tommy and Bill.''

''The Dazzlers investigation wasn't the only case they made mistakes on, it was just the only one the media learned about.'' Jack leveled a glance at Stone. ''I didn't agree with the way you hauled out the department's dirty laundry for the whole world to see, laddie, but I guess you felt you didn't have much choice. I play poker with Bill Trainor once in a while. It's like taking candy from a baby." He shrugged. "Tommy Knopf seems a tad quicker on the uptake but it's hard to know what makes him tick. He's an even surlier son of a gun than you are, McQueen."

"Then that's a yes?" Stone's grin flashed briefly. "You'll send the stuff I collected to the lab and tell them this one's off the record?"

"Dave Leung owes me a couple of favors." Jack nodded. "He'll keep it on the Q.T. if I ask him."

"It's in the car." Impatiently Stone shoved his chair back, getting halfway to the door before he checked his stride and looked over his shoulder at them. "Thanks, Jack. The Sox play New York next week. Two to one odds suit you?"

Jack's eyes gleamed wickedly. "How about we make it three to one? The Yankee pitchers are on fire lately."

"You're a bad man, Uncle Jack. Totally unscrupulous," Tamara said in mock reproof. She heard the front door close behind Stone, and her smile faded. "Are we doing the right thing, keeping evidence back like this? I don't want you doing anything that could get you in trouble."

"Don't worry about me, punkin, I'm on a pension." Her uncle laid a hand over hers. "McQueen's got nothing to lose, either. But promise me you'll keep a low profile on this, Tammy. Even though Trainor and Knopf aren't the brightest bulbs on the Christmas tree, they'd have every right to ask for your dismissal if they found out you were involved in an unofficial investigation with Stone McQueen, of all people. I always liked the guy, but he made more enemies than friends when he was in the department."

"Really?" She shot him a wry glance, and then sighed. "Most of the time I feel like throttling him, too. But he saved my life and risked his own to get Petra out, and it seems he's right about the fire being deliberately set. Why else would the dog have picked up on an accelerant?"

"Hair spray's an accelerant. Spot cleaners can be one hell of an accelerant," Jack said sharply. "If Claudie was trying to do some home dry-cleaning and spilled a little benzine, the dog would alert to that just as quickly as to the scent of gasoline." He rubbed his jaw. "But I'll admit McQueen always had a sixth sense where arson was concerned. Is there something I should know about the two of you, punkin?"

To her annoyance Tamara felt herself flush. "When it comes to Stone McQueen, that nurse in the burn unit and I see eye to eye, Uncle Jack. The only difference is that I'm not dating him." Too late she saw the trap she'd laid for herself. She swallowed. "He's just kind of living with me for a while," she finished weakly.

"He's *what?*" Now there was an ominous rumble behind the gruffness, and she went on hurriedly.

"He's staying at my place—and whatever you're thinking, forget it. It's strictly separate bedrooms," she added with some asperity. "Besides, Uncle Jack, I've been a grown woman for some time now."

He leveled a bright blue gaze at her. "I know you're not the little girl your aunt Kate and I brought home all those years ago, punkin. You grew into a woman who made both of us very proud and your personal life's your own, so I'll butt out of this one. But what about Petra? Won't family services want to vet your living arrangements before they place her with you?"

"I'm sure they will, but they won't even think of releasing her to me for a week or so. By then McQueen should have found a place of his own.'' She raked a restless hand through her hair. ''Even then it's not certain I'll be approved to adopt her.''

''Because of your work?'' Her uncle frowned. ''Most firefighters have families. They can't hold that against you.''

''I don't think they do. I'll have to find a reliable woman to come in for the nights I'm on duty, but Lieutenant Boyleston said that won't be a problem. She even gave me my vacation time early so I could deal with all this.'' Tamara's smile was lopsided. ''It's Petra herself. I don't think she *wants* me to be appointed her guardian.''

''You don't remember how it was when you first came to live with your aunt Kate and me, do you?'' There was a quizzical note in his voice.

''Not the first couple of weeks, no.'' Tamara heard Stone coming back into the house as she shook her head. ''That's always been kind of a blurry period. Why?''

''You acted the same way you say Petra's acting now.'' As Stone entered the kitchen, Jack stood, smiling ruefully. ''Katie was at her wit's end trying to make you understand this was your new home. You only started to settle in after the nightmares began to fade away, punkin, and that's probably what Petra's going through. Give her time. She'll come around.''

''The puppy thing seemed to help.'' Briskly Stone removed a sealed glass jar from the paper bag he was carrying. ''Make it damn clear to Dave Leung I want a mass spectrometry, Jack, not some half-assed gas chromo test that might miss something, okay?''

''In other words, tell him how to do his job.'' The older man shrugged into a sweater-jacket. ''Laddie, people skills were never your strong point. Leung's a perfectionist. If there's something there he'll catch it without me drawing him a map. What's this puppy thing you mentioned?''

''Yeah.'' Preceding the two men toward the front door, Tamara stopped suddenly. ''What *was* that puppy thing? What's a puppy got to do with Petra? Aw, McQueen, you *didn't*. Tell me you didn't.''

''Didn't what?'' His eyes widened as they met her scowl. ''Hell, I never said you were getting her one. When I was carrying her back to her hospital bed last night, she made some crack about she'd rather live in an orphanage. I said fine but they wouldn't let her have a puppy and she asked me if you would. I said it couldn't hurt to ask.''

''So she asks and I say no. Then I'm the bad guy again. Smooth move, Stone.''

Stalking outside ahead of him, she made her way to her car. He had the keys, she realized as she tried the driver's side handle and saw him unlocking the passenger door for her. The fact that her shoulder ached enough to make handling a car a chore probably wasn't why he'd taken over the driving. Stone McQueen was just the type of man who did take over, if a woman was fool enough to let him. She considered grabbing the keys out of his hand, but decided to conserve her energies for the next confrontation.

With McQueen there always would be a next confrontation, she thought in resignation. A *puppy*, for God's sake!

''It doesn't have to be a Great Dane.'' He sounded disgruntled. ''Hell, Tam, every kid wants a dog. We could take her down to the pound today and just have a look.''

About to get into the car, she stared at him in suspicion. "Did *you* ever have a dog, Stone?"

"Nah. I moved around too much when I was being fostered out. You getting in or are we just going to stand here all day?" He'd been holding the door open for her. Now he swung it impatiently back and forth on its hinges. She gritted her teeth.

"Stop that, it's irritating, McQueen. We might drop around to have a look at the dogs, okay? You're right, it's not a bad idea, although what I'm going to do about Pangor I don't know."

"He'll get over it." She froze him with a look. "*If* you decide to get one," he added. His growl lacked its usual conviction.

"When Dave has an answer for me I'll call you right away." The paper bag tucked under his arm, her uncle paused on the way to his own car, parked ahead of Tamara's. "I wouldn't be surprised if you get a call from Bill or Tommy, too, especially if someone saw you poking around that site, Stone. Watch your back. Those guys could make things uncomfortable for you."

"You worry too much, Uncle Jack." Tamara gave him an affectionate smile. "Didn't I just tell you I'm a big girl now?"

She saw her uncle's gaze narrow on the man beside her. "Do you think I'm worrying too much, laddie?" His voice was softly challenging.

"I hope so, Jack." There was an indefinable note in Stone's reply, and Tamara glanced at him in surprise. He didn't look at her. "I'll know better when Dave Leung tells me what's in that sample."

"You already know what he's going to find, don't you?" She looked from McQueen to her uncle and back again in sudden comprehension. "You *both* know, and you've been keeping it from me."

She heard the sharpness in her tone and attempted to rein her growing anger in. "No. That's not the way we're going to work this, boys. You know what Leung's going to find. I want to know, too."

"Now, punkin, I don't want you worrying about—" her uncle began, but McQueen stopped him.

"Hell, Jack, she's got a right to know—probably more of a right than we do. You're retired. I'm a has-been. Tam here still goes out every day and puts her life on the line as a firefighter. Last time I checked, cotton wool wasn't part of their equipment."

She stared at him, slightly mollified. "What's Leung going to find?" she asked more quietly.

"I don't know what he's going to find." Under the olive-drab tee, the broad shoulders lifted. "But I think I know who he's going to find."

Now he did meet her eyes, and as he did she felt a chill settle over her. He was the man in the rooming house again, she thought in sudden dismay. He was looking at her, but he was seeing something from his past, something invisible, something that had been waiting for him all along. He was looking at her, but he was seeing a—

"He's going to find a ghost," McQueen said harshly. "Leung's going to run those tests and he's going to find a ghost. The bastard's back, and he's killing again."

Chapter Eight

"Family services made it clear Petra should be returned on time, Ms. King. Even if a child's only with us for a short while, it's important to create a sense of routine. Come on, Pet, we're about to sit down for supper. It's macaroni and cheese with stewed tomatoes—doesn't that sound yummy?"

It sounded like pig-swill to him, Stone thought shortly. And the woman standing in front of them was a fool, despite the fact that the authorities had enough confidence in her capabilities to have parked Petra with her upon the child's release from the hospital. Out of the corner of his eye he saw Tamara's cheeks turn a dull crimson shade that went badly with the red and gold of her hair and the pistachio green he'd just noticed around her mouth.

It hadn't been the greatest day for her. It was over twenty-four hours now and Leung still hadn't gotten back to Jack with any results. Petra had insisted on going to her mother's lawyer with them and had put on such a performance that Stone had had to carry her out of the office. And the dog pound, for crying out loud, had been closed. Apparently it was disinfecting day, or some such thing.

They'd brought the kid back five minutes past the agreed-upon time, Stone thought in irritation. So sue them. He was just about to say something along those lines when Petra beat him to it.

"I already ate, so I'm not hungry," she said coldly. "We had pistachio sundaes."

This last was unnecessary, since like Tamara she had an Incredible Hulk thing going on around her lips, too. Stone wished he'd caught it on both of them earlier.

"Pistachio?" Her name was Mrs. Hall, but she'd told them to call her Mary. As one of her plump hands went to her mouth in dismay he decided he'd sooner step on a nail than be on a first-name basis with her. "*Pistachio?* Heavens to Betsy, didn't it occur to you that the child might be allergic to *nuts*?"

Beside him Tamara looked stricken. "I asked her first, Mary. I'm not an expert on children, but I do know that much. Maybe it was a little irresponsible taking her out for ice cream so close to suppertime, but there's no real harm done." Her smile was conciliatory. Stone wondered just how much self-control it was costing her not to tell Mary where she could get off, the way he would have if he'd been her. "She'll have her appetite back in an hour or so."

"That's not the point."

There was a patronizing tone in Hall's voice that set Stone's teeth on edge. Enough was enough, he decided. Yesterday he'd come to the realization that Tamara thought his manner was a tad blunt, and he'd made a pact with himself to soft pedal his comments for her sake. But he wasn't bucking for sainthood, dammit.

"You're not a mother yourself, so you wouldn't know how important it is for little ones to understand the rules of a household as soon as possible. It's not fair to the

other children in my care to keep Pet's dinner warm
for—''

''Her name's not Pet,'' Stone interrupted, and was
about to go on when he found himself being thrown off-
stride by the look Tamara was directing at him. *What
now?* he thought defensively. Wasn't he allowed to say
anything anymore?

''Yeah, my name's not Pet. A pet's an *animal,* for
cryin' out loud.'' Petra's green lips thinned and her small
shoulders squared pugnaciously. ''And I'm allergic to
fudgin' tomatoes, so there.''

''Hey, Tiger, watch the mouth,'' he growled automatically. ''Look, we'll come by at the same time tomorrow, okay? And if the freak—'' He saw Tamara's
eyes close in despair and corrected himself in midstream.
''—the fudgin' pound's closed again, we'll go to a pet
store and look at puppies. Deal?''

''Nuh-uh, Stone! I *told* you, I want a pound dog!''

It was the first time the kid hadn't looked at him like
the sun shone out of—

Stone cut the thought off abruptly. Okay, maybe he'd
become a little rough-edged over the past few years, he
thought guiltily. Cleaning up his act mentally as well as
verbally might not be a bad idea, at least while he was
around a little pitcher who'd just demonstrated she had
big enough ears to pick up on his occasional slips.

''Petra's right, pound dogs are better, McQueen.'' Tamara didn't meet his eyes. ''We'll give it another try
tomorrow, sweetie. How freak—how darn long does disinfecting a few cages take, anyway?'' she added in a
harried undertone.

''She can't bring a dog here.'' The woman smoothed
her plump hands over the ample apron. ''And I'm going
to have to clear it with family services before we have

another outing, especially since Petra's falling behind on her schooling every day she's not attending classes. Perhaps it would be best if you gave me a call tomorrow morning.''

''But they told me—'' Tamara stopped. ''I'll do that,'' she said, achieving a smile. ''Sweetie, if you want to talk or anything, you've got my number, right?''

''Somewhere, I guess,'' Petra mumbled, putting her hands behind her and toeing a sneaker into the edge of lawn lining the walkway hard enough to dislodge a clump of grass. Stone could see the scrap of paper Tamara had written her phone number on clutched in an ice cream sticky palm, but he kept quiet.

Tamara made a half movement, checking it as Petra turned away. ''Call me if you want,'' she said to the stiff little back retreating into the house.

''Whatever.''

Petra's reply was studiedly disinterested, and Stone's eyes narrowed. When they'd visited her in the hospital yesterday after leaving Jack, the staff psychologist's opinion had been that for now, at least, it would help if McQueen kept up a relationship with the child. Dr. Weller had bandied about phrases like ''security fixation'' and ''trauma bonding,'' but what it really boiled down to was that Petra seemed to have decided that the only person she trusted was Stone.

You picked a real loser to be your hero, kid, he thought as he and Tamara made their silent way to the car. *But since you did, you and me are going to have a little heart-to-heart about your attitude toward your mom's best friend. I've got to make you see she's not your enemy, no matter what you decided when you overheard us the other night.*

''It isn't going to work, McQueen.'' As they pulled

away from the curb Tamara snapped her seat belt into place. "It doesn't matter what Claudia wanted, Petra's never going to accept me, and I don't really blame her."

She leaned her head back against the headrest, closing her eyes as she did. "I don't know anything about raising a child. What was I thinking, giving her ice cream at this time of day?"

"You wanted to smooth things over after what happened in the lawyer's office," Stone said edgily. "Bribery's a perfectly acceptable child-rearing technique as far as I'm concerned. I felt like telling that Hall woman where she could put her damned stewed tomatoes. You notice I didn't, though."

"You showed remarkable restraint, for you. Thanks for not shooting your mouth off, Stone." She opened her eyes. "I didn't mean that the way it sounded. By the way, you've got pistachio on your chin. I nearly died when I saw it."

She flipped open the glove compartment. Peeling open a small foil square, she unfolded what looked like a damp tissue and handed it to him. "Moist towelette. Sometimes after I finish my shift I'm too wound up to go home so I drive somewhere and park for a while. These things are like instant washcloths."

They'd come to a red light. Stone peered in the rearview mirror and swiped at the dab of pale green on his chin before turning to Tamara.

"Open your mouth," he commanded. "You've got it all over you, too."

"For crying out loud." As he tipped her chin back she tried to move out of his grasp. "What must that woman have *thought* of me? Dammit, let me go, McQueen. I can do it myself."

"As Tiger might say, I don't give a flying fudge," he

said briefly. "For God's sake, stop jostling my arm. You nearly made me knock the gearshift into drive."

"I finally figured out what it is about you." Since his thumb was rubbing at her bottom lip, Tamara's words were slightly muffled. Stone raised an eyebrow.

"Oh?" If he hadn't gone and turned into Sir Lancelot the other night, he thought, he could have had this mouth all over him. And despite his dire prediction at the time, he was willing to bet he could have rocked Tamara King's world hard enough that she wouldn't have booted him out of bed when it was over. Hell, except for his inconvenient and uncharacteristic attack of conscience the two of them might *still* be tangled up in her sheets together.

Instead, he was sitting here at a red light getting all hot and bothered when he couldn't do a damn thing about it.

Because it wasn't just her mouth. It wasn't just the memory of how creamily perfect her breasts had looked when he'd had that all-too-brief flash of them in her kitchen. *Everything* about her seemed to get to him, Stone thought, scrubbing the last of the pistachio from her lower lip and wondering what she'd do if he suddenly decided to lick it clean.

Unconsciously he leaned closer to her, letting a single rebellious strand of her hair brush against his knuckles. The way she always scraped it back in that damn braid was a crying shame. Unbound it was like molten copper and gold, all flowing together in one incredible, silky mass. He knew because he'd seen it like that—just once, but the image was seared into his memory.

He was such a freakin' screw-up, he thought with sudden anger.

"The thing about you is that you're the complete

male. You're the prototype," Tamara mumbled around his fingers. "Are you trying to take my lips off completely, McQueen?"

Abruptly he released her chin and handed her the damp tissue. The light ahead of them was still red. Frowning, she tossed the tissue into a small waste container at her feet.

"You're the stripped-down model, like those performance cars companies test on the racetrack before they modify them and sell them as road vehicles. But you weren't ever modified." She looked over at him. "That's why you didn't think twice about going in after Petra. That's also why if you knocked the gearshift into drive and plowed into the car ahead of us you'd tell yourself I made you do it. You're so male it's not even—"

"You finish your shift and find someplace to cry, don't you?" Finally the light had changed. Stone accelerated slightly faster than he'd meant to. "Then you use your little premoistened washcloths and drive home like nothing's happened."

He shrugged without looking over at her. "If that's what you want to do now, we can go to a park or something and I'll take a walk. When you're all cleaned up again you can honk the horn to let me know it's okay to come back."

Out of the corner of his eye he saw her stiffen. "What I do or don't do is none of your business, McQueen. And despite the sensitivity of your offer, I'll pass, thanks. I'd like to get home in case Uncle Jack's been trying to reach us."

She inhaled sharply. "You know, that performance car analogy I just came up with was all wrong. Life's more of a demolition derby for you, isn't it? Other people try to steer around things, but you don't even bother to look over your shoulder to see who you just crashed into.''

Just ahead of them was an empty parking space. Pulling into it abruptly, Stone snapped the ignition off and turned to her.

"How the hell can you say I crash into you when there's no way you can feel it, honey? You're a damn tank, for God's sake. The armor plating's so thick no one gets through.''

"I don't think I even want to know what this conversation's about." Coolly she met his gaze. "We've been thrown together for a few days, McQueen, that's all. If and when we find out who started the fire that killed Claudia, whatever connection there is between us is over. Not that there's much of one now," she added. "A ghost from your past? You throw a cryptic remark like that at me without any further explanation and then tell me *I'm* sealed off?"

"Like I said yesterday, if it turns out I'm right I'll fill you in." He shook his head. "If I'm wrong then it's just ancient history, and I never liked history that much. But that's not what this is about and you know it. You've been hanging on to those damn letters like a drowning woman clutching a lifebelt since we left the lawyer's office, but you haven't glanced at them once. Hendricks gave them to you when I took Petra out into the reception area, didn't he? And if they hadn't made such a bundle, I'll bet you would have crammed them into your purse and never mentioned them to me or to anyone else.''

"What's to mention?" Her tone was edged. "Apparently Petra was right—her mom, for some unknown reason, wrote me every couple of months for the whole seven years she was gone. Except instead of sending the letters to me she mailed them to the lawyer who'd handled her own mother's estate and told Hendricks to keep them on file, along with her will and the instructions she'd left about contacting me in the event of her death. What do you expect me to do, McQueen—rip them open in front of you and start sobbing over them?''

She glanced down at the taped bundle of envelopes in her lap. With an impatient gesture, she twisted around and tossed them into the back seat of the car. When she turned to face him once more her face was expressionless.

''I wish she hadn't died the way she did, and yeah, I'll look through them in case there's anything in there that gives us a lead on why she was killed, although I'm not expecting to find any clues. But Claudia's a part of my past, McQueen, and history never was my favorite subject, either.''

She tucked the stray strand of hair he'd noticed earlier behind her ear. ''Like I seem to recall you saying once, the sharing's been swell. Can we go now?''

''You really can't stand it, can you, honey?'' Stone heard the whiplash of heat in his own voice, and was powerless to control it. She flicked him a disinterested glance and started to turn away, but swiftly he reached over and caught her by the shoulders.

''You just can't *stand* to have another human being catch a glimpse of tough Tamara King being vulnerable. Hell, you're probably still kicking yourself for almost letting a few tears escape when you realized your best friend had been killed, for God's sake. You don't cry in front of anyone, do you?''

Her gaze was so electric he could almost feel her fury. He was blowing it with her, he realized. With his usual unerring talent, he was going about this in the worst possible way, and with every word he spoke he could feel her withdrawing. The hell of it was, he didn't know what else he could do to get through to her. He plunged on recklessly, unable to stop.

"From what you said yesterday, your first week as a probie you got hit with a fire that the most experienced guys on the crew had trouble handling. You seem to be ashamed you even let it get to you. At the hospital two days ago you couldn't clam up fast enough when you realized you'd actually let your defences down for a second. Now you're trying to tell yourself that sad collection of letters from a dead woman doesn't mean squat to you."

He shook his head tightly at her. "You're a liar, honey. You care, all right. You care about what you see on the job, you care that Claudia never got up the nerve to send those letters to you, and it's tearing you apart that Petra told Hendricks today she didn't know if she wanted to live with you. But you'll die before you admit it. And if anyone comes close to seeing the real you behind that shell, you make damned sure they never get near enough to take a second look."

"Too bad you went in for arson investigation, McQueen." Under his hands her shoulders were rigid. "Obviously pop psychology's your forte. Maybe if you'd taken that up in the first place you wouldn't have crashed and burned the way you did. Maybe Donna Burke might even be alive."

Her words drove into him with such force that Stone felt as if he'd just taken an actual physical blow. His hands fell away from her shoulders and for a moment he found it impossible to get his breath.

"That was unforgivable of me." Her face white, Tamara stared at him in horror. "Unforgivable and stupid and—and *untrue.* Stone, I'm sorry. I just said the cruelest thing I could think of."

He opened his mouth, and was vaguely surprised to find his voice still worked. "Hell, no. I—I deserved that." He blinked, and her stricken face swam back into focus again. "It's like you said, I go through life crashing into people, honey. I pushed you and you pushed back, that's all."

He fumbled for the door handle. "Listen, there's something I wanted to ask Chandra about so I arranged for us to meet her at a diner not far from here, the Red Spot. You probably know the place since it's a hangout for you jakeys." He tried to smile. "If I get any information worth passing on I'll let Jack know, okay?"

He stopped pushing down on the door handle and pulled up, and with relief he felt the damned thing unlatch. He had to get out of here, Stone thought. He'd blown it with her and this time he wasn't going to get another chance to put things right, so he had to get away.

"You're leaving, aren't you?" As the door swung open he started to get out, but suddenly her hand was clamped around his upper arm, pulling him back. "Stone, you're broke and you don't have anywhere to stay. I—I don't want to think of you without a place to stay."

Her voice cracked on the last few words. He had no idea why it had, so he ignored that and addressed the one thing she'd said that he did feel capable of facing. "I'm not broke, honey." He frowned, wondering if he'd heard her right. "Where'd you get that idea?"

"You were living in a flophouse. You don't have to keep up any kind of pretence with me, Stone."

"I lived in places like that because I didn't want to

run into anyone I used to know," he said tightly. "But I've been working since I was sixteen, and I socked away a good chunk of my pay in investments. Honey, when you grow up on the mean streets, you don't leave anything to chance."

He saw her lips form a surprised little *o*. Her mouth looked like a pink velvet bow, he thought stupidly. It would feel like velvet, too. It was time to end this.

Luckily, he was good at ending things.

"Like you say, we were thrown together for a few days. But be honest, babe—most of the time I rubbed you the wrong way, didn't I?"

"Most of the time you drove me crazy." Her gaze still held his. Her voice was still uneven. Her mouth still looked like velvet.

"Hell, I guess if I was a gentleman I wouldn't admit it, but being a gentleman is one of the few things you haven't accused me of. You drove me crazy, too." He gave her a hard grin. "So we're both off the hook here. Take care of yourself, honey."

This time when he opened the door she didn't stop him. He gave her one last glance, taking in the live fire of the tendrils of hair curving into the ivory of her cheeks, the rounded firmness of her uplifted chin, the shimmering silver tracks that were making their way down her face.

It was fate, buddy, he told himself harshly. *This was never in the cards for you, and you knew it almost from the start. Say goodbye to the lady, McQueen.*

But he couldn't, and he knew that, too. Without another word he got out of the car and walked away as fast as he could.

He'd gone half a block before he stopped in his tracks.

"For God's sake, she was *crying*, McQueen," he said

out loud. "Tough Tamara King was actually crying—and you walked away from her, dammit!"

He made it back to the car in seconds. Wrenching open the door, he stared in at her, still sitting in the passenger seat where he'd left her. On her lap was a litter of torn foil packets and crumpled towelettes.

Streaming blue eyes met his in a glare.

"Yeah, you drive me crazy, McQueen." It would have been a pretty good facsimile of his own growl but for the hiccup. She tossed a tissue aside and ripped open a new packet. "I didn't say I didn't *like* it."

"You don't cry." It was the first thing that came into his head.

"I *know* I don't cry, McQueen. Not where anyone can see me, anyway. Do you blame me?"

She wiped angrily at a fresh torrent of tears. Helplessly he stood there, feeling as if his heart had ballooned up to about ten times its normal size, and was still swelling.

She didn't cry pretty. The tip of her nose was a bright pink. Her whole face was wet and shiny and red. She looked as if she was about Petra's age, and had miserably reached the tail end of a tantrum.

He still thought she looked beautiful, but of course that was because he was in love with her, Stone told himself impatiently. He'd thought she'd looked beautiful with a helmet crammed onto her head and her face streaked with soot. He'd thought she'd looked beautiful in those mismatched pajamas.

He'd known she was beautiful the night they'd—

"Stone?" She was looking up at him, and all at once he knew he was seeing the real Tamara King behind the tough mask. Her voice was a raw whisper. "Oh, Stone, I *hurt* you."

There was so much pain in the simple declaration that all he could think of was that he had to make it go away for her somehow. He shook his head, and started to get into the car.

"No, honey—" he began, but before he could get another word out he felt a heavy hand drop onto his shoulder and heard a gratingly familiar voice close behind him.

"I see he's still got the magic touch, Bill. They're either slapping his face or crying their eyes out. Tell me, McQueen, how come women always leave you like this?"

Chapter Nine

Slowly Stone turned to face the two men. Even more slowly he looked at the hand clamped on to his shoulder, and then at its beefy owner.

"Well, well, Trainor and Knopf. And still in each other's pockets, I see." There was no inflection in his voice. "Which one of you two clowns wants to take me on first?"

Judging from the tone of his voice, Tamara thought in alarm, she had roughly a two-second window of opportunity before Stone did something that would end up with her having to trot down to the police station later to bail him out.

She was out of the car and sprinting around it just as the window began to close.

"You giving us fair warning, McQueen? In the old days your streetfighting used to be dirtier than that." The heavy-set man with his hand on Stone's shoulder was wearing a plaid sports jacket. "You must have soaked up some religion in those church basements they hold the meetings in, huh? I hear you spent the last seven years soaking up something, anyway."

"Tommy, cool it." His companion moved hesitantly forward. "This isn't why we're here." Muddy brown eyes blinked behind round gold-framed glasses. He looked relieved as Tamara approached.

"Besides, there's a lady present," he added.

"Oh, please," she snapped, marching past him to the other two. Reaching up, she plucked the beefy man's hand from Stone's shoulder.

"Think of me as the recess monitor, boys," she said flatly. "You wanna lower those testosterone levels a notch before some nervous citizen calls the cops?"

"I know you." The beefy man's eyes were small to begin with. When he narrowed them they almost disappeared. "You're Jack Foley's little girl, aren't you?"

"If you say so." She gave him a cool stare. "I guess that makes you Mrs. Knopf's little Tommy then, doesn't it?"

"And you think *I'm* a jerk," Stone said. He nodded toward the younger man, who was still hanging back. "Bill Trainor, the other half of the daring duo. So how come you two master investigators aren't hot on the trail of some arsonist?"

"We dropped in at the Red Spot." Trainor shot Stone a glance of pure dislike. "You heading that way, McQueen?"

"Yeah, as soon as I get the gas can out of the trunk. Anybody besides me think the Red Spot's roast-beef sandwich is a little on the stringy side lately?" Stone patted his jeans pockets. "I was sure I had matches on me somewhere," he muttered.

Trainor's fair skin pinkened. "Watch it, Stone." He swallowed, and Tamara saw his Adam's apple bob. "You know damn well we could take you in on the strength of that."

"I know damn well you could try. And I know damn well you wouldn't succeed." Stone's reply was innocuous enough, but at the look in his eyes Trainor took an involuntary step back.

"Calm down, Bill, he's jerking your chain." Knopf threw his partner an impatient glance. "It's how he gets his rocks off. You always thought you were pretty smart, didn't you, McQueen?"

"Let's just say the competition didn't worry me, Tommy." Stone lifted his shoulders. "Look, this old lang syne crap's warmed my heart, but you boys probably have a dumpster fire or something like that to look into, so I'll see you around. Let's go, Tam."

"It's not a dumpster fire we're working on. But you knew that, didn't you?" Knopf planted his bulk in their path. "Imagine my surprise when I came across your name on the list of residents in that rooming house, McQueen. And imagine my surprise when I found that Chandra Boyleston had signed you out of the hospital."

His smile was unpleasant. "The lieutenant didn't want to tell us where you were until I reminded her of the penalties for obstructing an arson investigation. You make a habit of offering a bed to guys who get burned out of their homes, sweetheart?"

This last question was directed at Tamara, and at it she felt Stone's hand on her arm tense. She drew in a tight breath.

"If you've got a point, get to it, Knopf. Otherwise move out of my way." She kept her voice steady. "Because if you don't, imagine your surprise when I make you."

Knopf's small eyes blinked. "Okay," he said evenly. "I'll keep it short. You were seen near the site yesterday, McQueen. If I find out you're trying to cowboy in on this investigation, I'm taking you down and your firefighter girlfriend with you. Is that straight enough?"

"Straight as a die, Tommy." Without making a move that Tamara could see, Stone seemed somehow bigger, as if he'd shifted his weight to the balls of his feet. "And I'll be just as straight with you. If I even think you're trying to drag Tamara into our private little feud, I'll make sure the rest of your career consists of giving Sparky the firedog safety talks to grade-schoolers. The Dazzlers fire wasn't the only one you two screwed up."

"You're never going to let that go, are you, Mc-Queen?"

Unexpectedly, Trainor spoke. He moved slightly and the sunlight caught the thick lenses of his glasses, reflecting blindingly off them. Tamara was reminded of childhood experiments she and Claudia had performed with a magnifying glass and small piles of dried grass.

"This isn't the Dazzlers nightclub, so if you're looking to get back into the department in a blaze of glory you picked the wrong case. Right now it doesn't even look like arson, luckily for you."

He stopped abruptly, as if he'd said more than he'd meant to, and Tamara saw Knopf's face darken.

"What's that supposed to mean?" In the sudden silence Stone's question sounded startlingly loud. Knopf shook his head.

"Nothing, McQueen. Nothing at all. You just got Billy boy going, that's all." He didn't look at Trainor as he spoke. "Don't forget what I said. This was a friendly warning, McQueen. It's the only one you're going to get."

With a curt jerk of his head at Trainor he started to move away, but the younger man didn't follow him immediately. Instead his gaze sought Tamara's, and when he spoke the rancor he'd displayed a moment earlier was no longer in evidence.

"You and she used to be close, didn't you? I—I was sorry to hear about her death."

Above his collar his Adam's apple bobbed once more, and then with an awkward shrug he turned on his heel. As he and Knopf strode away Tamara saw the heavier man remonstrating with him, but Trainor seemed to be ignoring him.

"What was that about?" With a frown she turned to Stone. "How did he know I had a connection to Claudia?"

"I don't know." He was still watching Trainor and Knopf, now halfway down the block and getting into a nondescript sedan. "Jack said he played poker with him so I guess it's possible Claudia's name came up in the past." The sedan pulled out into the stream of traffic and some of the stiffness seemed to drain from Stone's posture. "But why offer his condolences?"

"He could have been trying to make it obvious his fight was just with you." She gave him a sharp glance. "Knopf was right, you *were* trying to jerk their chains."

"They were asking for it," he growled. "Besides, I figured if I made them mad one of them might let something slip, although I've got to admit my money was on Tommy, not Bill."

"They'd like to pin the fire on you, wouldn't they?" The notion was ludicrous. "You think those two ever heard of concepts like motive and means?"

"Trainor came close to buying the roast-beef sandwich motive for torching the Red Spot." He flashed her a grin before his expression sobered.

"But hell, they couldn't have picked a worse time to show up," he said huskily. "About Claudia's letters, Tam—I was way out of line there. I was out of line on everything I said. I just thought—" He stopped. "You know, that roast-beef sandwich is actually pretty good, and Chandra's probably wondering where we are. How about I buy you dinner?''

A corner of his mouth lifted, but she wasn't distracted. ''You just thought what?'' He didn't answer her, and her brows drew together. ''I want to know, Stone. What were you going to say?''

His gaze met hers directly. ''Just that I get the feeling you've spent your whole life trying to prove something, although what it is I don't know,'' he said. ''But you seem to need to keep up that tough facade at all costs. I want you to know I'm the one person you don't have to keep up the facade for, Tam.''

As if he couldn't help himself, his hand went to her chin. Lightly tipping it up, he ran his thumb along the fullness of her bottom lip, his gaze never leaving hers.

''Honey, I'm one of the world's great losers,'' he said softly. ''I hit rock-bottom years ago, and I just kept going down. Over the last few months I started climbing back up again, but I've still got a hell of a long way to go. I'm no one you have to impress, sweetheart. If you need someone to hang on to once in a while when being tough gets to be too much, I'm your man.''

Trust Stone, Tamara thought, staring speechlessly at him. Trust him to pick such an inappropriate time and place to disarm her so completely.

''You're such a jerk, McQueen,'' she said unsteadily. Five minutes ago she'd thought she'd used up her quota of tears for the next few months, at least. It seemed she'd been wrong. She felt a pinprick tingle behind her eyelids. ''You've seen what I look like when I cry. Why would you want to go and start me up again?''

Definitely a jerk, she thought as he smiled at her. It wasn't the sexy, hard-edged grin or the ironic quirk of his mouth she'd seen before, but a slow, guileless, incredibly sweet smile. Only a jerk would have kept that smile back until now. Only a jerk would have hauled that smile out at the exact moment when she was feeling almost vulnerable enough to fall in—

Hold it right there, King!

The voice inside her head was sharp enough to bring her musings to an abrupt halt—and just in time, too, Tamara thought, her sanity returning in a rush. For God's sake, her first and only foray into dewy-eyed romance had been a total disaster. If and when she gathered up her nerve to take the plunge again, she intended to make darn sure she was diving into a crystal-clear pool, preferably with depth markers plainly painted on its sides, rather than taking an impulsive header into some seductive lagoon that was probably chock-full of jagged, barely submerged rocks.

She tilted her chin higher and his hand slipped away.

"Believe me, McQueen, the waterworks were completely out of character." She managed a rueful smile. "I don't really see myself needing a manly shoulder to cry on, but I'll take you up on your first offer. You spring for the roast beef sandwiches and I'll chip in for the pie and coffee, how's that?"

For a moment she thought he wasn't going to answer her. Then that smoke-gray gaze changed almost imperceptibly, and she realized he'd taken a step away from her.

"Not bad." His tone was easy enough, she noted with relief. He put his hand lightly on her back as they began walking toward the diner.

"Damned impressive, in fact," he added. "In two sentences you not only managed to shoot me down in flames but you also stipulated we were splitting the tab for dinner. I just figured out why that neutered ex-tomcat of yours has such a pissy attitude...and hell, at least Pangor would have been anesthetized while the procedure was being performed on him.''

''The procedure?''

They'd reached the Red Spot, and she put her hand out to push open the diner's door. He reached past her, his expression unreadable, and suddenly she got it.

''For crying out loud, McQueen,'' she said, feeling swift color flooding into her cheeks. As they stepped into the crowded diner she automatically raised her voice. ''If I'd had any idea your masculine self-esteem was so fragile I wouldn't have said anything at all.''

''You think everyone heard you okay, honey?'' McQueen muttered.

''I know I did.'' The dry rejoinder came from a table a few feet away by the wall. Lieutenant Boyleston, an empty glass by her elbow, held out a wrist and tapped wearily at the slim gold watch encircling it. ''The big hand's on twelve and the little hand's on seven, McQueen. I'd just about given up on you.''

''Cut me some freakin' slack, will you, Chand?'' Stone's retort was edged. A waiter in what was obviously the eatery's uniform of black pants, white shirt and fire-engine red suspenders attempted to move by him without making eye contact, but Stone snagged him by one suspender. ''Not so fast, buddy,'' he growled. ''Another glass of red wine here.'' He raised an eyebrow at Tamara, taking her seat beside Chandra.

''House red's good for me,'' she said distantly.

''Two glasses of red,'' Stone corrected. ''And I'll have whatever's on draft, as long as it's not some watered-down microbrewery beer of the week. Got it?''

He began to pull out the chair beside Chandra, and

then stopped as abruptly as if he'd been shot. He turned back to the departing waiter.

"Instead of draft, make it coffee."

"Coffee?" The waiter looked confused, but at McQueen's glower he shut his mouth with a snap and hurried away.

"How'd you remember I liked red wine, Stone?" If Boyleston's question was an attempt at tactful diversion, it didn't work. He glared at her as he sat down.

"I'm an ex-drunk, Chand. We might forget our own names occasionally and apparently we even forget we're on the wagon once in a while, but we never forget a drink. Let's talk about something else, all right?"

"Sure." Boyleston smiled thinly at him. "We could talk about how I put my butt on the line trying to get that information you asked me for, McQueen. We could talk about how Trainor and Knopf have been putting the screws on me just because I know you. We could talk about the fact that I should be at home right now with a husband and a son I see rarely enough as it is, but instead I gave up my evening for you."

"And I guess we could talk about how did a sorry son of a bitch like me ever rate the friendship of someone like you." Stone reached across the table for Boyleston's hand. "Hell, I'm sorry for being late and for almost biting your head off, Chand. Why do you put up with me?"

"Maybe you've forgotten why, McQueen," Chandra said steadily, her gaze softening. "I never will."

Watching them, Tamara saw a flush of faint color suddenly appear beneath the tan of Stone's skin. As their waiter approached with the drinks he disengaged his hand from Chandra's.

"God, let it go, woman," he said uncomfortably. "That was years ago."

"Ten and a half, to be exact," Chandra agreed. She picked up her menu. "Are we all having the roast beef sandwich?"

"I've talked it up to Tam so I guess I'm going to have to." For the first time since they'd arrived, Stone looked directly at Tamara, his eyes darkening slightly.

"Tamara?" Chandra's voice held a note of inquiry. "The special for you, too?"

Disconcerted, she tore her gaze from Stone's. "What? Oh sure, Lieut. Sounds good."

The use of the other woman's rank was habit, but as soon as she'd spoken Tamara realized how stiffly formal it had sounded. As Chandra smiled at a comment of Stone's and he began telling her about their encounter with Knopf and Trainor, she pulled her glass of wine toward her and took a hasty gulp.

It was true, she thought in dismay. Why hadn't she seen it in herself before? She *did* keep the world at arm's length, from her insistence on addressing Chandra as a superior rather than a friend in a casual setting like this to the way she'd unthinkingly rebuffed Stone.

"I'm the one person you don't have to keep up the facade for, Tam."

He'd opened himself up to her and she'd shut him out. Why?

You know why, King. You've known from the moment you first laid eyes on him. He was a stranger, but all it took was one look and you felt as if he'd handed you his soul. All it took was one look and you knew you'd just given yours to him. Terrifying, isn't it?

"Sorry, Stone, I just don't buy it. It can't be, not after all these years."

Chandra's voice was firm enough to break into Tamara's thoughts. Seizing on any excuse to silence her own inner voice before it came up with further uncomfortable self-revelations, she switched her attention to the conversation that had been going on around her.

"I don't buy it either—not yet. But what if Leung's results show—"

Stone fell silent as their waiter came up to the table. Not until the man had placed their meals in front of them and left again did he go on, his tone low.

"What if his results reveal that the same accelerant was used, Chand? We'd never come across that compound before and since I resigned it hasn't shown up again."

"It's not exactly a fingerprint," Chandra said. "It's a bastardized version of rocket fuel, too unstable to be put to any legitimate use and probably developed in the fifties. You told me the retired scientist you talked to said he'd heard of people actually trying to cook stuff like that up on their kitchen stove, and blowing whole houses to smithereens." She picked up her fork and speared a French fry. "If there was enough of that around seven years ago to start half a dozen blazes then it's not impossible some other firebug might use it in the future. But your theory's a little too close to—"

She stopped. Popping the French fry into her mouth, she looked down at her plate, her face suddenly drawn.

"A little too close to paranoia, Chand?" Smiling crookedly, Stone picked up half of his sandwich and took a bite, his gaze on Chandra's bent head. "Don't you think I know that?"

Tamara felt her patience give way. "Would someone fill me in on what this is all about?" she demanded. "What theory? And why is it paranoid, dammit?"

"McQueen thinks the arsonist responsible for the string of fires he was working on when he resigned took a little holiday himself," Chandra said flatly. "And now he's back."

"You put it like that and of course it sounds crazy," Stone growled. "I told you, it's still just a hunch."

"If it's just a hunch, then why did you insist I find Glenda Fodor's current address for you, McQueen?" Chandra's lips tightened. "For God's sake, arsonists don't stop setting fires and then start up again years later."

She shook her head decisively. "We know he was never caught. That leaves only one explanation for why the fires stopped."

"For the same reason the authorities figure that rash of apartment fires in Baltimore ten years ago ended so suddenly," Stone said curtly. "I read the textbooks, Lieutenant. I know even arsonists get killed in car accidents or have heart attacks."

"And that's what had to have happened in this case," Chandra snapped back. "What *didn't* happen is that he took a time out and then decided to get back into the game."

Tamara picked up the massive slab of crusty bread and juicy roast beef, flicking a glance first at Chandra's closed features and then at Stone's shuttered expression.

"Why the hell not, Chandra? I don't think Stone's theory is crazy at all," she said, sinking her teeth into the thick sandwich. "Who's Glenda Fodor?" she added inelegantly, her mouth full.

Stone had been right. The Red Spot's roast beef on a bun was pretty good, if messy. Hastily she leaned over her plate and grabbed for her serviette.

He'd been right about the darn sandwich and he'd

been right about her. How someone so incredibly inept at social interaction as McQueen had managed to read her as unerringly as he had was more than baffling, it was annoying. But he had. He'd only known her for a little over forty-eight hours, and he'd put his finger on something she'd gone twenty-seven years without recognizing in herself.

Even her choice of career fitted. She rushed in and out of crisis points in other people's lives, and the next day there was always another emergency to focus on, another fire to put out. She never actually had to stick around and get involved, and that was the way she'd wanted it till now.

Arm's length had been comfortable. Arm's length had been safe. She was probably going to miss keeping the world at arm's length, Tamara thought resignedly. But it was no use. Stone McQueen had come crashing into her safely detached existence and even if she wanted to, she knew she would never be able to erect all her barriers again. She was involved—not only with the investigation but with the man.

And seeing as how she'd finally admitted it, there really wasn't any point in half measures.

McQueen had just gotten himself a partner. Partners backed each other up. She began to take another bite of her sandwich and then stopped.

Two pairs of eyes were staring at her. The narrowed brown pair belonged to Chandra. The gray ones were Stone's and they were fixed on her with a kind of uncertain hope. She gazed at him steadily, and slowly he smiled at her.

She smiled back at him. Her heart did a foolishly show-offish triple-gainer as it dived off the cliff and into the lagoon.

"I always suspected Glenda Fodor knew the arsonist's identity. I was pretty sure she was his girlfriend," Stone said huskily. His smiled faltered. "But maybe Chandra's right, Tam. Maybe this whole thing is crazy. Hell, for the past seven years the only thing I've investigated is the bottom of a bottle. Maybe I drank away whatever skills I used to have."

She was such a jerk, Tamara thought shakily. Who had she been trying to kid? She didn't think of him as her partner. A whole lot of the time they weren't even friends. He was an irritating, abrasive, exasperating man, and if she didn't do something right now to drive the last of the uncertainty from his gaze she was pretty sure she was going to start blubbing again.

"Big deal, Stone, you hit the skids there for a while," she said dismissively. "But you've been clean and sober for eight months now and no other essential McQueen elements like charm and personality got lost in the shuffle. Why would you suddenly have mislaid your ability to handle an investigation?" She picked up her sandwich again. "The pie here good, too?" she asked casually, taking an unladylike mouthful of roast beef.

It was the horseradish, she thought. That was her story and she was sticking to it. Everyone knew horseradish made your eyes water. It certainly wasn't because the damn man was looking at her as if she'd just handed him back something he'd lost a long time ago, for crying out loud. Even as she watched, his shoulders straightened belligerently and a corner of his mouth lifted in a grin.

"The coconut cream's not bad." His reply was as offhand as her query had been, and out of the corner of her eye Tamara saw Chandra watching both of them disbelievingly. "Pack that away first and then try a piece," he added. "Hell, I'm buying, honey."

She swallowed with difficulty. With even more of an effort she managed to glare at him.

"Of *course* you're buying, McQueen," she growled.

Chapter Ten

...and I've quit smoking! I wouldn't have been able to live with myself if I'd let Petra down. For a five-year-old, she can be pretty stern! I wish I could pick up the phone to tell you, Tam-Tam, since I know how unlikely it is that you'll ever read this. Remember when Aunt Kate took us to Cape Cod and we each put a secret message in a bottle and threw them into the ocean? That's what my letters to you are. Maybe a long time from now you'll be standing on a shore and the waves will carry one of my bottles in. You'll have every right to throw it back into the ocean, but just maybe you'll bend down and pick it up. It's always the same message. I love you, Tam-Tam. I've never stopped missing you. And there's not a day goes by that I don't wish I could go back and change the past.

All my love,

Claudie

Tamara folded the letter and slipped it back into the envelope. Even as she did a wet splotch fell onto the address, blurring the ink a little.

There had been similar blurs on the letter itself—some fresh and wet, and some that had dried long ago, before the missive had landed on Hendrick's desk to be filed away in accordance with Claudia's instructions to him. This one had been written two years previously, Tamara saw. It had been bobbing in the ocean for two years, and finally it had washed up onto shore.

"Message received, Claudie," she whispered. "I won't throw any of them back. They're all I have of you—the letters, and that little girl you left in my care."

She wiped her eyes. There were still at least a dozen letters she hadn't read, but they would keep. When she'd finished reading them all she would put them away in a safe place, to be taken out whenever she needed to feel Claudia's presence.

It wouldn't be like having her back. But after seven years of locking the memories of their friendship away, regaining them was a comfort.

Glancing up at the kitchen clock she saw with surprise that it was nearly eleven. Carefully she gathered up the pile of letters, but as she stretched the elastic band around them it broke, shooting across the room to bounce off the nose of an offended Pangor.

"I didn't do it on purpose." She released the elastic that confined her hair at the nape of her neck and used it to bind the letters. "I suppose you wish Mr. Wonderful were here. Don't worry, he'll be back soon."

She filled the kettle and plugged it in. Restlessly she boosted herself to the counter, her feet crossed at the ankles and bouncing idly against the cupboard doors.

Chandra still didn't buy Stone's theory. She'd said as much at the Red Spot, but that hadn't stopped her from handing him a scrap of paper with an address scribbled on it.

"You didn't get this from me, McQueen," she'd warned. "And any visit you pay to the Fodor woman is going to be strictly unauthorized, so if she doesn't want to talk just leave."

"I'll handle her with kid gloves," McQueen had protested. "But if her old boyfriend's back I've got a feeling our Glenda's not going to need much persuasion to talk."

He'd seen Tamara's incomprehension. "Sorry, I forgot you don't know the background. Glenda Fodor came to my attention in the first place because at two of the early fires I suspected as being this bastard's work, she should have been in the buildings when they were torched, and she wasn't. When I learned that a part-time salesgirl who'd called in sick half an hour before a fire started at the store where she worked and a tenant who'd moved out of the Alpine Apartments a day before *that* building went up in flames both had the same name, one hell of a warning bell went off in my head."

"Glenda's not that bright. That's probably why her story was so unshakeable," Chandra said dryly. "She just kept saying she must have been lucky."

"Yeah. I knew she was lying, but since she obviously wasn't the arsonist herself I couldn't press her." Stone shook his head. "But then I learned from one of her former neighbors at the Alpine that she'd started going out with a new boyfriend about a week before she'd moved. Glenda had told me she wasn't seeing anyone."

"And the sketchy description the neighbor gave of the boyfriend matched Robert Pascoe, a suspected arsonist for hire no one knew too much about," Chandra added. "But since Glenda denied having a boyfriend, that was the end of that lead."

"Only because I was hauled up on the carpet for suggesting we put her under surveillance,'' Stone said curtly. "She was on the edge, goddammit. I think she wanted an excuse to crack. If we'd given her that excuse, then maybe the Mitchell Towers blaze—"

Chandra's next words were quiet. "Someone made the wrong decision, Stone, but it wasn't you. One of these days you're going to have to realize you can't change the past."

His head had jerked up, the raw pain behind his gaze an almost tangible force. "Hell, Chand, I know I can't change the past," he'd said harshly. "I've even come to realize that it can't be blotted out. All I'm trying to do now is to make sure it doesn't repeat itself, and whether you buy into my theory or not, that's exactly what I think is going to happen."

Beside Tamara the kettle began to whistle. She reached over and unplugged it.

Stone had seemed unusually edgy after his dispute with Chandra, and when the two women had ordered more coffee he'd gotten abruptly up from the table, as if he couldn't stay still any longer.

"I'm going down to the Y, see if I can find a pick-up game of basketball," he'd said without preamble. "If I'm not home by the time you want to turn in, that's my problem."

He'd turned and gestured to their waiter on the other side of the room. Before he'd gotten more than a couple of tables away he turned back. His gaze had sought hers.

"I just have to do something physical, Tam," he'd said tightly. "Wear myself out. Do you understand?"

"I think so." She'd kept her own voice steady. "Do you understand that I'm behind you all the way on this, Stone?"

A fraction of the tension seemed to seep out of his

rigid posture. "I never worked with a partner before, honey," he said hoarsely. "Never thought I wanted one. I'm probably a real prick to work with."

"I'm sure you are, McQueen." She'd flapped a hand at him, her smile suddenly wobbly. "Go shoot some damn hoops."

"He's going to hit the bars." Chandra's comment had come as Stone had walked away, and although there had been no condemnation in it something in Tamara had flared.

"I'm getting real tired of hearing about how Stone McQueen's nowhere near the man he used to be," she said sharply. "Have you considered the possibility that after what he's gone through he might be even tougher than he was before, Chandra? For God's sake, that's how they strengthen steel—by putting it through fire. For a friend you seem awfully eager to write both him *and* his theories off."

"That's not true!" Chandra's eyes had widened in denial. "I owe Stone my *life,* dammit, and if anyone's stuck by him all these years it's been—"

She'd fallen abruptly silent, and her gaze had gone to her hands, tightly clenched on the table. When she'd looked up, her features had been etched with strong emotion.

"Maybe you're right," she'd said. "Maybe it's my own past, not McQueen's, that's the problem. Hank's my second husband. You didn't know that, did you?"

"No." Tamara had frowned in confusion. "But what's—"

"No," Chandra had echoed. She'd given Tamara a searching look. "You've never exactly encouraged confidences. I wonder why that is?" She'd looked away. "John had always been a drinker. I married him thinking

I could change him. When he started hitting me I thought that was somehow my responsibility, too.''

"You don't have to tell me this." Tamara's words were automatic, and she regretted them immediately. "But—but I'd like to listen if it's not too hard for you to talk about," she added haltingly.

"It's hard." Her companion's tone was brittle. "It was harder at the time it was happening. I didn't tell anyone that the man I'd once loved had turned into a terrifying stranger who used me as a punching bag. I kept telling people at work I'd walked into a door or slipped on a newly washed floor, and they kept pretending they believed me."

She looked up from her hands at Tamara. "One day I ran into McQueen for the first time since he'd transferred into the investigative division. I was sporting a shiner no amount of concealer had been able to cover completely, and I began to go into my usual routine. Everyone else had been polite enough to let me get away with it, but I'd forgotten McQueen didn't give a damn about polite. He told me to cut the crap and tell him who was beating me up so he could do something about it. I *wanted* to tell him, Tamara." Chandra's eyes darkened. "But I was ashamed to. I told him to mind his own business."

"I've noticed McQueen doesn't do that too well," Tamara said softly.

Chandra's smile was faint. "No. But this time his bull-headedness saved my life. That night John kept trying to pick a fight with me. When I told him I was tired and I was going to bed, that was all he needed."

The tightly clasped hands on the table were shaking, Tamara saw. She covered them with her own as Chandra continued, her voice uneven.

"I remember lying on the bedroom floor trying to cover my head with my hands. I remember wishing I'd told Stone the truth, and screaming out his name as if he could hear me and save me. I remember seeing John's boot drawing back to kick me in the face, and knowing I was about to be murdered by my own husband."

Her hands shook uncontrollably in Tamara's grip. "And then I remember seeing Stone race in. He knocked John halfway across the room and when John came charging back, Stone simply and methodically beat him to within an inch of his life. At the end he stood over him and said in the coldest voice I'd heard any human being use that if John ever came near me again he was a dead man. Then he picked me up and drove me to the hospital." She looked up at Tamara, her eyes bright with tears. "I found out later he'd taken it upon himself to keep watch outside my house that night. He'd been worried about me."

"That sounds like him." Her own voice was far from steady, Tamara noted, and of the two of them it was hard to tell who was clasping whose hand the tightest. "No wonder you didn't give up on him when his own life unravelled."

"But I did." Chandra shook her head. "I've been telling myself how noble I've been to stick by him, when all the while I've let my experience with John color my reactions. No one can stop someone else from drinking. I didn't acknowledge the fact that Stone obviously found that out for himself, and did something about it."

"He's been going to AA for about eight months now. He says he hasn't had a drink since, and I believe him."

"So do I." Chandra had bitten her lip unhappily. "Maybe that's why I don't want to believe he's right about Robert Pascoe coming back to haunt him, Tamara.

Maybe I'm afraid that if it's true, Stone will be destroyed all over again—and this time he might never recover.''

Was there any possibility Chandra's fears could be right? Tamara wondered now. She saw Pangor prick up his ears and a split second later she, too heard the sound of footsteps coming up the walk. Already she could recognize his step, she realized as she slid off the counter. But could she truly say she knew the man?

Never in a million years, she told herself resignedly, hearing him twisting at the doorhandle and then swearing in what he probably thought was a low tone. But she knew all she needed to know, and what Chandra had told her tonight only bore out the impression she'd already formed.

Beneath that rough exterior was a man who embodied all the old-fashioned and unfashionable virtues of his sex. McQueen would go to the wall for the people he cared for. He believed that justice sometimes included vengeance, and whether he admitted it or not, he was a protector—of a woman he considered a friend, of the victims whose lives were torn apart by evil, of a little girl who'd put her trust in him. And he was used to playing a lone hand.

Too bad about that last one, Tamara thought, unlocking the dead bolt and opening the door. *The man's got to evolve a little, for crying out loud.*

''I had to wait half an hour to get into the showers. I figured you would have turned in already.'' He raised surprised eyebrows at her. She gave him an appraising look.

''And you were hoping that if you made enough noise you'd get me out of bed?''

''Something like that.'' His grin was unrepentant. ''Our team lost. Spectacularly,'' he added, following her into the kitchen. "Probably because our cheering section only consisted of an old wino who'd wandered in by mistake and fell asleep, and the other side had a couple of hookers rooting for them. You should have been there to even up the score, honey."

"I would have been, except I couldn't find my thigh-high rubber boots and my special spandex firegirl's outfit."

This wasn't her, Tamara thought, opening the refrigerator and hoping the color in her cheeks wasn't too visible. She didn't *banter*, for heaven's sake. Behind her she heard him laugh, and ridiculous pleasure spread through her. Retrieving a carton of milk, she turned to the counter.

"Besides, I got the impression you needed to be alone," she said carefully. Pulling a saucepan from the cupboard, she measured out two mugs of the milk. "You weren't just playing basketball tonight, were you, Stone? You were wrestling demons."

She turned to him, wondering if she'd gone too far. He returned her gaze steadily.

"Just the one." A corner of his mouth lifted but his eyes were clouded. "I'm sure Chandra thought the demon had got the better of me. Is that what you suspected?"

"No." His gaze cleared, and she was glad she'd answered so immediately. "It only had power over you when you didn't admit it existed, Stone, and you don't strike me as the type to hide the truth from yourself for long."

She switched on the stove's burner, suddenly a little unsure of the intimate turn the conversation had taken— the intimacy she herself had introduced. She was breaking all her rules tonight, she thought tremulously.

"Don't I?" She had to have imagined the odd note in his voice, because when she glanced over her shoulder he smiled at her before gesturing at the elastic-bound bundle on the table. "Taking on a few demons of your own, Tam?"

"I thought I was." She'd bought a couple of bars of milk chocolate on the way home from the Red Spot. Now she unwrapped one and broke it into squares. "But as soon as I started reading them it was as if I could hear Claudie's voice, Stone, and I realized that there weren't any demons at all. There was just an old friend—a friend I'd missed."

"A friend who hurt you." He frowned as she dropped the chocolate into the simmering milk. "What the hell's that?"

"Real hot chocolate, and you're going to drink it and love it, McQueen," Tamara replied unconcernedly. She found a wooden spoon in the utensil drawer and began stirring the milk. "Yes, what Claudia did hurt me terribly. But that's all I've allowed myself to remember about her, and tonight brought back everything else we'd shared. I decided that those good memories outweighed the single bad one. Does that make any sense?"

Instead of answering her question, he asked one of his own. "So you'd forgive an unforgivable action if there was enough on the other side of the scale to balance it?"

She shrugged, a little taken aback. "It would depend on the circumstances, I suppose. That's just the conclusion I came to in this particular case." She moved the pan from the burner. "You know, it wasn't even what she did that stayed with me for all these years, it was how she did it. Of course, I realize now she must have felt she had no choice."

"You did the arithmetic on Petra's age, too?" Stone took the mug she was holding out to him.

"I did the math, but it shouldn't have been necessary." She grimaced as she pulled out the chair across from him. "The signs were there at the time, and I refused to see them. Claudia and I were closer than sisters—how could I not have guessed she'd fallen in love with Rick? And how could I not have realized he'd fallen for her, especially when I never really felt I was the right one for him?"

She frowned at the steaming mug in front of her. "Maybe Claudia and I were more alike than I ever knew. Perhaps we both were more in love with the idea of creating a family of our own than with Rick himself." She raised her gaze to his. "But at the time I thought what I felt for him was the kind of love poets wrote about, the kind people died for. When I found out the wedding wasn't going to take place I thought I *would* die. Being me, I wasn't about to let anyone know how I felt."

"Don't tell me you had your secret tissue stash back then." His teasing didn't camouflage the uncharacteristic gentleness in his voice. "How did you handle it, Tam?"

"I didn't."

She heard the dangerous brittleness in her answer, and hastily raised her mug of chocolate to her lips. Was she really going to tell him? she thought, swallowing a mouthful of the too-hot liquid. After never telling anyone, was it finally going to be to Stone McQueen, of all people, that she recounted the shameful details of that terrible night?

He's the only one you can tell, she thought with sudden certainty. *He knows what it's like to hit rock bottom, to sink lower than you ever thought yourself capable of sinking. You've carried this secret around for seven years, dammit, and he's the first person you've met who might understand.*

"I didn't handle it well at all. It just looked like I was handling it," she said, avoiding his eyes. "Our reception was to have been held in one of the big hotels downtown—no expense spared, Uncle Jack had said. I walked up the aisle in my wedding dress and told the whole churchful of guests that I planned to go ahead with the party and I hoped everyone would join me." She smiled shakily at him. "I think half of them thought I'd lost my mind, and the other half thought it was some kind of tasteless gag. But in the end most of them showed up at the reception, though my aunt and uncle refused to."

"Jack should have done more than that," McQueen said harshly. "Dammit, he was a firefighter. He knows what shock looks like. Didn't he see you'd gone over the edge?"

"His immediate concern was Aunt Kate." Tamara's reply was defensive. "She was already having trouble with her heart back then, and he wanted to get her home."

She paused. "You know, I've told other people this much of the story. You're the first who's ever seen that. But the fact that I was in shock doesn't explain why I ended the night the way I did."

"You got a little drunk? You went a little crazy?" He looked away, his jaw tight. "Hell, honey, you don't have to go into the details."

"That's my line, McQueen." She gave an unsteady laugh to cover her sudden discomfiture. She stared into her mug, and then raised it to her mouth. "But you're probably right—what do the details matter? If you've seen one jilted bride go off the rails, you've seen them all, I guess." She took a sip of her drink and managed a grin. "So what do you think of Hot Chocolate a la King? Admit it—it beats the pants off Omelet McQueen."

She looked up, and saw he was watching her. For a moment their gazes locked—hers wide and too bright, his dark with what she took at first glance to be anger, although she knew instinctively it wasn't directed at her. This time she was the first to look away, but even as she did he spoke.

"Tell me the details, Tam." His tone was low. "I didn't mean to shut you out. What else happened that night, honey?"

She shook her head and stared down at her hands. "It was like you said. I got a little drunk. I went a little crazy. Drink your hot chocolate, Stone."

She heard him sigh. Then out of the corner of her eye she saw him pick up his mug. He tipped his head back, the muscles of his neck working as he drained it at one go. He set it down again on the table with an audible click.

"You're right. Hot Chocolate a la King wins hands down," he said huskily. "But Omelet McQueen sucked, so don't let it go to your head. What else happened that night, Tam?"

She looked up at him, her smile uneven. "You jerk, McQueen," she said, her laugh catching painfully in her throat. He smiled back at her, and it was the smile he'd given her earlier in the car—the smile that had the power to undo her completely. Her vision blurred, and through the blur she saw him lean toward her and take her hands in his.

"Tell me, honey." There was an edge of pain in his voice. "Tell me and I'll make it go away."

"Oh, Stone." She shook her head. "I wish you could. But you can't. Nobody can."

"Then maybe telling me will make it hurt less, Tam," he said softly. "You got a little drunk. You went a little crazy. And then what did you do?"

She'd been wrong, Tamara thought, gripping his hands desperately. Not even Stone would understand. *She* hadn't been able to understand her actions, so how could she expect him to? The next morning she'd looked at herself in the mirror with total self-loathing. She'd hated the woman she'd seen looking back at her.

You're too damned afraid to trust anyone enough to fall in love with them.

He'd told her that the second day he'd known her. He'd been almost right, but not quite.

No, McQueen, she told him silently, feeling the tears slip down her cheeks. *What I'm really afraid of is that no one could love me back—not even a man who says he knows what it's like to go down as far as it's possible to go. And I'm about to prove that to myself right now.*

She blinked her tears away and met his eyes unflinchingly, her own gaze hardening.

"I went looking for a stranger. I found one—a man I'd never met before in my life, a man who didn't know me. When I'd found him I took him up to the bridal suite and let him give it to the bride all night long." She gave him a tight smile. "And I haven't been able to live with myself since, because as ashamed as I am about what I did, some part of me—"

Her voice faltered. Her gaze wavered. She forced herself to go on, and her words came out in a harsh whisper.

"Because some part of me just *loved* it, Stone."

Chapter Eleven

Lying on her bed, Tamara stared into the darkness, wondering what had possessed her to spill her tawdry little confession to Stone McQueen. She'd been wondering that for the past hour, ever since she'd spoken those last shameful words and had fallen silent, waiting for him to respond.

He hadn't. He'd looked down at his hands, still wrapped around hers. His jaw had clenched into rigidity.

Were you hoping he'd give you absolution? The voice in her head was mocking. McQueen's never been able to absolve himself, so how did you think he'd help you off the hook?

When she'd pulled away he'd let her go. He hadn't looked up as she'd left the kitchen.

He'd known what she wanted him to say, but he hadn't been able to give her the comforting lies she needed. She wasn't fool enough to think what she'd told him had wounded him personally in any way, or naive enough to believe a man like McQueen would have been shocked at her confession. But he knew her. He knew that what another woman might have been able to accept as a regrettable moral lapse had been much more to her.

You wanted to look into its face. You thought you might see yourself looking back.

Right from the start McQueen had seen into the most hidden corner of her soul, had guessed at her most dreadful suspicion. For as long as she could remember she'd lived with the fear that she couldn't trust herself—that the chaos she saw raging around her when she went up against the beast had somehow escaped from *her*. And on the morning following that night of uncontrolled passion, she'd known all her fears were true.

The blackness behind her closed eyes lightened suddenly to charcoal, and her pain was instantly transformed into trembling anger.

"Get the hell out of my bedroom, McQueen." She opened her eyes as she spoke, and saw him silhouetted in the doorway of her room. What remaining tears she hadn't yet had a chance to shed thickened her voice. "That's one of the house rules, remember?"

"I'm tired of the rules, honey."

He walked over to the bed. He was barefoot and bare chested, Tamara saw, suddenly all too aware that under the concealing bedclothes she herself was wearing a sleep shirt and nothing else. He looked down at her, his expression closed.

"And not just yours. I'm tired of my own, too." He flapped his hand impatiently at her. "Shove over. I'm coming in."

He'd actually reached down to flip back the sheets before she found her voice. "Are you out of your mind?" She scrambled awkwardly to a kneeling position, stiff with disbelief. "You even *try* to get in this bed with me, McQueen, and you'll wish you hadn't. What the hell's gotten into you?"

Even as the outraged question left her lips she knew
the answer. She felt the breath leave her body in a rush.

"You think the rules have *changed,* don't you? You
think if I'd do it once, what's the harm in seeing if I'll
do it again, this time with you. You total bastard!"

He was frowning at her.

"That wasn't *me,* do you understand?" She brought
her face closer. "That's why it tore me apart—why it
still tears me apart! What I did that night has nothing to
do with who I am, with *what* I am, McQueen. I don't
even *know* the woman who slept with that stranger."

"It's not the woman who slept with him you don't
want to know, honey." Slowly he locked his gaze with
hers. In the light from the hall it was possible to see the
dark glitter behind his eyes. "It's the woman who still
thinks of that night, the woman who loved what he did
to her, what she did to him. And that woman's you,
whether you admit it or not."

Until this moment, she'd never raised her hand to anyone in her life. Blindly she brought it up, but he caught
her wrist just as her palm reached his face. He shook his
head.

"I won't be your whipping boy, Tam. I'll let you use
me just about any other way you want, but I won't be
that." The muscle in his forearm flexed as she tried to
pull her wrist away from his grasp. Instead of releasing
her, lightly he dragged her hand along the unshaven line
of his jaw. "For what it's worth, I didn't come in here
for the reason you think. I came because I couldn't make
myself stay away any longer. I came because I just
wanted to hold you."

His breath was warm on her skin. He bent his head,
and for an instant she felt his mouth against her palm.

He curled her fingers into her hand and released his

grip. Swiftly she pulled away from him, the words spilling from her.

"You let me walk away from you in the kitchen. You didn't say a damn thing, McQueen." She heard the raw edge in her voice. "Now you tell me I'm exactly the woman I don't want to be, as if you're bestowing some kind of accolade on me. Is *this* how you make it all go away for me? Because as far as I'm concerned, you've only made things worse."

"That's why I let you walk away." His tone hardened. "Dammit, I *know* you. The possibility that you might not really be that closed-off Tamara King sitting alone in her car with her little packets of tissues is something you just can't face. As for the other…"

His words trailed off. He straightened to his full height and with an impatient gesture raked his hand through his hair.

"I can make it all go away, all right. Hell, I can make you forget everything, and you know it. I'm down the hall if you decide you want me to."

She'd been expecting comfort from Stone McQueen? Tamara asked herself in incredulous fury. She'd been insane. He'd prowled in here with all the battered arrogance of some back-alley tomcat, he'd flashed an acre of tanned skin and hard muscle at her, and after proving he'd lost none of his trademark abrasiveness he'd as much as offered himself as stud to her.

And now he was walking away from the wreckage. In one blurred movement she threw back the sheets and swung her feet to the floor. Before he'd gotten halfway to the door she was right behind him, her hand on his arm, roughly spinning him around to face her.

"Go ahead, then," she said tightly. "Show me your moves, McQueen."

"What?" That wayward strand of dark brown hair had fallen into his eyes again, and he shook it aside. "What do you mean, my moves?"

"Drop it," she snapped. "You can't carry off dumb and innocent, so don't try. You know what I mean, Stone. You keep telling me you can make me forget what I did with another man. Prove it."

"For crying out—" He sounded nonplussed. "Right here? Right now? Just like this?"

"I take it back, you can carry it off." She gave him a hard look. "The first part, anyway. Yeah, right here and now, McQueen."

She felt his arm tense under her hand. He narrowed his eyes at her. "I don't think so, honey," he said slowly. "I don't think you really want anything I could give you tonight. That's not what you're looking for here."

"Then make me want it." As he started to turn away she tightened her grip on him. "Unless you're backing down, of course," she added. "Was it all just talk, McQueen?"

He stared at her. Then he gave a short laugh. "It isn't fair," he said evenly. "I get the rep for being so damned insensitive, and all the while you've got me beat hands down. What's this about, Tam?"

"You just said it—your reputation." She smiled thinly at him. "You look good. You've made my heart beat a little faster once or twice. But can you make me forget?" She tipped her head to one side. "Nah, I don't think so. Whoever he was, he was a son of a bitch, but he was fabulous, McQueen. And the woman you say I am went *crazy* in his arms that night."

Her flow of words stopped as suddenly as it had begun, and in the abrupt silence that fell between them

Tamara thought she could hear her heart crashing in her chest. All at once it seemed as if the only thing keeping her upright was her hold on his arm.

He'd wanted her to open up to him. He'd wanted her to share her emotions. She'd known it was a bad idea, known she didn't do touchy-feely well, and yet she'd let him talk her into it.

This was the result. He'd forced her to face the woman in the mirror. He'd forced her to admit that woman had been a part of her—was *still* a part of her.

This time his destructiveness had gone too far, she thought dully. This time he had to know what he'd done.

"For years the only way I've been able to handle the memories is by telling myself there was no way I could act like that again." She realized she was still clutching his arm, and she let her hand slip away. "I think the most I'd ever had to drink in my life before then was a white wine spritzer or two, and I'd been putting away the champagne like it was water since I'd arrived at my so-called reception. So I told myself it had been the alcohol and the pain that had made me behave so out of character. That was true, up to a point."

She shook her head, her eyes squeezing shut. "I never even got a good look at his *face*. Some time during the evening I went to the ladies room and on the way back I took a wrong turn. I ended up in one of the hotel's bars—a dark cave of a room—and by then I was drunk enough to decide I preferred to pass out there so I plopped myself down at a secluded table in the corner. I must have stood out like a beacon, of course. I was still in my wedding dress. But it wasn't until I heard someone ask me what I was drinking that I realized there was another person at the table with me. By that time the room was already going round and round."

She opened her eyes. If she simply stared straight ahead she could focus on his chest. It looked solid. Just enough light filtered in from the hallway to delineate the slabs of muscle beneath that expanse of hide, and there were just enough shadows in her bedroom to turn the sprinkling of hair arrowing down to the fly of his chinos into a dark, mysterious tangle.

She blinked. She went on, her tone low.

"I told him I wanted more champagne. I told him I'd never been drunk before but that I liked being drunk, if being drunk meant you felt kind of numb and floaty. He said he liked it, too, but that maybe I'd better be getting back to my husband. When he said that I fell completely apart."

"You told him what had happened." McQueen's voice was emotionless. She nodded.

"I think it was what's commonly called a crying jag. That's when he offered to get me up to my room. The next thing I remember I was lying on an enormous white satin bed, and he was standing in the doorway, about to leave."

"What a freakin' hero." Now there was some emotion in Stone's voice. It took a moment for her to identify it as cold rage. "Obviously he didn't follow through on his noble impulse."

"Because I wouldn't *let* him," Tamara said gratingly. "I told him I'd already been rejected by one man that day, and I didn't think I could stand it if a second one walked away from me. I asked him what it was about me that made me so undesirable that no one seemed to want me. Then I started crying again. I didn't stop until he put his arms around me and kissed me in the dark. As soon as he did it was just—"

She stopped. She heard him take in a tense breath.

"It was just what?"

"It was just like he set me on *fire*," she rasped. "God help me, McQueen, he did things to me I'd never even let myself imagine before, and I was a more than willing participant. I fell asleep in the end in his arms, completely satiated. It would have been just before dawn that I woke up, because it was still dark. I remember being thankful it was."

She remembered more than that, Tamara thought. She remembered the soft darkness pressing in on her, the unfamiliar weight of a man's leg thrown over hers, his heartbeat under her palm. She'd never woken up in a man's embrace before. She'd never felt so totally and absolutely *secure*, so completely safe. She'd felt his hand spread wide against the back of her head under the unbound fall of her hair, snugging her into the hollow of his neck, and with a little sigh she'd closed her eyes again and breathed in the warmth of his skin.

And then her eyes had flown open in shock. In the darkness she could just make out the white glimmer of yards of crumpled satin spilled across the floor, and everything had come rushing back—Claudia's note, the travesty of a reception she'd fled from, the stranger she'd fled to. With stark clarity every erotic moment of the past few hours had tumbled through her mind, and a wave of incredible shame had washed over her.

She'd heard herself moaning in incoherent denial, felt herself struggling against the strong arms holding her, and for a second those arms had tightened. She'd thought she felt the hand cradling the back of her head stroke gently down the length of her hair and for the space of one heartbeat, perhaps two, her panic had halted. Then it had come back in full force and her moans had become a jumble of desperate phrases, guilt-ridden self-accusations.

She couldn't remember everything she'd said, she thought now, her burning gaze fixed on the vee of coarse hair bisecting the solid chest in front of her. She could recall pleading hysterically with him to go—to just go—and entreating him over and over again never to tell anyone, never even to mention what had happened between them to a living soul. She'd told him she didn't think she could live with herself if anyone else ever learned how shamefully she'd behaved, that she wished she could erase her own memories of the past few hours.

He'd said nothing. In the middle of her torrent of words she'd felt his hand lightly against her lips, cutting off the desperate flow. In silence he'd risen from the bed, and just as silently he'd gotten dressed in the darkness. She'd felt his fingers gently touch her eyelids, and even more gently close them.

Then he'd uttered the only words she could clearly remember him saying throughout that whole night. They'd come out in a low whisper, as if he were speaking more to himself than her.

"He was a goddamned fool. But I'm a bigger one."

An hour or so after he'd left she'd gotten up from the bed. Averting her gaze from the dress on the floor, she'd stumbled to the shower, turned on the water as hot as she could stand it and had stayed there until her sobs had finally subsided.

"So you see why I don't think you can make me forget, McQueen," she whispered. She raised her hand, and with one finger she traced the arrow of hair between his pectorals down to the bottom of his rib cage. She heard him inhale sharply, and she looked up into his face. His features seemed carved into immobility. "But you made me remember. And for that I don't think I'll *ever* forgive you."

His lips hardly moved as he spoke. "I already knew that."

She held his gaze for a moment longer. McQueen was McQueen, she told herself. He couldn't help it that he wasn't the man she'd imagined him to be for a few foolish hours today. Looking for healing from a man whose own scars ran so deep had been her mistake.

She wouldn't make it again. Turning away from him, she walked over to her bed.

"It's late, and this conversation is over."

"But that wasn't the deal. You're right. If I don't at least give it a shot then it was all just talk, Tam."

"What deal are you—oh, for God's sake." Incredulity sharpened her voice. "You've got to be joking."

His eyebrows drew together. "I'm no good at jokes, honey. I suppose that's another of my limitations. I'm not that funny, I'm a washout in social situations and my cooking skills seem to have gone downhill. On top of that, like you said, I'm probably a lousy lay." He walked over to her with a shrug. "So there's a good chance you might get to kick me out of here in three or four minutes, max."

"Try immediately, McQueen," she snapped.

"You told me to make you want it. How about you give me that much, dammit?" he said, his voice taking on an edge. "Come on, Tam, one kiss. I might not be able to drive everything out of your mind, but let's see if I can make you forget just how much you hate me right now. If I can't, then no harm, no foul."

She stared flatly back at him. "I don't see it happening but just for the sake of argument, what if you can?"

His smile was brief and humorless. "Now you're the one playing dumb."

She stiffened. Her gaze narrowed. "Fine. One kiss. Rock my world, McQueen."

"I intend to," he said shortly, pulling her toward him.

When he'd kissed her two nights ago he hadn't been hesitant or subtle. But a split second before his mouth came down on hers Tamara knew instinctively that what little control he'd exercised then had now been discarded completely. Even as she parted her lips to voice an unsteady protest his mouth was over hers. The words never left her throat.

His tongue was immediately in her and immediately deep, and immediately she knew what was going on.

The antagonism that had been crackling between them like a downed electrical wire had finally found something to ground itself in. McQueen had stripped what he wanted from her and what she'd said she wanted from him down to the barest essentials, and he was beyond caring that what was left might be too basic.

She placed her palm flat against his chest. It felt as if she were pushing against concrete.

On the job she had to meet the same requirements as any man. She'd gotten used to shoving aside a six-footer who was pounding up a flight of stairs too slowly, of seeing no difference between herself and her fellow firefighters. She wasn't fragile. She wasn't helpless. She wasn't the kind of female who pretended to be.

Which was why the notion of being protestingly swept into Rhett Butler's arms and carried up the grand staircase at Tara had never figured largely in her fantasies— or if it had, she would have been altogether too embarrassed and appalled with herself to admit it, she thought dazedly. That wasn't any woman's fantasy anymore.

Even in their fantasies, women wanted their dream lovers to be gentle, didn't they? They wanted them to be accommodating, to be considerate enough to curb the rougher edges of their maleness.

Maybe there was something wrong with her.

She *liked* that he was a big man. She liked feeling hard muscle surrounding her. She liked that there was nothing of him that was yielding or accommodating right at this moment, and she liked the edgy thrill that was spilling through her at the realization that his sex was something it would never occur to McQueen to apologize for.

Casting aside the last of her inhibitions, she let herself sway against him, her fingers curling into her palms on his chest. He lifted his mouth just enough that his kiss trailed to the corner of her lips, to the edge of her jaw, to the exposed line of her neck.

Raw desire slammed through her.

And Stone McQueen rocked her world.

Chapter Twelve

Tamara gasped as immediate heat lapped at her breasts, licked at her inner thighs, violated the most private recesses of her being. Even as her limbs went completely boneless she felt her feet leave the floor, felt herself being swept up in Stone's arms, hazily saw that gray gaze, half-hidden behind the dark veil of his lashes, meet hers.

Her sleep shirt had slid up as he'd lifted her. It was one of her less embarrassing ones, pale pink with darker pink snaps marching all the way down its front. Right now the bottom snap was somewhere near the top of her legs and she was pretty sure she was even more exposed at the back.

He positioned his grip securely under her. Her suspicion became a certainty as she felt the muscles of his forearm flex slightly against the curve of her derriere.

"You said one kiss. That makes it your call now." His tone was edged. "I want to see you on me and under me, honey. I want those gorgeous legs wrapped around me and I want to be in you so badly I can taste it. I want to feel myself going out of my mind while you're making me prove to you that I'm your man. But it's your call."

Hot desire spilled through her, and with it a jumble

of lushly carnal images flashed across her imagination—images that started with the acts he'd just described and took them to the limits of possibility. Vintage McQueen, Tamara thought, biting down on her lip. If his words had been any more bluntly erotic… She bit down harder.

It was a moment before she could speak.

"I—I think I called it the first time I saw you," she said unsteadily. "I kept telling myself you were everything I didn't like in a man. You're too big. You're too aggressive. You're a loose cannon. I think you'd probably be like that in bed, McQueen." She took a shallow breath. "I think in bed I'd like it," she whispered.

"Do you, now?" he said huskily.

With no visible effort, he lowered her to the bed and himself with her, so that he was kneeling with one leg on either side of her thighs as she lay back against the pillow-cushioned headboard. His expression was unreadable in the shadows.

"It was the same for me, honey," he rasped. "One look and I was willing to sell my soul to have a night with you."

"It's night, Stone. We're both here in my bed." She reached up to the top snap of her shirt and slowly undid it. "Are you sure you didn't sell your soul after all?"

"Hell, I'm pretty sure I did. Maybe you can help me get it back someday." His voice roughened. "But right now I just want to watch you do what you're doing."

"What am I doing?" Tamara breathed. She unpopped two more snaps, her eyes never leaving his.

"Stripping for me," he said hoarsely. "Teasing me. Making me wait."

That was *exactly* what she was doing, she thought hazily, unfastening another tiny snap. She saw a muscle jump at the side of his jaw.

He was the one.

She'd been certain this evening at the Red Spot, she thought, drinking in the sight of him watching her. She'd been certain, but that very certainty had frightened her. She hadn't shared her past with Stone, she'd thrown it at him as hard as she could in an effort to prove to herself that she couldn't trust him.

And it hadn't worked because he was the one—the one she could reveal herself to, the one she could trust, the one man she'd been looking for all her life. She hadn't felt anything like this with Rick—as if she and he had been lovers in another reality, and were just picking up where they'd been forced to leave off a lifetime or two ago. And whatever intimacy she'd had with the man who'd stood in for her groom had come from the liquid drug she'd taken to numb her pain.

But Stone McQueen was the one. He was the man she could be a woman with—unselfconsciously, unhesitatingly, passionately. Maybe she *was* drunk, Tamara thought. Whatever was fizzing through her veins felt like champagne.

"It just feels like I'm making you wait, Stone," she murmured, her fingers sliding to the next snap. "We both know patience is one of those virtues you don't possess. This might be a good time to teach you one or two of them."

"I've always wanted to be a better man, honey. It's a damn shame you have to be such a bad girl in order to help me out."

How did he do that? she thought agitatedly. Her fingers slipped and two snaps popped open at once. How did he switch from that throaty growl to that dangerous purr in the space of a few sentences? Did he know what that did to her?

She gave a little tug to the edges of her shirt. The row of tiny snaps popped open down to her waist, and she saw his gaze darken. Leaning back a little against the propped up pillows, slowly she slid the two edges of the shirt aside.

"Uh-uh, no touching, McQueen," she said reprovingly. "You were the one who first brought up teasing."

"You're going to make me pay for that, aren't you?" He was still straddling her. Moving forward, he braced his hands on his knees, as if to keep them occupied. "I dreamed about you last night, honey. You were a whole lot more accommodating, as I remember. You let me hold them and stroke them and kiss them. You begged me to lick those perfect pink peaks, and when I did you arched your back and dug your nails into me. You were a little wildcat in my dreams, and when I woke up I almost expected to see the claw marks to prove it."

"That was just a dream. This is real." She gave him a glance of wide-eyed innocence. "But tell me more, Stone. What happened next?"

"I was wearing what I'm wearing now," he said hoarsely. "A pair of chinos and nothing else. You unzipped my fly."

"That—that's within the rules." Her own voice wasn't too even, Tamara noted, and no wonder. Heat now seemed to be licking every part of her. Almost nervously her hands went to the zippered front of his pants.

"Oh." The shocked gasp escaped her before she could stop it. She looked swiftly up at him, her lips still parted.

"Okay, the freakin' bet's off, sweetheart. You win, I lose." Stone's voice was strained. "Stop looking at me like that or I'll totally humiliate myself, honey. By the way, that was cheating."

She'd told him she liked big and aggressive. She'd just had very hard evidence that he was the former, and from his tone it seemed as though he'd reverted to the latter. Her laugh was shaky.

"Just admit it McQueen—you're never going to be a patient man."

"I'm never going to be a patient man."

His hands spanned her waist. Almost before she knew what he intended, Tamara found herself being lifted up from between his legs and into a kneeling position facing him. Out of the corner of her eye she caught a shadowy movement a few feet away. Looking toward it, she saw the two of them dimly reflected in her dresser mirror. Stone followed her glance.

"Now it's your turn to watch," he muttered tightly.

He grasped the two edges of her shirt, not tentatively as she had, but almost roughly. In the same impatient movement, as the rest of the snaps opened and the pink sleepshirt parted completely he slid it over her shoulders and down her arms.

It fell to the pillows behind her unheeded. In the space of half a heartbeat he'd totally disrobed her. Her stunned gaze flew from the mirror to his face, but at his expression whatever she'd intended to say went completely out of her mind.

Stone McQueen was looking at her as if he was a blind man who'd just been given back his sight.

"You're so beautiful," he breathed.

Slowly he brought his hands to the sides of her breasts, cupping their outer curves. Even more slowly he slid his palms downward, his thumbs brushing against her suddenly hard nipples and going past them to her rib cage, her waist, the flare of her hips.

She was kneeling naked on a bed and allowing a man

to touch her wherever he wanted, Tamara thought dazedly. Shouldn't she be feeling some small flicker of modesty? Shouldn't she be trying to retain some scrap of demureness?

And wasn't it just the tiniest bit sinful to let him make her feel this wanton?

Maybe it was, she told herself helplessly. But that just made it more exciting.

She shifted slightly, her legs moving fractionally farther apart. Bringing her arms up, she scooped the weight of her hair from the nape of her neck and piled it carelessly into a dishevelled mass at the top of her head, her breasts tipping upward with the gesture. Slanting a glance through her lashes at Stone, she saw the tanned column of his throat move reflexively as he caught his breath.

"You're bad, Tam." His tone was raw. "You know damn well what you're doing to me."

Even as he spoke he was lowering his head to her, his hands wide and cupping her uplifted breasts, but instead of feeling his mouth on them as she'd expected, with a small shock Tamara realized he'd gone lower.

She felt his tongue flick into the tangle of curls at the top of her thighs. Immediate, liquid heat poured through her.

She arched herself toward him, her own hair tumbling free as her outstretched fingers sank into the coarse silk of his, her other hand clenched tightly at her lips to hold back the moan she could feel rising in her throat. She felt his tongue circling slowly downward, felt it move between her parted thighs.

His mouth opened. She felt him take her gently in, felt the hypnotically circling strokes of his tongue probe deeper, felt it find the sensitive spot it was searching for.

"Oh, no," she gasped. "Stone, that's too *much*."

He lifted his head, and for an instant his gaze met hers. "I know it's too much, honey. I want it to be too much for you, over and over again. I just love the taste of you, Tam."

Without waiting for her response he bent his head again, and this time when she felt his tongue slowly circling and teasing her she didn't try to stifle the low cry that came from her throat. It *was* too much, she thought hazily—too much sensation, too much exquisite torture. The rest of her body no longer existed, except as a conduit for the pleasure she could feel mounting steadily in her. Her whole consciousness had focused down to what Stone was doing to her.

She felt his tongue lick deeper. She felt his mouth open wider. She felt him take her completely in, and as he did an outrageous thought tore shockingly through her mind. It was as if he was drinking her, she thought disjointedly. He'd said he loved the way she tasted, and he'd been telling the simple truth.

And he was *loving* it.

The sensations building in her exploded into shattering, overwhelming ecstasy. From somewhere far away she heard her own slurred voice calling out his name, and then she felt him holding her and repeating hers in her ear.

A shudder ran through her, and then another, like tiny aftershocks.

"Tamara, honey, Tamara, sweetheart, Tamara, baby." His whisper seemed to wrap the endearments around her. With an unsteady hand he stroked her hair back from her closed eyes, his murmur barely audible. "Sweetheart, you're perfect. Honey, I'm yours."

It couldn't be McQueen holding her, Tamara decided

hazily—not the tough, abrasive McQueen she knew. Whoever this man was, he sounded as if he'd found his heart's desire, and was determined to keep it at all costs. Slowly she opened her eyes and met Stone's smoky gaze.

Her heart skipped a beat.

"I was loud." It was the first foolish thing that came into her head, but somehow she didn't feel foolish saying it. He lifted a strand of her hair to his lips.

"I like you loud."

A final tremor ran through her, and her fingers curled into fists on his chest. "You drove me crazy," she said softly. "I didn't know anything could be like that."

He was pressed hard against her. She felt him harden even more. Uncurling one fist, unhurriedly she let her fingers trail down his ribs and past the washboard tautness of his abdomen to the button at the top of his zipper. She undid it, and heard his suddenly indrawn breath.

"What did I taste like, Stone?" Her fingers found the tab of his zipper. Gently she drew it down a quarter-inch or so, conscious of the pressure straining against it. She saw his eyes glaze slightly.

"Like jasmine, honey," he said hoarsely. "Like jasmine and sex. You're all over me."

Earthy carnality. Unexpected romanticism. The first ambushed her, the second totally disarmed her. The fact that they'd both been delivered by the man the rest of the world saw as hard-living, hard-bitten Stone Mc-Queen conquered her completely.

Slowly she slid her palm over the straining seam beneath her hand. Through the heavy cotton of his chinos she felt the outlined shaft bulge more turgidly until it seemed to be overflowing the cup of her palm.

"Oh, no. Honey, that's too much."

The low gasp sounded as if it were being torn from his throat. Raising her eyes from his obvious need, in the half-light, half shadow she saw that McQueen's eyes were closed and his bottom lip was cruelly caught between his teeth. The heavy sheath of muscle that defined his neck and bulked out those broad shoulders was accentuated by a gilding of moisture.

"I want it to be too much." Even to her own ears, her whisper sounded ragged. A frisson of desire ran through her, dangerously close to the core of her being. "But I want it to be too much in me, McQueen. I want you in me now."

Her fingertips closed over the tab of his zipper once more. As she slowly and carefully drew the metal slide downward his grasp on her shoulders tightened convulsively. She bent her head to focus on her cautious task, and her hair swung forward to brush against his belly.

She heard him inhale sharply, saw the flinching shock that passed through him. She had the power to do that to him, she thought with sudden fierceness. He had the power to melt her, but she had the power to bring him to this. From now on, wherever they were, whatever they were doing, she would be able to look at him and know that Stone McQueen's one weakness was her. Anytime she wanted to, she could remind him of that with a glance.

Because he knew it, too.

He moved. The zipper was forced fully open. He was in the circle of her hands, and he was far too big.

She swallowed dryly, her mesmerized gaze travelling along the length of him, taking in the size of him, finally coming to rest on the dark tangles spilling forth from the tightly stretched vee of the chinos, the shadowed fullness nestled close to the base of that shaft.

"This—this isn't going to work, Stone," she murmured unsteadily. She felt his grip slide from her shoulders to her arms, and then his hands were around hers and around himself.

"Trust me, Tam?" His question was terse, as if even the act of speaking held potential risk. "I won't hurt you, I promise. I'll make it good for you, honey."

She raised uncertain eyes to his face. His sheened gaze met and held hers.

His mouth had teased her into readiness. What would it be like to have this most blatant manifestation of his maleness deep inside her?

It seemed suddenly as if thousands of tiny sparks were raining onto her skin, raising her temperature to fever-pitch, sizzling like fragments of stars in her hair, on her face, down her limbs. She swayed toward him. He steadied her.

"Will I burn, Stone?" she breathed, her lashes dipping to her cheekbones and slowly lifting again.

"Yeah, honey, you'll burn." His tone was broken glass. "We're both gonna burn, little darlin'. And you'll love it."

"Then yes," she said hoarsely. "I want it, Stone."

A line of color rose and almost instantly ebbed under the hard angles of his face. His eyes searched hers. Then he drew away from her, his gaze not leaving her face.

He moved from the bed. With no self-consciousness at all he stepped out of his pants, pausing only to retrieve something from the back pocket. He tossed back a recalcitrant strand of hair that had fallen into his eyes, brought the object to his mouth, and ripped it open with his teeth. The smile he directed her way was wry.

"I'd rather feel you than latex around me, Tam. But I don't want you worrying about anything tonight."

She wasn't worried. In fact, she hadn't even thought of protection, and that had been recklessly careless of her, Tamara thought with swift compunction. Aside from anything else, she was on no form of birth control.

But McQueen was the type of man who came prepared. She should have known he would be, but that didn't completely satisfy her curiosity.

"You carry one around just in case?" She couldn't help the tartness in her tone. She also couldn't seem to help the flicker of jealousy it stemmed from.

"From the time I was a way too optimistic fourteen-year-old until seven years ago." He didn't appear to have identified the edge of emotion in her tone, and she felt suddenly grateful he hadn't. "I started carrying one again two days ago. And it wasn't because I'd gotten the hots for Chandra out of the blue, either, so pull in your claws, honey," he added with soft amusement.

He had identified it. She lifted her chin. "Good thing for you that you don't, McQueen. You should know that I'm a very jealous woman."

"And you should know that I'm a very jealous man," he said evenly, his head bent to his task. His palms flat, he skimmed the condom tight along his length, and then looked up. "I'm even jealous of your memories, honey. Let's see if I can make them disappear."

She was still kneeling on the bed, fully expecting him to return to it. Instead, he scooped her up beneath her haunches and swung her to him. Instinctively her legs went around his waist, her arms went around his neck and her lips parted in surprise.

After everything they'd already done she would have guessed she was beyond blushing. But somehow this pose was so intimate. Her breasts were pillowed against his chest. The softness of her inner thighs was skin-to-skin with him. And if she adjusted her position very slightly, she realized, she could feel the hardness of him nudging up between her wide-spread legs.

She hadn't known it could be done like this, Tamara thought in brief confusion. Probably it couldn't be—not unless the man was big enough and strong enough to not only hold his partner throughout but to lift her and release her while the two of them moved toward a climax together.

Stone McQueen was strong enough. Even now with her arms clasped so loosely around his neck that it was obvious he was taking her whole weight he seemed to be expending no effort at all. She leaned back, and saw the reflection of her movement in the dresser mirror beside them.

The light cutting in from the hall grayed out the darkness in the room enough that she could easily make out his expression. His eyes were shadowed with desire— desire and something else.

"Maybe I've made you forget a little." The something else was pain. It bled through the huskiness in his voice, and at it her heart turned over. "But I want it to be like it never happened, honey. I want you to remember this as the first time you were ever with a man— because I already think of you as the first and only woman for me. Do you understand, honey?"

Even as he murmured the question she could feel him raising her slightly, his outspread hands laced and clasped under her derriere, his thumbs around her hips. She nodded tensely, supremely aware that the nudging pressure she'd felt between her legs had become more intense.

He was about to enter her. She wouldn't be able to

take him. She squeezed her eyes shut in sudden panic, and all at once she felt his mouth on hers.

"Relax, baby," he whispered against her lips. "I'll take care of everything. All you have to do is guide me home, honey."

So ridiculous, she thought shakily, opening her eyes and meeting his gaze. Didn't he know men weren't like this anymore? She didn't need a too-big, too-aggressive, too good-looking hunk of male to take care of her.

"You're so damned old-fashioned it's sexy, Mc-Queen," she murmured back. "Go ahead. Take care of me."

His mouth covered hers. She felt his teeth gently nipping her bottom lip, and then his tongue lapping at it to take away the tiny pain. He nipped her again, licked her again, and farther down she could feel herself opening as he began to move into her. She felt him lowering her, felt herself opening wider.

Wrapping her arms tightly around him, she bit down on his lip to stifle the shocked little cry that issued from her throat. She felt him pause, and then he was moving carefully upward and into her again.

Her bite on his lip had drawn blood. She was *glad* she'd drawn blood, Tamara thought frantically. She felt herself expanding to receive him, felt him expanding her farther, felt the pressure becoming unbearable. Her breath was coming in shallow gasps against his mouth and those strands of her hair that had fallen across her face were already plastered damply against her skin. She nipped him again, and this time she didn't let go.

It was all darkness. There was nothing else but that and the tang of salt in her mouth and the man moving into her. She felt him fill her completely and stop.

He was in her. She was surrounding every last inch of him. He was all hers.

She released his lip. She let her breath out in a cautiously shaky sigh.

Heat pooled in her, swirled in her, seemed to spill over her open thighs and splash down between them. Heat dripped from her hardened nipples, her suddenly-swollen breasts. She felt Stone lift her, felt his biceps tauten against her, felt herself sliding slowly up along his length. She opened her eyes and saw he was watching her, his own gaze unfocused.

"I hurt you, honey." His words were thick. "I tried not to."

"I hurt you, too." The tip of her tongue flicked against the split skin of his lip. "You—you deserved it."

"Everyone's gonna know how you keep me in line, Tam," he breathed, lowering her onto him and thrusting into her with tantalizing deliberation. "Everyone's gonna know that big bad McQueen has to answer to a spitfire of a redhead now."

"And you like it that everyone will know," she said unsteadily, feeling him filling her and then withdrawing again. She tightened her legs around him, and saw his lashes dip briefly down, saw the hard color mount in his face.

"Yeah, I like it," he admitted on a gasp. "I love it, honey."

This time when he thrust into her he was more forceful. She felt herself gripping the smooth length of him, opening again as he pushed inside. The heat inside became more insistent, and a soft moan escaped from her lips.

He'd promised her fire. He'd said they would burn.

Desire was already licking its way through her, and with every sliding stroke it was getting hotter. Her head felt too heavy for her neck, and dizzily she tipped it backward, feeling her hair brushing damply against her spine.

"Look at yourself, baby." His voice was so slurred his words were barely intelligible. "You're pure sex, all open legs and wet hair and such a sweet, soft rump. Look how you fit me."

Through half-closed eyes she slanted a dazed glance at the mirror beside them, and saw what he was talking about. The last of her control slipped away, and she felt the fire flare inside her.

The reflection was of a massively built man, heavy muscles gleaming in the dim light, his eyes dark with need. The woman he was holding seemed to have no inhibitions at all. Her lips were parted, her legs were wrapped around him, her hair was tangled and loose.

This was what Stone did to her, she thought breathlessly, watching the dark shafting shadow move upwards to disappear between her spread thighs, feeling it moving in her. And this was what she did for him. She was the need he had to fulfill, she was the fire that was even now beginning to consume him. He moved into her again, and then again, each time harder, each time tighter, each time more aggressively, and she dug her nails cruelly into his shoulders. Even as the darkness rushed over her, she heard his voice, raw and low.

"This is the first time for me, honey." His lashes were spiky fans against his cheekbones. "No matter what I've done before, this is the first time."

She nodded mutely, feeling him inside her, knowing she was about to go over the edge. The dark lashes lifted.

"Tell me." The words seemed dragged from him. "Tell me it's the first time for you, too, Tam."

"You're the only man who's ever done this to me, Stone," she whispered. "And this is my very first time."

The shadows behind his gaze cleared. The tenseness in his expression eased. He brought his mouth to hers, and she could feel the warmth of his breath on her lips.

"I want to be kissing you when we come, baby," he said hoarsely. "I want to be as in you as I can be. You know I fell in love with you the moment I met you, don't you?"

Her eyes flew open but before she could say anything her head was bending back with the force of his kiss and his hands were tightening convulsively into the softness of her flesh. He pulled her completely onto him, thrusting deeper into her than ever before.

It felt as if she was being *consumed*—as if everything nonessential was being burned away, leaving only the essence of her, the essence of the man in her, the shuddering explosions that were gripping them both. The two of them had flown straight into the sun, Tamara thought crazily. That had to be what all this heat and light was that she could feel filling her, surrounding him. They'd flown into the sun, but she wasn't afraid because he was with her and he would bring her back safely....

It seemed like hours later that the last tiny explosion ran through her. She gave one final gasp, and when she eventually opened her eyes she saw his were still closed. As if he knew she was looking at him, his lashes lifted and he smiled faintly at her.

"I said it because it's true, Tam," he said huskily. "I said it because I do."

Chapter Thirteen

Jack Foley had chosen one hell of a time to drop in unannounced, McQueen thought, grabbing a clean pair of chinos and a shirt from the guest bedroom dresser.

They'd been in the shower together. He'd been soaping her breasts and her eyes had already taken on that glazed look that made his knees go weak when the doorbell had buzzed. It had continued to buzz and a hint of alarm had broken through the glaze in Tam's eyes.

"That has to be Uncle Jack," she'd said in an appalled whisper. "He's got a key. If I don't answer the door he'll imagine I've fallen down the basement stairs and let himself in just to make sure I'm all right."

He'd seen her point, McQueen thought wryly. Jack wasn't her father, but he was the nearest thing to it. Probably not even his friendship with Stone or the fact that his darling Tammy was a full-grown woman would have made much difference to him if he'd caught sight of a randy, bare-assed male stepping out of the same shower as his little girl. Tamara had raced into her bedroom and seconds later she'd reappeared at the bathroom door, dressed in a sweatsuit.

"We've both got wet hair. Don't come out too soon or he'll put two and two together, Stone." She'd blushed, and that had made his damn knees go weak, too. "I know I'm being stupid about this."

"You're not being stupid, honey." He hadn't said what he'd really been thinking—that as soon as he could get to a hardware store he intended to buy chain-locks for all the doors in the house. "I don't blame you for not wanting to spring this on him."

He hadn't been able to resist pulling her to him and giving her a quick kiss. It had been harder to resist giving her a second one, especially when he'd felt her tongue dart into his mouth and then out again, but he'd turned her around by the shoulders and given her a swat on that gorgeous rump.

"Go on and answer the damn door. He won't suspect a thing."

But Jack Foley wasn't blind, McQueen thought, staring at his reflection in the full-length mirror affixed to the back of the guest bedroom door. He was going to know exactly what his adopted daughter's no-good houseguest had been up to.

The broken skin on his bottom lip looked like what it was—a love-bite, delivered with enough passion so that it was still swollen. She'd done that to him, he thought. When they'd made love the second time he'd felt the rounded tips of her nails desperately scoring his back, and they'd left marks on him, too.

He hadn't been able to get enough of her. He was never going to be able to get enough of her. Just before dawn she'd breathlessly told him that this time she was going to be in charge, and he'd felt her binding his wrists with a silken scarf to the bedposts behind him. What she'd done next had driven him out of his mind, and when she'd delicately nipped the top of his thighs, pursed those pink lips together and lightly blown on him he'd gone completely crazy.

The tiny marks she'd branded him with were evidence that she'd made his body hers last night, but whether she'd known it or not she'd already owned his heart.

Maybe there was a chance for him after all.

Heading down the hall toward the sound of her voice and Jack's deeper rumble in the kitchen, he nearly fell over Pangor, who'd obviously decided to forgive and forget the indignity of being locked in the guest bedroom all night. On a sudden inspiration, McQueen scooped up the cat and continued into the kitchen.

"Old flea-bag here nailed me a good one in the mouth when I went to toss him off the bed," he growled. "Stings like a bastard. What the hell's the holdup with Leung, Jack?" he growled.

"And a good good morning to you, too, laddie." Jack Foley lifted a cardboard cup of coffee in wry salute, his blue eyes narrowing as he glanced at Stone. "I brought breakfast, Stone, so sit down and grab a coffee while I bring you up to speed."

He nodded at the open box of donuts on the kitchen table. "Leung's a perfectionist, like I told you. He wouldn't accept the results of the test until he'd run it three times."

"But all three times it came back the same." As Tamara spoke, Stone looked over at her with what he hoped was studied casualness. "The accelerant was what you suspected, McQueen."

She was standing by the counter with a barely nibbled donut in her hand and a light dusting of powdered sugar on her top lip. Desire slammed into him, hot and immediate, along with the insane impulse to hustle her into the bedroom, lock the door behind them, and then proceed to lick not only those sugared lips, but every other part of her body. Their eyes met. He saw the heated flush that mounted her cheeks. She went on hastily.

"Leung says it's some flawed variant of rocket fuel. Apparently if it had been the legitimate stuff there wouldn't have been much more left of the structure than ash."

"And neither of you would have gotten out of there alive." Jack set down his coffee. "Leung wasn't around when you were hunting Pascoe seven years ago, McQueen, so he didn't make the connection. But Knopf and Trainor did."

Stone stared at him. "How did those two find out?" It was an effort to keep his voice even. "You told me Leung would keep this quiet."

"Isn't it obvious? They saw you and me together." Tamara exhaled. "That would have led them to Uncle Jack, and they guessed you'd go to him if you needed outside help. They must have suspected you'd found something at the site."

"That's the way I figure it. Then Tom Knopf put the strong-arm on Dave Leung, according to Dave." Jack looked disgusted. "Told him he could kiss his job goodbye if he didn't hand over the results of his tests to them instead of a maverick who'd had no business using official resources in the first place. I let you down," he said with a grimace.

"It wasn't your fault, Jack. I can't blame Leung, either." Frowning, Stone pried off the lid of his coffee container. "You said Trainor and Knopf made the connection to the fires of seven years ago. But like everyone else they don't believe Robert Pascoe's still alive. They're connecting those dots to someone else, aren't they?"

"You got it, laddie," Jack said quietly. "They're connecting them to you."

"Are they crazy?"

Tamara pushed herself away from the counter, her eyes blazing. His spitfire, Stone thought as she glared at Jack. No—his partner, he corrected himself. So this was what it was like to have someone who would stand back to back with him and take on the whole world, if necessary.

He felt suddenly able to take on all comers.

"Come on, Jack, hit me with the rest of it. Maybe when you've got five cards in your hand you can keep a poker face, but right now I'm reading you like a book. What's their theory?"

"Tammy's hit the nail on the head, McQueen, crazy's the only word for it." Jack Foley's normally good-natured features were tight with anger. "Those clowns aren't just trying to pin the rooming house fire on you. They're saying there never was a Robert Pascoe, and that you set that series of fires seven years ago yourself, including the Mitchell Towers blaze."

He'd been half expecting it, Stone thought. But that was like half expecting a kick in the stomach—it still knocked the wind out of you when it landed.

"I hope those two have medical insurance." The emotion that Tamara had displayed a moment ago was gone. Her voice held a deadly calm. "Because I fully intend to rip both of them new—" She stopped. "Sorry about that, Uncle Jack," she said in the same flat tone. "What are they basing this insane theory on, for God's sake?"

"It's not so insane. It's not even original." Stone felt his jaw tighten. "I heard a few whispers before I resigned, but at the time I had more important things on my mind. Like going to five funerals," he added harshly.

"That's all they ever were, laddie—whispers. Cowardly whispers and rumors, dammit," Jack said heatedly. "Even your worst enemies never believed them."

Stone shrugged. "Bill and Tommy do."

"What rumors?" Tamara was looking frustratedly at them.

"I wanted to fast-track myself to a promotion, so I created a fictional arsonist. The way I heard it, Robert Pascoe was the man who never was."

He was aware of Jack shaking his head and looking away, but Jack's reaction wasn't the one he was interested in. "Supposedly I patched together a bunch of old unsolved arsons and attributed them to him so he'd have a history. Then I started setting fires myself and blaming them on the bogeyman I'd created."

"I don't get it. What about Glenda Fodor?" Tamara's shoulders lifted impatiently. "How could the man have a girlfriend if he didn't exist?"

"She always denied she had a boyfriend, remember?" The whole thing made a crazy kind of sense, Stone thought, if you accepted the initial premise. "Since I was the only one who could claim to have laid eyes on the man I had to be making that up, too. The clincher is that the arsons stopped when I left—"

"Hold on." Jack was frowning at him. "You actually *met* Pascoe?"

"On a crowded subway platform in the Charles Street station," Stone said curtly. "He was a stranger standing beside me, and when we heard the train coming he turned to me as if he was going to ask me the time. Instead he told me he was Robert Pascoe, the man I'd been hunting, and he just wanted me to know that he was building up to something so big the fire department would never forget it. Even as I moved he pushed the pregnant woman standing in front of him off the platform. I managed to grab her before she fell. By the time the excitement died down he was long gone."

He shrugged, feeling again the old frustration. "I finally had a name for my mystery arsonist, but I knew a name wouldn't convince anyone the man was real, especially since when I ran it through the computer I didn't get any results. He was right—the Mitchell Towers blaze won't be forgotten by the Boston jakeys. Not when four brothers and one brave sister lost their lives in it."

Once this conversation would have had him out of here and prowling for the nearest bar, Stone thought, seeing the shimmer in Tamara's gaze. Unself-consciously she reached over and laid her palm softly on his unshaven jaw. Bringing his own hand up, he gripped her fingers with sudden fierceness. If Jack hadn't known before, he'd probably clued in now, he reflected. That was fine by him. If it were up to him, the whole damn world would know how much he was in love with her.

He didn't need a drink. He just needed the woman beside him.

"I resigned. The arsons stopped. That added fuel to the rumors. The theory went that I never meant anyone to die in the Mitchell Towers fire, I just wanted to be the big hero who warned them in the nick of time and when I screwed up I was crippled by guilt. I guess Trainor and Knopf figure I'm looking to get back into the limelight again."

"I set them straight pretty quick," Jack said. He went on pugnaciously.

"I was almost glad they'd found out you'd contacted

me. Since that particular cat was out of the bag, I didn't see any reason not to read them the riot act, especially that bully boy Knopf.'' He picked up a donut. A spray of powdered sugar punctuated his next angry sentence. ''I told them they might consider the possibility that you'd been right all along, and try talking to Glenda Fodor.''

''Did they think it was worth a shot?'' Stone asked carefully. He felt a muscle in his jaw twitch, and wondered if it was visible. Whether it was or not, something seemed to alert Jack. The blue eyes widened at him.

''I shouldn't have mentioned the Fodor woman to them, should I?'' he said hollowly. ''You think they'll scare her off. Dammit, McQueen, I didn't think of it that way.''

''You went to bat for me to stop them from resurrecting the rumors, Jack,'' he said quietly. ''I appreciate it. Hell, who knows—maybe Knopf will let Trainor do the talking when they call on her. Bill doesn't come on so strong.''

''He didn't strike me as the type women confide in,'' Tamara said shortly. Slipping her hand from his, she leaned over and chose another donut from the box—not, Stone saw regretfully, a sugared one. She bit into it, catching the cream that oozed out with her tongue.

Hastily he swallowed a mouthful of lukewarm coffee, nearly choking on it. Whipped cream on the next grocery list, he decided abruptly. Deadbolts on all the doors and whipped cream on Tam. Hell, on him, too, if it meant having that tongue licking it up.

''...not only that she'd been my friend, but it seemed that he'd known her, Uncle Jack. Has he ever spoken of Claudia to you?''

While he'd been indulging in a quick hot fantasy Tam

had been asking about Trainor, Stone guessed. Jack's reply proved him right.

"You never knew? He was obsessed with her, for God's sake. I had to talk to him about it."

"But how did he even meet her?"

"He saw her here, whenever it was my turn to host the poker games and she was spending the evening with you." Jack's lips thinned. "He never took his eyes off her. He was years older than you and Claudie, and it just didn't sit right with me. I told him I'd always seen myself in the role of a surrogate father to her, since her real dad wasn't around to protect her. He got the message."

Arithmetic wasn't Jack Foley's weak subject, Stone thought wryly. Although he was looking at his Tammy as he spoke, there was no doubt as to whom his words were really directed to. He'd put two and two together, he'd come up with four, and he was telling the man whose life he'd once saved that it was going to be one-on-one if he suspected his little girl wasn't being treated right.

"You must run at about what, Jack?" He kept his tone casual. "Two-thirty? Two-forty?"

Blue eyes turned his way. "Two-thirty-five, laddie," Foley said. "And most of it's still hard muscle."

"That's what I thought." Stone allowed a faint grin to cross his features. "I wouldn't want to go up against you anytime, would I?"

Slowly Jack grinned back at him. "We'd both do some damage, McQueen. But it's not something we have to worry about, is it?"

"No, Jack, you don't have to worry." Suddenly serious, Stone met the other man's gaze directly. "You've got my word on that."

"What are you two talking about, anyway? Arm-wrestling?" Tamara sounded peeved. "I thought we were discussing Bill Trainor. I wonder how he felt when he heard that Claudia had run off and gotten married?"

"He'd probably gotten over her by then, punkin." Turning back to Stone, the older man continued. "I probably blew the Fodor lead. How do you want to approach this now?"

"I'll check out the address I have for Glenda, but if Bill and Tommy have gotten to her already I'll question anyone I can find who lived at the rooming house, see if they noticed anyone suspicious hanging around." Even to himself it sounded futile. "I never saw the rocket fuel as a solid lead to Pascoe. It was his calling card, sure, but that was because he was the only arsonist nervy enough to use it. When I was investigating this the first time I was told that anyone with access to equipment and the chemical formula could cook the stuff up, if they didn't kill themselves doing it."

"Not anyone, surely." Tamara frowned. "Just because you hand me some eggs and a recipe doesn't mean I can whip up a cake like the kind Aunt Kate made. You'd have to have some idea of what you were doing."

"That still doesn't narrow it down any," Jack said. "Even Tommy Knopf's probably got enough rudimentary knowledge to concoct it if he had to. I seem to recall he was in some kind of demolitions unit in the army. McQueen's right, it's not a case-cracking lead."

"Then we start with what we do know about Pascoe." Leaning back against the counter, Tamara crossed her feet at the ankles and jammed her fists into the kangaroo pocket at the front of her hooded top.

She looked tough, and determined, and with her pocket rounded out like that, pregnant, Stone thought.

He blinked, disconcerted by the heat that rushed through him at the notion, but he couldn't dispel the image— Tam pregnant with their child, getting gradually fuller with the seed he'd planted deep inside her, day by day displaying the evidence more and more clearly of what they'd created together.

He *wanted* that. The certainty slammed into him with such force that it almost took his breath away. He'd probably drive her crazy, he thought shakily. Knowing Tam, she'd sail through pregnancy with all the unruffled aplomb of a mother cat, while he'd be racing around helping her into cars, going into spasms if he saw her lifting anything heavier than a nail file, treating her as if she was more fragile than porcelain. And he'd insist on being there beside her, feeling her squeeze down on his hands, when the child they'd made came squalling lustily into the world.

Petra would go nuts, he thought, smiling a little to himself. She'd be a bossy, adoring big sister, and he'd make sure she always knew she was his Tiger, and just as much loved as any of his other children.

He wanted to be Tam's husband. He wanted to be the father of her children. He wanted to be allowed to love her for the rest of his life and beyond. That was the future he wanted.

There was a good chance that wasn't the future he was going to get.

"It's a lot harder for city council to turn down the department's budget request when there's a retired jakey standing there in his uniform and medals."

It seemed he'd missed yet another chunk of the conversation, Stone thought, forcing himself back to the here and now with an effort. Jack was on his feet. He pushed back his own chair and stood, wondering if there was some response he was supposed to be making.

"Don't worry about it, Uncle Jack. You go look brave and noble at your meeting and shame them into throwing wads of cash at us." Tamara was smiling. "If something comes up, you've got your cell phone with you, right?"

"That thing. Half the time when I hear it ringing I can't find where I put it." Jack was moving toward the door. "It's in the car, punkin. I'll make sure it's on just in case."

He turned to Stone, and once again his manner shifted subtly. If anyone saw Jack Foley as a retired duffer whose time had passed, Stone realized, they'd be making a big mistake. The man standing in front of him was suddenly as formidable and tough as he must have been in his prime.

"Good hunting, laddie." He clapped a hand on Stone's shoulder and fixed him with a glance. "A word of warning—don't underestimate Knopf and Trainor. They've been wanting your blood for a long time, and Tommy, at least, can hold a hate forever. He'd have liked to have seen me go down, and that was just because of my friendship with Chuck."

"With Dad?" Tamara looked startled. "How in the world did their paths ever cross?"

"They didn't really." Jack shook his head. "But even when Tom was still hauling hose he knew he wanted to be an arson investigator someday, and his mentor was Harley Perkins. Harley had been a good jakey. He'd even hauled me to safety once when a floor gave way underneath me. But he never should have been made an investigator."

"He was pensioned off before my time, but I've heard

the stories.'' Stone raised his eyebrows. ''His sloppy techniques were legendary.''

Jack nodded. ''Tammy's dad was an insurance investigator, and his company sent him out to check into a restaurant blaze Harley had written off as an accident. Chuck's investigation not only proved the owner had paid to have the place torched, but it raised some pretty strong suspicions about Harley. Nothing was ever proven, but within months Perkins had taken the hint and retired. Knopf never forgave Chuck for that.''

He tapped the side of his nose. ''So watch your back, McQueen. And call if you need me.''

''Trainor knew Claudia. Knopf held a grudge against my father,'' Tamara said moments later as Jack drove away and she closed the door. ''Sometimes I feel like I took on a second family when I joined the department. Did you ever see it like that?''

He pulled her into his arms. ''I don't usually let myself think too much about the past, honey,'' he said, inhaling the scent of her hair. ''But talking about it today brought everything back.''

''That's a bad thing?'' Her question was quiet. ''I don't know exactly what happened, Stone. I guess I could have asked Chandra but I wanted to hear it from you, and I only wanted to hear it if you wanted to tell me.''

He was one sorry-ass son of a bitch, Stone thought, tightening his embrace around her. He'd been a screwup for most of his life, and he'd come too damned close to letting the only thing that mattered to him slip through his fingers.

But no more. She was the woman he loved. She deserved to know everything. Or at least as much as he could find the courage to tell her right now.

"I didn't see the department as my second family, honey," he said huskily against her hair. "I saw it as the only one I'd ever known, and Robert Pascoe tore my family apart."

He felt the pain lance through him, as fresh and as sharp as the first time, and he had to fight to keep his voice even.

"Five went in," he said, too harshly. "They didn't come out. And I've never stopped wondering if somehow I couldn't have prevented it."

Chapter Fourteen

"Hell, sometimes I wondered if the rumors might be true."

They'd moved into the living room, and as Stone sat down on the sofa Tamara began to settle herself beside him. Without looking up he caught her wrist and pulled her onto him.

"It's very simple, honey," he said tightly. "I always want you as close to me as you can get, okay? In my arms. On my lap. Surrounding me."

He'd felt the way she had while Uncle Jack had been with them, Tamara realized—as if keeping even the barest distance between them was intolerable. She felt the warmth of his breath on the corners of her mouth.

"Like I say, once in a while I'd wonder if what they were saying was true—that the murderous bastard whose trail I believed I'd picked up was just a figment of my imagination. Then I'd read another PNI report and know I'd stumbled across his handiwork again."

"I'm a firefighter, not an investigator, Stone," she reminded him. "What's a PNI report?"

"Perpetrator Never Identified." He twined a strand of her hair around his finger. "I must have been the first one to have the accelerant analyzed, or maybe earlier investigators were simply told the lab was unfamiliar with the compound. I didn't see the term 'rocket fuel' in any of the old reports, and more often than not it was obvious from the descriptions of the burns that it hadn't been used.''

''He didn't always use the same method?'' She frowned. ''I just said this isn't my field, but isn't the theory that once arsonists find a method that works, they stick to it?''

''Theories are like rules. There's always an exception,'' McQueen said. ''Some of the arsons were just jobs to him—contracts he was paid to fulfill. He only used the rocket fuel for his own fires. He gets off on what he does,'' he added savagely.

Shaken by his intensity, Tamara tried to steer the conversation back on course. ''How far into the past did his trail go?'' she asked in a matter-of-fact tone. ''When you eventually came face-to-face with him, did Pascoe seem to be in the right age range?''

''The man on the subway platform was a good ten or twelve years older than I was. That would have put him in his mid-to-late thirties, and the first PNI I felt could be his related to an arson from about fifteen years before. His age fit.''

Her question seemed to have taken the edge from his anger, leaving hard implacability beneath. ''Bracknell Curtiss was a tycoon who'd made his money out west before coming to Boston. He was into real estate development in a big way, though it wasn't until forensic accountants were called in after his death that anyone knew just what shell companies had been controlled by him—which was why no one ever pointed the finger at him while he was alive. But when the pencil-pushers finally figured out what he'd owned, it was obvious how he'd gotten the prime pieces of property he'd wanted at such fire-sale prices.''

"Pun intended?" She didn't smile.

"Pun intended." Stone didn't smile, either. "If he wanted the land and not the building and the owner wouldn't sell, it was a safe bet that Joe Landlord would wake up the next morning and find that his comfortable little rental income had gone up in smoke, because the offices or apartments he'd been collecting it from no longer existed. At that point he'd be glad to unload his few thousand square feet of smoking ruins to Curtiss. If the property itself was valuable, the owner would find himself and his family standing on his own front lawn in the middle of the night, watching his home burn to the ground. Those guys signed on the dotted line when Curtiss handed them his fountain pen the second time.''

"And Curtiss's torch was Pascoe." She didn't phrase it as a question.

"Right up to and including the night Bracknell Curtiss's own mansion burned down," Stone agreed. "With Curtiss and one of his servants trapped inside. The way I figure it, Pascoe must have parted ways with his employer over something, and for that particular fire he used the rocket fuel as an accelerant. The servant shouldn't have died," he added. "He went back in to save his boss."

"The fires continued even after Curtiss's death?" Tamara prompted.

"Yeah, they continued. An arsonist like Pascoe could probably name his price, and I'm sure most of the fires he set were written off as accidents—gas leaks, careless smoking.''

"Petra was right. Claudia quit smoking for good at

least a year ago," Tamara interjected. She felt her throat tighten. "I—I came across it in one of her letters."

"You gonna tell Tiger?" A moment ago his gaze had been hard with remembered anger. Now it was fully focused on her, and shadowed with compassion.

"As soon as I see her. Although I guess that might not be today, from what Mary Hall said," she said, catching her lip between her teeth. "But I shouldn't have interrupted you, Stone."

"We won't call, we'll just show up after we check out Glenda Fodor. I'll persuade the Hall woman to let us take Petra out for an hour or so." He tipped her chin up. "I wasn't trying yesterday. But baby, when I want to I can pour on the charm like you wouldn't believe."

"You jerk, McQueen." She smiled at him, feeling suddenly weak with desire and knowing if she gave in to her weakness they might never leave the house. "I know it's hard for you to talk about it," she said softly, her smile fading. "But I'd like to hear the rest. When did you begin to suspect there was a master arsonist at work?"

"When Jimmy Malone tried to swing a deal after he was caught for the Dazzlers blaze." With his arms around her, it was impossible not to sense the tension that had seeped back into his muscles. "People had died in that fire. I wasn't about to let the prosecutor cut a deal, but I'm not real sure anyone conveyed that information to Jimmy. The one time I went to see him in prison he told me he was small fry compared to the man he'd tried to model himself after."

"Pascoe was his hero?" She felt repulsed.

"In my job I lifted up rocks. There were some freakin' weird things scurrying around beneath them," he said curtly. "Yeah, Jimmy hero-worshiped Pascoe, but he didn't know much about him, not even his name. All he knew was that he'd set more burns than Jimmy had ever dreamed of, but that was enough to get me searching for a pattern. It didn't take long to find it when I knew what I was looking for. And one day I arrived at an investigation scene and knew at once that Pascoe had struck on my watch. I could practically smell the bastard all around me in the ruins.''

"That was the first of the series of fires leading up to the Mitchell Towers blaze, wasn't it?''

"Yeah, and each one of those six fires were started with the rocket fuel, as it turned out, so they were strictly for his amusement.''

With a pang she realized that he was reliving those desperate months—months when he'd realized he was pitted against a ruthless killer, months during which he'd gradually come to know he was racing against time.

"I don't know who leaked it to the press that I not only suspected the first two of the series of fires were caused by the same person, but that I was convinced my mystery man had been operating for years and had once been associated with Curtiss, but the *Globe* got hold of the story and the other papers picked it up. The next day Pascoe introduced himself to me on the Charles Station platform, like I said. The day after that an old hotel burned down and a pensioner who lived on the top floor was killed. I knew what the accelerant was going to be even before the lab got back to me with the results, but what I wasn't expecting was the melted remains of some unidentifiable plastic contraption a member of my crew found in the rubble.''

He exhaled. "It was obviously meant to be some kind of triggering mechanism, but we didn't find anything it could have triggered and Pascoe always started his fires by hand anyway. When we found the next one I took that back to my office, too, but I couldn't figure out why he'd planted them. They were about as deadly as an alarm clock, but I knew I was missing something, because they just shouldn't have been there. It was like Pascoe was taunting me by leaving them for me to find."

"And by then the whispers had started," she said, more to remind him that he wasn't alone than to second-guess him. A corner of his mouth lifted.

"Yeah, the whispers had started. McQueen was losing it, McQueen was trying to get his name into the papers, McQueen had created his own personal Lex Luthor so he could be a hero. I started sleeping at the office, and I started belting back a couple shots of bourbon to help me sleep. I was sober on the job, so I told myself it was okay. It seemed even more okay when Pascoe's next fire was knocked down before it took hold."

"Then you *were* closing in on him." She couldn't keep the frustration from her voice. "Why didn't they see you were on the right track after that?"

"Because I'd had nothing to do with it, honey," he said harshly. "An anonymous tip was phoned in to the nearest stationhouse. The caller said he'd seen someone carrying what looked like a gas can around the back of a community center. The firetrucks were there even as the first flames started coming out of the ground floor windows, everyone got out safely and we recovered another of the plastic devices. It hadn't had chance to melt. It was obviously an activation device of some type, but again with nothing to activate."

He took a breath. "The biggest thrill for an arsonist is to blend into the crowd gathered around the fire he's started. I knew Pascoe had to be no different from the rest of his kind in that respect. The next night I was at the office poring over the structural plans of the buildings he'd torched in the last few weeks when I heard over the scanner that crews were responding to a massive blaze at the Mitchell Towers, and even before the report had finished I was in my car. All I could think was that there was an outside chance I might actually come upon him just standing in the crowd.''

He closed his eyes. He opened them again, and although his arms were around her Tamara felt as if he was a million miles away. When he spoke again it was in a dead, flat tone.

''I had my radio with me. There was a lot of static but I could make out the crew chief's orders as he gave them. I heard the outside hose crew reporting they'd knocked down the fire on the upper storeys, and I heard the chief ordering the first unit in. I heard him mention Burke by name. I was only a couple of blocks away when I suddenly knew what Pascoe had been planning all along.''

How often over the past seven years had he raced in his nightmares toward a disaster he knew he was powerless to stop? Tamara wondered wrenchingly. How many times had he heard a staticky voice over a radio give the last orders five brave firefighters had ever heard? Had he been reliving that doomed race against time and hearing those orders when she'd first seen him only two days ago, standing with his back to her and looking sightlessly out of a window?

''I'd assumed the devices we'd found were incendiary triggers. I'd thought Pascoe had been toying with the idea of starting his fires remotely, and testing the toughness of the casings while still using his old method. Instead he'd been testing me. He'd wanted to see if I could figure out his plan before he armed his devices. I failed the test,'' Stone said softly.

"Even while I was screaming into the radio to be patched through to the chief's frequency so he could hear me, I got to the scene. I pushed my way through to the chief and yelled at him to get his people out of there. I'd actually gone past him and was a few feet from the main entrance, intending to go in after them myself, when the whole thing just blew. This time Pascoe's device had been operational. It had triggered the bomb he'd planted near one of the crucial supports of the building. From wherever he was watching he'd brought the entire building crashing down, knowing full well there were firefighters inside.''

This time when he closed his eyes he kept them squeezed shut. His whisper was ragged.

"Terry Cutshaw. I went to his funeral first. Max Aiken's and Larry Steinbeck's were held on the same day, one in the morning and one in the afternoon. In between the two services I went back to the hospital, and they told me Monty Stewart had been taken off life support and had died. Two days later, while I was sitting at her bedside, Donna finally slipped from the coma she'd been in since the night she'd been pulled from the wreckage of the Mitchell Towers. After I'd attended her funeral I came back to the office, handed in my badge and ID, and went out and got drunk. I stayed drunk for the next seven years, but being drunk didn't change anything.''

"You'd looked into its face, McQueen.'' Her own whisper was a thread, Tamara noted dispassionately. But thready or not, the words she had to say needed to be spoken now. "You thought you saw yourself looking back. You were *wrong,* dammit.''

He shook his head. "No, honey, I was right. I should

have gotten there sooner. Thirty seconds earlier and I would have made it into the building. I might have gotten them out.''

She stared at him. ''You wouldn't have gotten them out. That was never a possibility, and you know it. You'd have been killed, too.''

Suddenly it seemed as though a giant hand was gripping her heart. ''Dear God—*that's* what's been tearing you apart all these years,'' she breathed. ''You think you should have died in there with them, don't you?''

His gaze met hers emotionlessly. Sudden fury tore through her.

''You did your *job*, McQueen! You were hunting a monster no one believed in except you! Any other man would have knuckled under, but you told the rest of the world to go to hell and you kept hunting Pascoe—and came closer than anyone ever had to catching him. The fact that he got away wasn't your fault. The fact that you survived isn't a reason for guilt, either. I should know, dammit!''

Her voice shook with emotion. ''I was five years *old*, for God's sake! I was five years old and I woke up in the middle of the night and I had to go to the bathroom. I didn't want to be a baby and wake up my mom and dad, so I found my way there in the dark, even though I was in a strange motel room and I was scared.''

She could feel the tears welling up in her eyes but she didn't care. All that mattered was the man watching her. All that mattered was making him understand.

''I closed the bathroom door—not all the way, but almost. I thought I could hear sounds from outside—a car door closing, voices from one of the nearby units. The next minute my whole world exploded in a ball of fire.''

Impatiently she knuckled her eyes. Gently he pushed her hand aside and thumbed away her tears himself.

"Don't talk about it anymore, Tam," he said tonelessly. "I can't bear to see you hurting like this."

"And I can't bear to see *you* hurting either!" She glared at him through her tears. He looked away.

"There's not much more to tell," she continued. "When I was older I told Uncle Jack I needed to know how they'd died. He said it had probably been almost instantaneous, and from the explosion of the room's gas heater rather than from the fire. It helped a little, but it didn't take away the memories—that towering ball of fire coming toward me, myself screaming out for my parents and Mikey, the tiny window in the bathroom that I could just reach when I stood on the toilet tank. I was sure I was going to die. I knew I didn't want to. I wriggled out through the bathroom window and dropped to the ground, and I don't really remember much more after that."

She smiled tightly at him. "You're wondering what this has to do with your situation, aren't you? After all, I was just a little girl. Who could hold me responsible for something that wasn't my fault?" Her voice took on an edge. "I'll tell you who, McQueen. *You* do."

His head jerked up. Behind the opaqueness of his eyes she saw a spark. "That's crazy, honey. How could you think that?"

"I think it because it's true." She held his gaze with hers. "If you're guilty, then I'm guilty, because we both committed the same crime. We *survived*, dammit. Others died. We lived. If you can blame yourself for that, then you blame me, too. And all the while, the one really responsible for those five deaths is still out there tearing lives apart."

"I know Pascoe set the bomb," he said tersely. "I should have found some way to stop him."

His arms were no longer around her. It took no effort at all to slip away from him. Tamara stood.

"There was no way you could have stopped Pascoe then, and deep down you know it. But we can stop him now." She lifted her shoulders helplessly. "You've been handed a second chance to put the past right."

"You really believe that, Tam?" He looked up at her, his face unreadable. "You think that sometimes we get to change the past, to wipe out our mistakes and start all over again? Do you swear you really believe that?"

His tone held an odd intensity, and just for a moment unease stirred in her. Then she nodded. "I swear I believe that, Stone. The past can be changed."

You changed mine, she thought tremulously. *You took away the pain and regret I'd been carrying for so long by replacing the memory of a night in a stranger's arms with the reality of the passion I found in yours.*

Slowly he stood. He took a step toward her. His hand reached out and she felt his fingertips lightly touching her hair.

"I'd hoped it could be," he said huskily. "I was afraid I was lying to myself, honey."

She saw the shadows fade from his eyes. She saw his jaw set and his mouth straighten to a hard line. He took a deep breath.

"Robert Pascoe's out there somewhere, Tam. Let's get our butts in gear and go hunt the bastard down."

Chapter Fifteen

Robert Pascoe was out there somewhere, Tamara reflected hours later. They'd just had no luck today in picking up his track.

Glenda Fodor, her landlord informed them, had done a midnight flit weeks ago. Tempting as it was to blame her disappearance on Trainor and Knopf, even Stone admitted it was obvious they'd had nothing to do with it—though from the landlord's description of the men who'd been asking for her earlier that day, the two investigators had been there.

They'd had a single lead. Now they had none. Stone had phoned Chandra at the office, only to get her voice mail. He'd left a message for her to phone them.

"If she can get my old files I can go over them," he'd said. "I don't see any other option."

So investigation-wise, the morning had been a complete bust. But as if to compensate, the last few hours had turned out to be about as perfect as possible.

"It's the dog, isn't it?" In the driver's seat beside her, Stone grinned. "'Fess up, honey, you fell in love with him even more than Tiger did. That's why you've got that big smile all over your face."

"I'm sitting here with a big smile all over my face

because I'm happy," she replied simply. "Happy that I got to see for myself that Joey was doing fine, happy about how it turned out with Petra and happy just to be here with you." She felt her smile widen. "But Strawberry *is* adorable."

After they'd paid a brief visit to the hospital and she'd been allowed to look in on a sleeping Joey, they'd headed straight to Mary Hall's home. What Stone thought of as his fatal charm Tamara been more inclined to call bulldozing, but finally the woman had let them take Petra for the afternoon. When the child had come out of the house she'd promptly thrown her arms around Stone when she'd heard where they were going.

As she and Petra had gotten out of the car at the entrance to the animal shelter while Stone found a parking space, it had taken all Tamara's courage to broach the subject she knew they needed to talk about.

"Remember you said your mom had written me letters?" she said, squatting down on her heels so that her face was on a level with the carefully blank expression turned on her.

"I remember. But now I think I was wrong." The words dropped from the little mouth like stones. "She wasn't writing to you at all. She was writing to her *real* best friend."

For a moment Tamara's will failed her. Stone had a rapport with the child, she thought desperately. Maybe it would be better to wait until he was here to mediate this conversation. Sighing, she was about to stand up when she caught the furtive gleam of tears in the angry green eyes watching her.

Her heart cracked.

"I *was* her best friend, Petra," she said softly. "I just forgot that for a while, that's all. But I read all her letters yesterday, and they helped me remember how much I loved your mom. I read she quit smoking. You must have been pretty proud of her when she did.''

"It was hard for her. She chewed a special kind of gum that wasn't for kids.'' Petra looked away, as if she wanted to make it clear she was keeping a distance between them.

"And for the first few weeks she always had candy bars in the house,'' she added. "We used to sit on the sofa after she'd finished washing the dishes and I'd done my homework, and we would each have half of one while I watched television for an hour before bed. It— it was fun.''

She swung her gaze back to Tamara's. Her eyes were wide and shadowed. "Stone said it was just like she fell asleep. He was telling me the truth, wasn't he?''

"Let me tell you something about Stone, sweetie.'' Tamara reached for Petra's hands. After a slight hesitation, the child allowed her to take them. "He always wants his own way. He's kind of big and loud. And sometimes he drives me crazy.'' She gave the fingers in her grasp a squeeze. "But he never, ever lies. He told you the truth, sweetie. Your mom didn't suffer at all.''

"I should have stayed awake, Tam-Tam.''

Tamara wasn't sure what was more poignant—the agonized whisper that rushed from Petra or the fact that she was calling her by the pet name Claudia had always used. She pulled the stiff little body closer.

"We'd gone to the park and I'd been playing all afternoon. After supper I just fell asleep, and I didn't wake up until—until—''

Suddenly her arms were around Tamara's neck, and her body was shaking with sobs. Tamara pulled her fiercely into her embrace, her own eyes overflowing.

"Mom's gone, and I'm never going to see her again, am I?" The anguished question poured from her with her tears.

Over Petra's shoulder, Tamara saw Stone approach and pause. She tightened her hold on Petra. "You won't see her, sweetie, but she'll be there. She loved you more than anything in the world, so how could she ever really leave you? She'll be there when I read you her letters, she'll be there when I tell you stories about when she was a little girl like you and she'll be there on the sofa with you and me and Stone, when we watch movies and have popcorn and laugh together. And she'll be watching to make sure you pick out the very best pup in the shelter. She's here right now, sweetie. Moms never really go away."

She was tough and a scrapper, Tamara thought now. But she had the loving heart of her mother, and that heart had finally opened to let her mother's best friend in.

Her face had lit up with joy when she'd seen the gangling black and white pup she'd promptly chosen for her own. She'd christened him Strawberry, for his strawberry-pink tongue, and only the promise that they would pick him up the next day after the veterinarian had checked him over had persuaded her to leave him for the night.

"This looks like trouble. Slide down in your seat, honey."

Startled from her thoughts, Tamara glanced up and saw they were approaching her house. There was a police car in the driveway. Behind that was the nondescript sedan she'd seen Trainor and Knopf getting into outside the Red Spot.

Which wasn't surprising, she thought, seeing as how the pair were right now pounding on her front door. She ducked quickly out of sight, and saw Stone avert his head as they cruised by.

"You can get up now. I don't think they spotted me, but we've got to call Jack." Stone's voice was grim. "I want to know what the hell's going on, and I want to know now."

"You know what's going on. They were there to have you arrested," Tamara said tightly. "For the rooming house fire and whatever other trumped-up charges they think they can hang on you, McQueen. But you're right, we'll call Uncle Jack and see if he knows what they think they've got on you."

"They can't have anything on me because I didn't do it. But somehow I don't think those clowns are really concerned about annoying details like proof," he growled. "And while I'm cooling my heels in a holding cell and all this is being sorted out, Pascoe could be planning another damned fire."

"Turn left here." One minute she'd been daydreaming about the best day of her life, she thought angrily, and only seconds later it seemed to have turned into a nightmare, thanks to a pair of incompetent and vengeful fools. "There's a phone outside that convenience store. If Uncle Jack's not at home, let's pray he's still got his cell on him."

"Give me both his numbers, and while I'm phoning lock the doors," Stone said as they pulled into the parking lot. "This isn't exactly the safest-looking place for a woman now that it's getting on for evening."

She shot him an exasperated look. "For crying out loud, McQueen, where do you think I go at night when I've run out of milk?"

"Humor me, honey," he said firmly. "And next time

you run out of milk in the middle of the night, I'll get it, okay?''

She was in love with the man, Tamara thought in resignation, watching him stride across the parking lot. The door latch locked with a solid-sounding *thunk*, and out of the corner of her eye she saw a couple of scrawny loungers look toward the car at the sound.

She was in love with the man, and that meant the whole package—his occasional overbearingness, his protective manner toward her, his insistence on being the man for his woman in a world that had tended to blur those distinctions. And he was right, she admitted with reluctant honesty. She'd never felt entirely comfortable coming here after dusk.

He didn't compromise. He didn't pretend. That was the key to his whole character. She loved that about him, but it was what had turned Knopf and Trainor so against him they could believe him capable of the crimes they wanted him booked for.

''They want to take me in for the rooming house fire, all right.'' As soon as she opened the door for him Stone was in the car and sliding behind the wheel. He reversed out of the lot, his face hard. ''Jack says they've been going over my old reports. Already there's scuttlebutt going around about the Mitchell Towers blaze.''

''What kind of scuttlebutt?'' She was almost afraid to ask.

''That I not only set the fire myself but I rigged the explosion that resulted in the deaths,'' he said, his mouth tightening. ''The theory is that it was on a timer and it went off sooner than I'd calculated. Damn those two bastards anyway,'' he muttered. ''As if the families of those firefighters need the trauma starting up all over again.''

"What does Uncle Jack suggest we do?"

"Lay low while he tries to pull some strings," McQueen said dryly. "I said that sounded good to me, since my only other option was to turn myself in. When I told him Knopf and Trainor had practically staked out your house, he nearly blew a gasket. I think the first thing he intends is to get them the hell off your property unless they can show him a warrant, so I should be able to drop you at home in an hour or so."

"Oh, good. Because I'd like to do my nails and have a bubble bath before I go to bed," Tamara drawled. She leveled an impatient look at him. "Get real. We're in this together, McQueen, like I've told you about a dozen times. Even if you end up handing yourself over to the authorities tonight I'm going to be right there beside you, dammit."

"You kiss your boyfriend with that mouth, lady?"

The thread of amusement in his tone contrasted with the edginess it had held moments ago. She smiled, glad she'd taken his mind off his problems, if only briefly.

"Yup," she said promptly. "He likes bad girls."

"He likes one bad girl," Stone corrected, reaching over and slipping a hand between her jeans-clad thighs. "He can't wait to teach her a couple more bad things to do with that mouth."

Slow heat spread through her, and with it a spark of frustration at the knowledge that no matter how much both of them wanted it, at the end of the evening it was unlikely they'd be in each other's arms as they had been last night. On impulse, she brought his hand to her mouth and pressed a kiss to his palm. Folding his fingers closed, she gave him a shaky smile.

"That's for later," she said unevenly. "Just in case."

Just in case it all goes bad tonight, she thought, staring unseeingly out at the lights and the traffic. *Just in case they try to tear your world apart again.*

She leaned back against the headrest, her thoughts unsettled. He'd need a lawyer. She'd have to come up with some kind of explanation for Petra if he wasn't with her tomorrow. She and Uncle Jack would have to—

"I don't freakin' *believe* it."

Even as Stone's exclamation broke the silence he was pulling over to the curb. Opening her eyes, Tamara saw they were in an area of small commercial buildings, the flickering neon of an eatery far down the block the only sign that the business district had any life at all after office hours. But someone had faith in the possibilities here, she realized. Across the street was the skeleton of a five-storey building set in an otherwise empty lot. In front was a large sign with what appeared to be an architect's ambitious rendering of how the as-yet barely started structure would look.

It wasn't the picture that Stone was staring at in disbelief, she knew a second later as she read the banner-like notice at the bottom of the board.

"The new Mitchell Towers now accepting rentals!!! Desirable office suites still available, construction to be completed September this year!!"

"They didn't even have the decency to change the name," he said tightly. "I'd hoped they'd never find a developer willing to construct here again."

He was out of the car and heading across the street before she'd unclipped her seat belt. Scrambling out herself, Tamara caught up with him as he halted in front of the edifice. Only its bottom two storeys were covered in some kind of weatherproof sheathing, she saw. The top three were still little more than supports and framing, although temporary floors had been installed to make it easier for the construction crew to get around.

"A couple years from now no one's gonna remember that five firefighters gave their lives here," Stone rasped. "I know you can't stop progress, Tam, but it just doesn't seem right."

"I heard tell there was talk of putting up some kind of memorial plaque. That you, McQueen? Long time no see."

The shabbily dressed old man coming from the alleyway beside the half-completed building was carrying a white cane and wearing dark glasses. He stopped a few feet from them.

"In my case, a real long time. But I'm pretty good with voices and footsteps. It is you, isn't it?"

"Katz? Harry Katz?" The street lighting in the area was sparse, but the security floodlight affixed to the building illuminated the surprise on Stone's features. "For crying out loud. Don't tell me you still live here."

"New cardboard box, same location, McQueen," the other man said. "I'm too old a dog to change, although I'll admit I hit the shelters a little more often than I used to. The booze acted like antifreeze, I guess. I've been off the sauce for five years come this summer."

"That's great, Katz. Just great." Stone took the old man's heavily-veined hand, wringing it with real affection. He hesitated. "You probably saw me a little the worse for wear when I used to drop by here after the fire. I've cleaned up my act, too."

"I could tell. If you'd touched the stuff anytime recently I would have smelled it on you. Eyes like a mole, nose like a bloodhound, hearing like a fox, that's me." The old man grinned. "Which means I know she's pretty, whether I can see her or not. You scared I'll steal her away from you if you introduce us, McQueen?''

''Sure I'm scared, you silver-tongued old devil.'' Stone laughed softly. ''Tamara, this is Harry Katz. He was a friend when I didn't think I wanted one. Harry, this is Tamara King. She's a firefighter. She's also the heart of my heart, so back off.''

He had to warn her when he was going to do that, Tamara thought shakily, taking the hand the old man extended to her. He couldn't go roaring along in his normal McQueen style and then drop an extravagance like that into the conversation.

Heart of his heart. She felt herself blushing with pure pleasure before turning her attention to what he was saying.

''Did I ever ask you about it, Harry? Or was I even coherent when I used to come around here during that period?''

His question was tentative. The old man took his time before replying.

''You were hurting bad, that was obvious. For those six or seven months after the fire, you couldn't seem to stay away, but you didn't want to talk about it. None of the other investigators that tramped around the site while it was still fresh ever asked me any questions, either. They figured since I was blind, I wouldn't have anything to tell them.''

He rubbed his white-stubbled chin with a suddenly trembling hand. ''And since they didn't ask, I didn't volunteer. I was a homeless drunk. If they hadn't believed you, why would they believe me? He's back, isn't he? I was sure it was him.''

Stone stared at him in stupefaction. ''Who's back, Harry? And what do you mean, you were sure?''

"Not here." The old man dipped his head in the direction of the shadowy alleyway. "I told you, I'm a mole. I feel safer in the dark."

Tamara felt Stone's hand on her arm as they picked their way along the cracked pavement of the alley, but she wondered if it was her or himself he was attempting to steady.

"Down here." Unerringly the blind man grasped a rusted metal handrail flanking the short downward flight of concrete steps in front of them. At the bottom was a basement entrance to the building beside them, she realized, with just room enough for the three of them.

By craning her neck she could see past the steps they'd just descended and down the alleyway to the street. From this angle, only the back of the billboard was visible.

"You've seen him, haven't you?" McQueen's voice was unsteady. "Robert Pascoe. He's been here, hasn't he, Harry?"

"I haven't seen him." Katz seemed to take no offence at the slip. "I've heard him. He comes by every couple of nights to look at the site. The only other person who ever did that on a regular basis was you," he added. "And I don't know what his name is, I just know he's the son of a bitch I always suspected of torching the place. He started coming round a few weeks ago, but I recognized the sound of his footsteps right away. When I heard his voice, that clinched it."

"Back up there, Harry," Stone said tersely. "You're saying you had a pretty good idea of who started the Mitchell Towers fire and you never told me? You never told *anyone?*"

"I'm saying that the night before the fire I was sleeping off a drunk in this stairwell here, and I woke up to hear two men talking," Katz retorted. "Arguing, more like, even though they kept their voices down. In the state I was in, what they were arguing about didn't make much sense to me, so I rolled over and went back to sleep. It was only when the whole place went up in flames the next night that I put the pieces together, and when I did I was scared spitless."

He paused. "So I was real glad when no one asked me if I knew anything, McQueen," he went on in a lower tone. "And when you started haunting the place I'd already overheard what everyone thought of the nutcase who'd cracked up and resigned before they could fire him. Even after I got to know you, I decided to keep my mouth shut. I knew no one would care about any witness you said you'd found."

Stone let his breath out in a sigh. "You're right, Harry, they would have told me to get lost. But maybe they won't now. What exactly did you hear the night before the fire?"

"What woke me up was the sound of something metal being set down on concrete." It was hard to see Katz's expression, but from his voice Tamara knew he was frowning. "The old Mitchell Towers had the same kind of stairwell as this one, and that was where the voices were coming from. I heard a man say something about all it would take was a spark, so not to make him nervous. He's the one who shows up here now."

"Pascoe," Stone said. "Go on."

"The second man was angry. He seemed to be threatening this Pascoe, telling him he was going to turn him in, but Pascoe, if that's who he was, seemed to find the whole thing funny. He said Jake had a lot more to lose than he did and that both of them knew he'd keep quiet, just like he'd always kept—"

"Jake? The other man's name was Jake?" Stone interrupted.

"That's what I seem to remember Pascoe calling him," Katz replied. "I was drunk, though, so I might have gotten it wrong. Anyway, that's when the conversation got weird. Pascoe laughed again, and—"

Tamara stiffened. "Harry, could Pascoe have been calling him *jakey*?" she asked numbly. "Is it possible that's what you heard him say?"

"Jakey. Yeah, that's right." The old man snapped his fingers softly in the dark. "I remember it sounded like a kid's name, not a grown man's."

"He was a firefighter." McQueen's tone was flat. "Goddammit, he was one of *us*. A firefighter knew what was going to happen, and he stood by and let five of his comrades *die*."

"You know this Jakey guy?" Katz sounded confused.

"I hope not," McQueen said grimly. "What do you mean, the conversation got weird after that?"

"It coulda been the booze." The old man sighed. "But the one you figure as a firefighter said something I didn't catch, and Pascoe's voice got real cold. He said the Chinese man was wrong and this Jakey guy wasn't responsible forever, because if that was true and Davidson was still alive, the poor fool would still be watching Jakey's back. The firefighter—Jakey, I guess—said Davidson might not have been the brightest guy, but he'd taken what he'd known to the grave even though he could have saved himself by implicating Jakey. Jakey said that if Davidson had, he wouldn't have hesitated to take Pascoe down with him."

Katz made a small movement that could have been a shrug. "It was two guys having an argument, McQueen, and an argument that didn't make sense to me. I musta dozed off again then, because that's all I remember. It wasn't until the fire the next night that I realized—''

His head jerked up. As McQueen started to say something Katz waved him urgently into silence.

He took a cautious step backward, deeper into the stairwell. His whisper was almost inaudible.

''Those footsteps—can you hear them? Someone's coming.''

Again he fell silent, and this time Tamara heard it too—the faint sound of shoe leather on concrete, unhurriedly getting nearer. It was a man's step, she thought, but it was beyond her ability to discern whether he was old or young, fat or thin, tall or short. To know any of those details she would need to see him.

But to the blind man beside her, individual footsteps were as readily identifiable as faces were to her. She felt him tense.

''It's *him,* McQueen,'' Katz said under his breath. ''It's the man you call Robert Pascoe.''

Chapter Sixteen

It never worked this way in movies, Tamara thought, keeping her gaze fixed on the figure half a block ahead. Even driving at the speed of a funeral cortege Stone had to keep pulling in behind parked cars to avoid closing the distance between them and the man on the sidewalk, but they hadn't been able to risk the chance that Pascoe had a car waiting nearby.

If he *was* Pascoe.

Katz had said it himself—he'd been in a drunken stupor when he'd overheard the argument. How could he say with certainty that the voice and footsteps he'd heard that night belonged to the man who'd recently taken to visiting the site? It wasn't as if the rest of his impressions had been rock-solid. He himself admitted that the argument as he remembered it obviously owed some of its outlandishness to his condition at the time.

The man who'd paused at the site and then walked on had been wearing a hat pulled down low over his eyes and his collar turned up, but even those features that weren't actually obscured were impossible to make out in the shadows.

"He's dressed like the invisible man, goddammit,

even down to the gloves,'' Stone had muttered in frustration. "Wait for me here, Tam.''

"What do you think you're doing?'' she'd whispered.

"Taking the bastard down. What am I supposed to do, just let him walk away?'' he'd replied in an angry undertone.

She'd shot an apologetic glance at Harry, forgetting for the moment that he couldn't see her. "If he's not Pascoe, that's exactly what you're supposed to do, McQueen. And if he *is* Pascoe, he'll be off and running as soon as he sees you. Harry says these walks of his are a regular thing. He probably knows every shortcut within a five-block radius.''

"And your plan is?'' There'd been an edgy note in his voice.

"Follow him. Find out where he lives,'' she'd said urgently. "Then we call Uncle Jack and get some reinforcements in.''

If there'd been no doubt in his mind about the man's identity, he would have done it his way, Tamara thought now. The only reason he'd gone along with her suggestion had been because he'd seen the same problems in Harry's story as she had.

"If nothing else, we've got a name to check into,'' she said. "A Davidson who died sometime prior to the fire. Harry seemed pretty sure about that part.''

"That's quite a lead,'' McQueen growled, slowing the car to a crawl. "We don't know when he died, we don't know if he was connected with the fire department and Davidson isn't exactly an uncommon name. Even if we found out who he was, what does that get us? The guy once took the fall for Harry's mystery jakey and no one ever learned about it. If you want to stamp a big red

'Case Closed' across the file on the basis of that, honey, be my guest.''

"It's not a good idea for you to tighten your mouth like that, McQueen," she said coldly. "Your bottom lip's split open again."

Automatically his thumb went to his lip. He touched it gingerly, and then glanced her way.

"What a dirty fighter you are, honey," he said softly. "Are you keeping me in line?"

"Only when you step over it." She saw sudden color mount his cheekbones. "And only when you need me to, McQueen," she murmured huskily.

"Oh, I need you to, sweetheart." He held her gaze. "I think I need it right now."

Her own cheeks felt hot, Tamara thought. In fact, she felt hot all over. In any other circumstances she would have urged him to turn the car around, head straight for her house, and probably neither of them would have made it to her bedroom before giving in to the heat.

But this wasn't the time or the place. He knew it as well as she did.

"When this is all over let's go to bed and not come out for three days," she said, her voice suddenly uneven. "We'll turn off the phone, lower the blinds and let the rest of the world go by while we make love. We can do that, can't we?"

"We can do that, honey." He reached over and touched her hair. "When this is all over we won't let anyone stop us from doing that."

For a moment his hand rested on her hair. Then he sighed, and took it away.

"Sorry I snapped at you, Tam." His knuckles tightened around the steering wheel. "But I knew Harry when he was drinking. The whole thing sounds pretty damn flimsy.''

"It's all we've got," she reminded him, her gaze narrowing on the figure up ahead. "But you're right. I can't even guess what that reference to a Chinese man—hey! Where'd he go?"

She'd had her eyes right on him, she thought. One minute he'd been there. Now he wasn't.

"He has to have slipped into a hidden entrance or a doorway." McQueen let the car coast to a stop. "I'm going to take it from here myself, honey. If I'm not back in five minutes, go call Jack. Understand?"

"I understand, Stone." She watched with wide eyes as he exited the vehicle. As soon as he started down the sidewalk she began counting under her breath.

"One…two…three…four…*five*."

Grabbing the keys from the ignition, she jumped out of the car and caught up with him.

"I told you I understood," she said as he spun around to face her. "I didn't say I agreed."

"Listen to me, Tamara—" he began furiously, but she cut him off.

"No, you listen to *me*, McQueen. I don't stand around outside a burning building waiting for the guys on the crew to give me the all-clear. I go in and take the same risks they do. Let's get moving."

"You drive me crazy," he muttered, striding down the sidewalk as she trotted to keep up with him.

"Ditto," she snapped. She jerked her head at the darkened storefront they were approaching. "There's where I lost sight of him."

"At least let me be point man," he growled, stepping in front of her. Recessed into the wall beside the store's dingy window was a door. "I was right. This must lead to an apartment over the store. Got a credit card on you?''

When she shook her head McQueen shrugged.

"Let me know if you see anyone coming." Grasping the doorknob, he braced himself and put his shoulder to the door.

In her line of work she'd kicked open more than one locked door, Tamara thought. She saw his biceps bulge with tension. But that procedure depended on abrupt force applied to just the right place, and resulted in the lock popping open loudly and the door smashing back on its hinges. Surely it took more strength than was humanly possible to do what he was attempting—to push inexorably against the lock itself until it gave way. She heard metal grind against metal. McQueen grunted, checking the sudden inward swing of the door as it opened.

"My hero," she breathed, impressed.

His grin was briefly white in the gloom of the unlit entrance. "And don't you forget it, baby." He squinted into the darkness. "There's probably just the one apartment up there. Stay to the sides of the stairs."

This wasn't the way she usually entered a stranger's home, Tamara thought. The one component of a firefighter's job that the public never comprehended was the noise. She stepped on something soft, and stifled a nervous gasp.

"Stone, look…a leather glove," she whispered. "Okay, that clinches it. This is where he came in, and this must be where he lives. Let's get out of here and find a phone."

They'd reached the miniscule landing at the top of the stairs. From under the only door facing onto it came a crack of light, enough to see his expression as he took the glove from her.

He frowned. Slowly he shook his head, and met her suddenly suspicious gaze.

"I can't do it, honey." His voice was edged. "I just can't walk away now. I have to know if it's Pascoe. I have to look the son of a bitch in the face."

Fear and anger flared in her. Just as instantaneously, it died.

Robert Pascoe had destroyed his life. He'd killed five of McQueen's colleagues and countless other innocent victims. And it was possible that he was just behind that door. She'd known all along what McQueen intended to do.

"If it's him, can you take him?" she asked foolishly.

"Honey, please." His tone was wry. "Yeah, I can take him. I can take most guys, and Pascoe's not what I'd call physically formidable. He's a handsome bastard and I'm sure he's never had any trouble getting the ladies, but he's just medium build, at best. But I want you to keep back, and this time it's not negotiable, okay?"

"Okay." Even on the one word her voice had shaken, she realized. Her mouth suddenly dry and her palms suddenly damp, she watched as McQueen stepped up to the door.

"If he asks who it is, let me talk," she said urgently. "He's more likely to open up for a woman."

He hesitated, and then gave her a curt nod. Turning back to the door, he rapped lightly on it with one knuckle.

"Hold on." The casual command was called out from somewhere in the apartment, and a moment later came the sound of muffled footsteps crossing the floor. "Who's there?"

McQueen was to one side of the door, out of range of the security peephole, Tamara saw. She swallowed.

"I—I'm looking for Claudia Anderson. Do I have the right place?"

Silence greeted her words. Then she heard the rattle of a chain-lock sliding back, and she shrank against the wall.

"Come on in, McQueen." The voice on the other side of the door sounded amused. "What took you so long, buddy?"

The door opened. Light from the apartment spilled out into the small hallway. Tamara looked at the man in the doorway.

Horror swept through her.

She'd seen burn victims before. Despite their scars, she found it easy to look past the destroyed tissue and cruelly stretched skin to the courage and humanity of the person inside. Maybe that was why Robert Pascoe's disfigurement was so nightmarishly monstrous, she thought numbly, staring at the barely human face confronting them.

His mask had been melted away. Now his outward appearance reflected the soulless evil that had always been there. Sometime in the past seven years the beast he'd unleashed on so many others had turned on him.

"A pretty woman at my door used to be a common occurrence. Now I'm lucky if they don't scream when they see me on my evening walks, so maybe it's better if I leave the hall light off." He glanced at the bare and unlit bulb above them. "You look shaken, McQueen. Don't worry, it's really me."

"I know it's you, Pascoe," Stone rasped. "But how

did you know it was me, even before you opened the door?''

The sound from Pascoe's throat might have been a laugh. ''As soon as I got back into town a few weeks ago I just had to stroll over to take a look. I thought, hey, if I can't stay away from it, I bet my old buddy McQueen can't, either. Can you believe they're building on the site again?''

''I'm not your buddy, I'm the guy who's taking you in.'' Stone's expression was shuttered. ''Let's go.''

''You sure you want to play it that way?'' Pascoe didn't move. ''Because they're not going to let you near me once you hand me over, McQueen, and you know it. You were an embarrassment to them. I'm even more inconvenient, because I'm the man they insisted was just a figment of your imagination. The way I see it, they'll dig up some restaurant grease fire to pin on me just to get me locked up, and then they'll wash their hands of the two of us. They won't ask me the hard questions. They won't ask me the questions you want to ask me.''

His ruined mouth achieved a smile. ''They don't want to know the answers. If you don't, either, then let me get my coat and I'll come quietly.''

''Stay where you are.'' McQueen's tone was sharp. ''I don't know what your game is, Pascoe, but I know you're playing one. You weren't willing to let yourself be caught seven years ago and I'm not stupid enough to think you don't have something up your sleeve now.''

''Seven years ago I was a man. No—a *god*.'' With shocking suddenness raw fury filled Pascoe's voice. ''Whenever I wanted I could light up the night with my flames and watch the rest of you trying to save yourselves while your world burned around you. Do you understand how that *felt*, McQueen?''

He brought his hands up in front of him. The terrible scars covering his face contorted into a grimace of anguish.

Protruding from the sleeves of his sweater were two clawlike appendages. The fingers of his right hand were completely gone. His left hand seemed to be only a knob of flesh.

"They're useless. I can't even hold a match! That's why I'm willing to turn myself in, McQueen—because there's nothing left for me anymore."

"You looked into the face of the beast, Pascoe," Tamara grated. "Finally it looked back and saw you. I call that justice, not a tragedy."

He let his hands drop to his sides, the emotion he'd just displayed fading as if it had never been. When he spoke his voice once again held a note of amused affability.

"She's a looker, buddy. Feisty, too. But then, you never had any trouble finding them, you just couldn't hang on to them. To be honest, that's a problem I've been running into lately myself. Thought I'd call on an old girlfriend the other night, but it was obvious when she saw me I wasn't her dream date anymore. I went back the next day and found I'd scared her right out of town. Do I scare you, little lady?"

McQueen stepped swiftly forward, his face dark with anger, but Tamara put her hand on his arm.

"Yeah, you scare me," she said softly. "You scare the spit out of me, Pascoe. I'm not a little lady, I'm a firefighter, and you scare me because I've seen lives destroyed by crazy bastards like you. But I'm not afraid to have that chat with you."

She turned to McQueen. "He's right, Stone. Once you

hand him over they're not going to allow you access to him.''

Even before she'd finished he was shaking his head. ''I don't like it, Tamara. I *know* him. I know what he's capable of.''

''You know what he used to be capable of,'' she said urgently. ''He's not a threat anymore. Dammit, there's a jakey walking around who stood by and let five fire-fighters die. I'm not willing to risk that being covered up.''

She turned to Pascoe. ''We know you had a contact in the department. Who was he?''

''A business associate from the old days.'' Pascoe slanted a glance at her. ''Nice name. What do they call you, Tammy?''

''The old days when you worked for Bracknell Curtiss? The old days before you killed him?'' McQueen moved, forcing Pascoe's attention on to himself. ''Are you saying you've had a jakey feeding you information and protecting your back all that time? What in the world would turn a jakey against his own so completely that he'd betray them like that?''

''He had a problem. Curtiss made his problem go away. I told Curtiss he was playing with fire, so to speak, but he didn't listen.'' Again Pascoe's mouth stretched into a parody of a smile. ''The jakey didn't turn against his own, McQueen. In the end he turned against Curtiss. He was the one who killed him, not me.''

''Now I know you're lying,'' Stone said tightly. ''That fire was one of your rocket fuel specials.''

''Of course he used the same accelerant,'' Pascoe snapped. ''He wanted to make it look as if I'd done it, just like he wanted to make it look like I torched that rooming house. You're not tracking, McQueen. Do you really think these things were capable of setting a fire three days ago?''

He held up what remained of his hands. ''He knew where I stored it. He knew I only used it when everything had to be just right. Some crackpot inventor in the desert near Vegas when Bracknell and I used to operate out west came up with the formula for it. He was another one who had a problem, only in his case Bracknell had no reason to make it go away. When he couldn't pay off his debts I was sent in to make an example of him, and when I saw how perfect his invention was for my needs, I took what was left with me when we relocated in Boston. He stole a whole can of the stuff from me. Do you know how many fires he robbed me of by doing that?''

''I don't give a damn how many friggin' fires you think you lost out on,'' McQueen ground out. ''All I'm interested in is a name. Who was he?''

''I'm telling this my way or I'm not telling it at all,'' Pascoe said flatly. ''This is all I've got left, McQueen— talking about my fires.''

''So he's still in the department and still operating.'' Tamara closed her eyes briefly. ''Dear God, is he trying to take up where you left off?''

''We were never best buds. We were enemies who had enough on each other to make a working relationship possible, but he still thought of himself as one of the good guys. It's all justifiable to him. Bracknell never understood that about him. I didn't either at first.''

Pascoe's gaze lingered for a moment on her. ''Anyone ever tell you you've got hair like fire, Tammy? Bet the other kids teased you about it when you were growing up, but there's something sexy about a woman with red hair.''

"You don't talk to her. You don't even look at her, Pascoe." McQueen's tone was ice.

"I didn't mean to step on your turf, buddy." To Tamara's relief Pascoe took his gaze from her. "Like I said, I came close to going down the same way Bracknell did, but me and the jakey came to an arrangement. I wouldn't tell what I knew and he wouldn't blow the whistle on me. It worked okay until the Mitchell Towers blaze. I pushed him over the line on that one. That's why I had to leave Boston."

"Why did you do it?" McQueen's jaw was clenched so tightly he could barely force the question out. "I know you get off on the fires, but that was deliberate murder. You waited until they went in before you detonated that explosion, didn't you?"

"No, McQueen. I waited until I saw *you,*" Pascoe said softly.

"You waited until you saw—" Stone's voice was harsh with shock. Glancing swiftly at him, Tamara saw terrible comprehension enter his gaze. "It was all about *me,* wasn't it?" he said hoarsely. "I was getting too damn close to you, and you needed to derail me. For the love of God, you killed five firefighters just so you could remain a ghost, a man no one believed existed."

Under his tan his skin was ashen. He took a step forward. "If that's what you want, I can give it to you," he said thickly. "Dammit, I can take away your existence right—"

"You're too *late,* McQueen!" Pascoe snarled, the mask of affability he'd been wearing finally stripping away completely. Tamara saw hatred flare in his eyes, and fear flashed through her. "I'm one step ahead of you, just like I've always been. I've arranged it myself, and I'm taking you with me!"

The knob of flesh that had once been his hand moved so swiftly that it was a blur. Tamara saw it knock the hall light-switch upward. She saw Pascoe's mouth open wide in a scream of unholy triumph. She saw the bare bulb above them brighten like an exploding sun—

"Tam!"

Even as McQueen shouted out her name his arms were around her, and he was diving from the landing into space, his body shielding hers. They hit the steps halfway down with a crashing jar and then they were tumbling down the rest of the stairs.

Tamara barely noticed. Her stricken gaze was fixed on the ball of fire that was rushing down the stairwell toward them.

They hit the bottom of the stairs, and immediately Stone was on his feet again. She caught an instant glimpse of his face, bloodied and grim as he scooped her up, pulled open the door to the street, and took a last desperate leap.

The pavement smashed up to meet them. His body still around hers, McQueen kept rolling, like a paratrooper making a dangerous landing. The ball of fire raced out of the doorway and across the sidewalk, and heat slammed into her like a wall. She tasted oil and dirt and asphalt, and then, blessedly, cool air flooding her lungs. She felt them stop rolling.

"Tam, honey, are you okay? Say something, baby!" Blood ran from the gash at his hairline into his left eye as he lifted his head. His gaze was dark with fear. "Talk to me, honey."

"I—I'm okay. But you, Stone…" She took in the graze on his forehead, the bracketing of pain around his mouth.

"I'm fine," he said tersely. "Dammit, you could have

been killed. How could I have put you in danger like that? I should have *known* he had some insane plan in mind.''

Abruptly he gathered her to him again, as if he was afraid of letting her go. ''I lost you once, baby. I found you and I lost you all in one night. When I walked away from you, I knew I'd just destroyed anything I might have had with you. I swore if I ever got another chance I'd *never* lose you again, but when I saw that maniac reaching for that switch I—''

''What do you mean, you found me and lost me in one night?'' Tamara looked up into his face. ''What night are you talking—''

She froze. Her gaze widened. She tried to take a breath and found she couldn't.

''It was *you*.''

The words felt torn from her. She saw brilliant pain flicker behind his eyes, heard him start to say something, and suddenly a terrible fury poured through her, burning away everything she'd thought was real, everything she'd thought she'd known about him. She put her trembling hands against his chest and shoved herself away.

''It was you, wasn't it? The night of my wedding, the most shameful night of my life, it was you,'' she rasped. Behind him the flames engulfed the begrimed storefront, and the display window shattered into blades of falling glass. She could feel every one of them piercing her heart.

''You were the stranger, weren't you, McQueen?'' she whispered hoarsely. ''You were the stranger I slept with that night!''

Chapter Seventeen

"He's gone," she said out loud, not looking at Pangor as he ran past her to the door looking for his beloved McQueen. "He's gone and he won't be back, so it's no good looking for him."

It was funny, she thought, sitting down at the kitchen table. The stupid cat had spent his life distrusting people and avoiding affection. Then a big man with a loud voice and rough manners had crashed into his sealed-off little world and the animal had fallen for him just like that.

"Stupid cat," she said dully. "Stupid woman."

As she'd gotten stiffly to her feet outside what had only moments earlier been Pascoe's apartment he'd grasped her arm to help her, and she'd fixed him with a flat stare.

"Don't touch me, McQueen. I don't want your hands on me," she'd said. "We'd better get out of here."

Without looking to see if he was following her, she started walking to the car. Soon one of Robert Pascoe's fires would again have a contingent of firefighters pitting themselves against the blaze, she thought. This time it would be his own charred body that was pulled from the ruins. Hers might have been found there, too, except for McQueen.

He'd saved her. He'd destroyed her.

"You're wanted for arson. The last place you want to be found is in the vicinity of a fire," she said tonelessly, pulling her keys from her pocket. "Tell me where you want me to drop you."

"I'll drive you home." He took the keys from her. "I can call a cab from your place."

"No, McQueen." As he opened the passenger door for her she shook her head. "I owe you a lift. But I want you out of my sight as soon as possible."

He closed his eyes, as if from a blow. Then he opened them, and the past three days disappeared. He was the man standing at the window again, the man who'd reached rock bottom and was still going down.

"I know you do, honey."

As they pulled away from the curb she saw the fire trucks approaching, the crews already bracing themselves. She said a silent prayer for their safety, as she always did, and then she spoke, her voice too loud.

"Would you ever have told me?"

"I kept telling myself I would." McQueen turned the car onto another street. "I hope I would have been man enough to."

"What was it like, McQueen?" There was nothing but detached curiosity in her tone. "Was it every blue-movie fantasy come true—the jilted bride, still dressed in white, with you as the randy stud giving her the wedding night she might have missed out on? Too bad I was so damn drunk most of it was a blur." Her perilous detachment cracked slightly. "You *bastard*. You saw me at my most vulnerable, and you moved in on me."

"It was your vulnerability I never could make myself forget," he said harshly, his gaze on the traffic ahead and his hands tight on the wheel. "Your vulnerability and your pain. Everything I did that night was wrong, Tamara, but it wasn't for any of the reasons you think. You sat down at my table in that bar. I looked at you…and just like that I needed to take everything bad away for you.''

Ahead of them was a red light. ''I needed to take it away for myself, too,'' he added emotionlessly. ''I'd gone to the last of the funerals that day. I'd watched them lower Burke's casket into the ground and then I'd found the nearest bar and started drinking. But that doesn't justify anything I did.''

He'd been to Donna Burke's funeral that day. That had been the day he'd handed in his resignation and started down the self-destructive road that had nearly torn him apart. Just for a moment a thin sliver of understanding broke through her own pain. She hated herself for her weakness immediately.

''Even if it did, it doesn't stretch over seven years. You knew who I was as soon as you saw me in that rooming house. You knew who I was when you came to my bed last night.''

Her voice had risen. ''You knew who *I* was. You knew I didn't know who *you* were.''

''I thought I'd been given a second chance with you,'' he said, almost to himself. ''The one unforgivable action,'' he added huskily. ''I thought I might be able to balance it. I thought I might be able to make you love me.''

She stared at him in angry disbelief. ''That's just it, McQueen—you *did*. That's what tears at me so! I *did* fall in love with you, dammit!''

''No, honey.'' The light ahead of them was still red, and he reached for the door handle. ''I think you came real close, but one vital part of you held back. I told you once you couldn't trust anyone enough to fall in love with them, and for a while I thought it was because of the way you'd been betrayed by Claudia. But it's not that.''

He opened the door. He stepped out of the car. He glanced at the neon sign over a nearby bar, and looked back at her as she slid across the seat and behind the wheel.

''You were expecting something like this all along. That's why you never said the words.''

She looked up at him, startled. Before she knew what he intended to do his hand went around the back of her neck and he brought his mouth to hers in a hard kiss. Just as swiftly he released her.

''That's why you never told me you loved me,'' he said softly.

He'd closed the car door behind him and had strode across the street to the sidewalk without looking back. As the light had turned green she'd accelerated from the intersection, her eyes staring sightlessly ahead of her.

''Of course I told him,'' she said to the empty kitchen. ''I must have.''

He'd told her. He'd told her when she'd been lying in his arms. He'd told her all through the night, sometimes gasping the words out just before he came, sometimes whispering them into her ear as he held her. She'd woken this morning to find him watching her, and it had been the first thing he'd murmured as she'd opened her eyes.

I want it to be like it never happened. I want you to remember this as the first time you were ever with a man, because I already think of you as the first and only woman for me.

He'd told her that, too, she thought, clenching her

hands in her lap. And she'd told him that the past could be changed.

One or both of them had been lying. It didn't matter who and it didn't matter if they'd been lying to each other or themselves. It *had* happened. The past *couldn't* be changed. She'd trusted him, and he'd betrayed that trust in the most complete way imaginable.

She needed to phone Uncle Jack and tell him what they'd learned, Tamara thought, getting stiffly from the chair and walking over to the phone. She needed to sever the last link between her and the man she wanted to forget.

She lifted the receiver, realizing even as she did that she'd interrupted an incoming ring. With immediate certainty she knew it had to be him.

"Hello? Hello?"

It wasn't McQueen. She closed her eyes. "Who's this?"

The voice on the other end of the line sounded hesitant. "It's Bill Trainor. Tamara?"

Her eyes flew open in shock. "What do you want, Trainor? If you're looking for McQueen, he's not here."

"I know he's not. We were at your house today, Tom Knopf and me, hoping we'd find him there."

"You were at my house with the police." It felt good to have an outlet for her rage. She went on, her voice a whiplash. "If you ever show up here again I'm calling the cops on *you,* get it?"

"I don't blame you for being angry. We had no right to show up there. We had no right to go looking for McQueen at all, and that's why I'm calling. Do you know where I can reach him? It—it's important."

About to lay into him again, she checked herself.

There was something wrong here, she thought. The man sounded *frightened*.

"What do you mean, you had no right to go looking for him?"

She could almost see him on the other end of the line, brown eyes blinking in indecision behind the gold-rimmed glasses. When he finally answered her, his words came out in a rush.

"We've got nothing on him, not a single scrap of evidence tying him to that rooming house fire. But Knopf's going to bring McQueen down, even if it means he has to manufacture a case. I've gone along with a lot of things, but this is where Tommy and I part ways."

"Are you trying to tell me your partner intends to frame an innocent man?" She gripped the receiver more tightly. "Is he out of his *mind?*"

"He might be," Trainor muttered. "God help me, I think he's finally cracked. He's hated McQueen since the Dazzlers fiasco—hell, I hated him, too, for what he made us look like."

"Stone didn't make you look incompetent," she interrupted. "The two of you did that all by yourselves, from what I hear. But that's old news, Trainor. What's happened to suddenly make Knopf go off the deep end?"

"I don't *know.*" Frustration bled into his voice. "But I think it's because McQueen's on the trail of Robert Pascoe again. I—I don't think Knopf wants Pascoe caught."

"I thought Knopf didn't believe in Pascoe. I thought his theory was that McQueen created Pascoe as some kind of publicity-getting ploy."

"That's what he's always said, and I believed him. Now I don't. I think he knows there's a real Robert

Pascoe, and I think he's afraid if Pascoe's caught, he'll talk. That's why he wants McQueen stopped.''

"You think he's been working with the arsonist all these years.'' It was falling into place, Tamara thought, closing her eyes and remembering Harry Katz's account. "You think he was Pascoe's contact in the department.''

"I think he was more than that." Trainor's tone hardened. "I think he hired Pascoe to kill a man.''

"Dear God." She braced herself against the kitchen counter. "Who did Knopf have killed?''

"I don't know his name. It was way before my time, when Knopf was still a jakey. An investigator he looked up to got shafted by some hot-shot insurance dick and had to resign in disgrace. Knopf didn't tell me any of this, but it's no secret. Everyone who was around at the time knew how he felt about the man who'd brought his friend down.''

A dull roaring sound seemed to be filling her ears. It grew louder, until Trainor's voice on the other end of the line was just a tiny buzz.

She'd known. She'd always known. When the beast had come rushing at the child she'd been then, she'd known she wasn't alone when she'd escaped the fire and stood bewildered in the motel's parking lot. She'd seen them, or the shapes of them—two men, each standing by their own car. They'd seen her, and one of them had laughed softly.

"Anyone ever tell you you've got hair like fire, little lady? Bet the other kids tease you about it, don't they?''

She'd heard two car doors slam, and she'd fainted dead away.

She'd known. She'd blocked it out all these years.

"What else did Knopf say about the insurance investigator? What were his exact words, Trainor?'' Her lips felt frozen, but at least the roaring sound had lessened a little.

"I asked him why he was gunning for McQueen, and at first he told me I didn't need to know," Trainor said grudgingly. "Then he muttered something like, 'Let's just say it all goes back to a nosy investigator who should've cut Harley a break instead of the guy he did.' I don't think he realized I knew what had happened to Perkins or to the insurance investigator who brought him down."

But you don't know who that insurance investigator was, do you? Tamara thought numbly. *You don't know that his wife and son were killed along with him, and you don't know you're talking to his daughter—the only one of his family who didn't die in that fire.*

"...ended up a damn hero and Harley's remembered as a joke. If I'm right McQueen could get railroaded straight into an arson conviction. For God's sake, half of the department suspected him seven years ago, and if Knopf takes the stand and swears that the evidence he's trumped up against McQueen is solid no one's going to give much weight to anything I say." Trainor sounded strained. "Pascoe's the only one who can clear McQueen. You tell your boyfriend he'd better catch his arsonist before Knopf catches *him.*"

"I'll get word to him somehow. I don't know how, but I'll find a way to warn him. And Trainor—thanks."

She'd stopped shaking, Tamara saw as she hung up the phone and immediately lifted the receiver again. She wasn't shaking, but that only meant she'd imposed enough control over herself to keep functioning right now.

Or maybe that wasn't true, either, she thought a split second later. Instead of calling Uncle Jack's home she'd unconsciously punched in the number of his cell phone. Pressing her lips together in quick irritation, she hung up once more, but not before she'd heard the staccato burring sound that meant she'd connected and the call had gone through.

From somewhere in the house she heard a muffled ringing. It broke off abruptly.

The tiny hairs on the back of her neck rose. Very slowly, she replaced the receiver in the cradle. She turned.

Uncle Jack was standing in the shadows of the hallway. Frowning, he shoved his cell phone into his coat pocket.

"Hate these things," he muttered to himself. He lifted his gaze to her frozen one. His face was devoid of expression.

"You know, don't you, punkin?" he said heavily.

"I know." She wasn't sure if the words had come out. She tried again. "I think I've always known it was you."

"*...other kids tease you about it, don't they?*" *It had been the slimmer man who'd tossed the teasing words at her. But her gaze had been fixed on the bulkier of the two silhouettes. Even as she'd tried to choke out his name, his hands—the same hands that had bounced her on his knee at her parents' house—flew to his face, as if he couldn't bear to look at her or as if he didn't want her to look at him. His shoulders had shaken, and that had frightened her enough that she changed her mind about calling out to him. Why wasn't he running over to her, lifting her up, getting her to safety and then going back in for Mom and Dad and Mikey?*

Uncle Jack was a fireman! He was a hero! Why was he getting into his car and driving away?

She knew why. She didn't want to know.

Just before her terrified mind slid into unconscious-ness, five-year-old Tamara King decided she wouldn't ever let herself know....

Tamara opened her eyes. She darted a quick sideways glance at the phone, and Jack Foley sighed. His step was reluctant as he approached, but it didn't falter.

"I can't let you do it, punkin," he said softly. "I never wanted to hurt you but you've left me no way out, Tammy."

Her legs weren't working right. He came closer, and now she could see that in his hand he had a wad of cotton cloth. She backed up against the counter and felt her feet slip on the small rag rug in front of the kitchen sink.

She struck her head hard on the steel edge of the sink as she went down. Her back against the lower cupboards and her legs splayed awkwardly in front of her on the floor, Tamara stared dazedly at Jack Foley's face as he bent toward her, but for a moment it wasn't him she was seeing at all.

"I *didn't* tell you," she whispered, her eyes wide with pain. "I never told you I loved you, did I, McQueen?"

One strong hand gripped her by the shoulder. The other pressed the chloroformed rag to her face. Darkness rushed in and her world went completely black.

"BOURBON AND SODA. ICE."

As McQueen strode into the bar and growled out his order, the bartender's head jerked up. He took in the bloodied graze on his forehead, the aggressive set of the big man's shoulders.

"How about we do this the easy way for once, McQueen? I tell you to go. You leave. That way Cyrus and Eddie and Joe don't hit me up for their medical bills.''

From the vicinity of the pool table in the corner, three muscular necks swivelled their way. Three faces registered identical antagonism as they recognized the big man at the bar, and three hamlike pairs of hands tightened on their pool cues and began sliding them edgily between thick fingers.

McQueen pulled a stool toward him and straddled it. ''Hold the bourbon. Hold the rocks.''

''Hold the bourbon, hold the—'' The man behind the bar frowned. ''You ordering plain soda water, McQueen?''

McQueen threw a bill on the bar. ''Yeah, I'm ordering soda water, Virgil. I'll pay for the booze if that's a problem.''

The bartender set a glass on the bar, brought a bottle of mix from under the counter and filled McQueen's glass with a colorless, effervescent liquid.

''Stone McQueen, on the wagon,'' he said with an unpleasant smile. ''It won't last, buddy.''

Stone lifted the glass and stared at the bubbles fizzing through it. He lifted it to his mouth and took a swallow. He set his glass back down on the bar.

''It's been eight months, Virgil. I intend for it to last.''

As he turned around, McQueen saw the thin man in the tweed jacket sitting in the booth behind him, a glass of beer at his elbow and a book open in front of him. Extending his hand, the man peered over the top of his half-moon glasses with a smile. ''McQueen? How've you been, man?''

''I get by, Professor.'' McQueen's answering smile was genuine.

There'd been a time when he'd spent most of his time

in places like this, he thought as he slid into the booth across from the man whose nickname stemmed from his scholarly demeanor. There'd been a time when the object of coming into a bar had been to get as drunk as possible as fast as possible, in the hope that some son of a bitch might take a swing at him and give him something to take his mind from the emptiness and futility of his life, if only for a while.

The emptiness and futility were back again, and this time for good, he thought, listening to his companion's casual conversation and once or twice managing a response. But the drinking was a part of his past.

It hadn't blotted out the memories of her before anyway, only dulled them a little. But this time he had the feeling even that wasn't a possibility. He had the feeling that ten years from now, forty years from now, the pain would be as sharp and piercing as it was at this moment.

His whole world was a silken swath of red-gold hair tumbling across his face, pink-velvet lips under his, blue eyes staring up at him, sometimes in exasperation, sometimes in annoyance, sometimes—he closed his own eyes and felt the heat running through him—sometimes glazed with passion, wide with anticipation, dark with desire.

His whole world was her. She was the heart of his heart. He hadn't deserved her, and so he'd lost her.

"She must have been something."

He opened his eyes. The Professor was watching him.

"What?" McQueen said stupidly.

"She must have been something, the woman you lost," his companion repeated. "You look like a man who's been barred from heaven forever."

McQueen nodded. "Yeah, Professor," he said softly. "That's about right. But if I live to be a hundred I'll never forget that just for a while I was allowed in. She wasn't something, she was everything.''

"People say you get over it," the other man murmured absently. ''You don't. And that's one of the few things I didn't learn out of a book, my friend,'' he added, lifting his glass to his mouth.

He set it down on the table with a click. ''You back investigating fires, Stone?'' His voice was brisker, as if he needed to dispel some memories of his own, and McQueen made an effort to respond in kind.

''Not officially, but I've been looking into one on my own time. There might be something you can help me with, Professor,'' he said with a frown. ''What could make a man feel he was responsible for another person's life forever? What would someone have to do to put you under such an obligation?''

The other man shrugged. ''Many religions teach that we're our brother's keeper. And the Chinese have a saying that if you save a person's life you're responsible for him forever. Of course—''

''What was that?'' McQueen's voice was sharp. ''You save a guy's life, you gotta cover his butt forever?''

''I'm not sure if that's the exact translation, but yes, that's the gist of it.''

''The jakey was arguing with Pascoe over setting the Mitchell Towers fire,'' McQueen said slowly. ''He knew it would destroy a man whose life he'd saved, a man he felt some liking and responsibility for. But Pascoe said if the saying was true, someone called Davidson would be under the same obligation, because he'd saved the jakey's life,'' he said under his breath. ''Except Davidson was dead.''

''Sorry, McQueen, I missed that,'' the Professor said

mildly. "If we're now on the subject of motorcycles, I'm afraid I can't be of much use to you in that area."

"Motorcycles?" McQueen frowned impatiently. "Who the hell said anything about—"

He stopped. His gaze swung over to the bar and the middle-aged bikers standing there.

"Harley," he said hoarsely. "Katz remembered it wrong. The dead man was Harley, not Davidson. Harley saved the jakey's life, and the jakey saved another man's life sometime later."

"Harley even hauled me to safety once when a floor gave way underneath me."

Jack Foley had told him that this very morning.

And Jack Foley had saved McQueen's sorry butt at the Corona fire.

McQueen got to his feet and strode toward the pay-phone on the wall. Jack, who always knew the latest scuttlebutt, would have heard by now about the mysterious blaze and that a man and a woman had barely escaped from the fire.

"You're no slouch when it comes to putting two and two together, Jack," McQueen muttered as he listened to the ringing at the other end of the line. "You're going to figure Tam and me found Pascoe, and since we didn't contact you you're going to think there's a chance he talked."

No one picked up. He let the receiver drop from his suddenly-numb fingers and strode back to the table.

"I need to borrow your car," he said tensely. "I don't have time to explain why, but it's an emergency. And if you're a praying man, Professor, this is the time."

His eyes blazed with pain and his jaw tightened. "Pray that I don't screw this one up," he said huskily. "Pray that this time I make it come out right."

Chapter Eighteen

She and Stone were flying into the heart of the sun. His arms were around her and he was telling her the truth—that he'd fallen in love with her the moment he'd met her.

Why hadn't she seen it before? Tamara wondered hazily. It hadn't been a stranger who had taken her that night, it had been the man who loved her so much he'd wanted to take away all her pain, the man who'd tried desperately to change the past for them both, and make it come out right this time.

It had been Stone.

She opened her eyes and saw darkness. She tried to move and found she was bound hand and foot.

"Watch out, Tammy. You're pretty close to the edge, and it's a long way down." Uncle Jack bent over her. There was just enough light from the street below to illuminate the concern on his familiar features. "You feeling a little sick, punkin? It should be okay to take the gag off now. There's no one around to hear you except the blind man, and I saw him toddling down the street a while ago."

Everything came flooding back. As he untied the knot

at the back of her neck and the gag fell from her lips she spoke, her voice a rusty croak.

"Why?"

The man who'd wrapped her around with the protection of his love from childhood until today misunderstood her.

"I'd give my life for you, punkin, and you would have betrayed me. You broke faith with me first." He squatted beside her, his hands on his thighs. "When our own turn against us, they leave us no choice. Claudia thought she could simply walk back into your life after she'd destroyed it. I'd once loved her like a daughter, too."

It's all justifiable to him... Pascoe's words came back to her, and she choked back a nausea that had nothing to do with the chloroform she could still taste in her throat.

"Dear God, you thought you were doing it for *me*, Jack?" She couldn't bring herself to call him by the affectionate term she'd used all her life. She knew she'd never call him that again. "Did she come to you first?"

"She phoned me and asked if I thought you'd see her." Foley's voice was hard. "I went to her room that night. She hadn't told me she had a child."

A flicker of emotion crossed his features. "I hadn't planned on that, punkin, believe me. As soon as Claudia turned to close the door behind me I hit her hard enough to knock her unconscious. It wasn't until I had her arranged on the bed with the cigarette and went back into the hall to get my can of fuel that I saw the cot set up by the bathroom. By then I couldn't turn back."

"You killed a woman in cold blood. You were willing to let a child die," Tamara rasped. "You couldn't turn *back*?"

She took a trembling breath. "My father was your best friend. What did he find out about you that made you kill him—him and my mother and my seven-year-old brother? What made it impossible for you to turn back *that* night?"

"For God's sake, Tammy, I didn't kill your family!" Horror filled his voice. "How could you think that of me?"

She stared at him. He'd been able to function all these years because he kept the two halves of his persona in separate compartments, she thought. He'd been the decorated hero, the loving husband to a good woman, the father figure to the little girl he himself had orphaned. No one had ever suspected there was another side to Jack Foley—an implacably murderous side that brooked no opposition, forgave no wavering of loyalty.

Tonight the compartments had split open. He wouldn't be able to function much longer, she thought. But it would be long enough for what he planned to do with her.

"If you didn't strike the match, you handed it to the man who did," she said. "I just want to know the truth before I die. My whole life's been based on a lie, and it's caused me more pain than you'll ever realize."

"I never wanted that for you, punkin. I never wanted any of this, but once it started there was nothing I could do to stop it." He heaved a sigh.

"I had a gambling problem that got out of hand. Bracknell Curtiss was a millionaire with a shady background who bought up my debt, and when I couldn't pay him he proposed a deal. I was to help him out with information about properties he wanted torched, and in return he would tear up my marker. I was desperate. Kate had warned me about the gambling, and I couldn't face losing her. So I agreed to be Bracknell's contact in the department, and that meant I was Robert Pascoe's contact, too. He was Curtiss's hired arsonist," he said heavily.

"I know some of this," Tamara said steadily. "McQueen's file on Pascoe was extensive, and tonight I actually talked to the man himself. Before he turned into a human torch," she added harshly. "You probably realized we'd tracked him down when the report of the fire came in."

"I had the scanner on," Foley admitted.

"He didn't tell us it was you. You might have gotten away with it without me ever finding out." Tamara shook her head. "But that's not important now. My father discovered your connection to Curtiss, didn't he?"

"He never knew who I was working with, just that I was connected with a fire that gutted a rental property." Jack rubbed a hand across his forehead. "Chuck told me he was going to have to turn me in. I asked him for time to break the news to Kate, and he agreed to hold off on his report for forty-eight hours. That was the weekend of the hockey tournament."

"He cut you a break because you were his friend. You repaid him by having him murdered." Tamara's voice shook.

"I told you, I wasn't responsible for that. I thought Curtiss might threaten him, maybe have his thugs pull a little rough stuff. When I informed him we had a problem, I made it clear I wouldn't stand for anything more than that."

He'd told himself that particular lie for so long he probably believed it, Tamara thought sickly. But he'd known when he carried the news to Curtiss that their whole operation was in danger of being exposed he was signing the death warrant of a man who'd been his friend.

"I needed to contact Pascoe the next day, and I was told he was out of town on business," Jack went on. "I realized then what I'd done. I went to the motel to try and stop him, but I got there just seconds too late. I—I saw you coming out of that window, and I vowed I'd spend the rest of my life being the father to you that you'd just lost."

"I saw you there." She saw a flicker of shock in his eyes. "The memory didn't come back until today, but some part of me always knew. You told me when I first came to live with you and Aunt Kate I kept trying to run away, remember? I grew up knowing deep down that I couldn't trust anything in my world, Jack. *You* did that to me."

"I *protected* you," Foley said swiftly. "You and Kate were my family, and I *protected* you. After what happened at the motel I realized that whenever Curtiss felt my usefulness to him had come to an end, he wouldn't hesitate to eliminate me."

"So you stole some of Pascoe's accelerant and set fire to Curtiss's house. But you still weren't free, were you? You found you'd tied yourself to Robert Pascoe."

She gave a short bark of laughter. "Do you realize just how much blood you have on your hands? You could have stopped him years ago. You could have prevented the deaths of those five firefighters, Jack. But you stood by and did nothing in the end. You stood by when Stone was trying to persuade the department that Pascoe existed, and you watched him crash and burn when no one would believe him. How did you live with yourself after Donna Burke's funeral?"

She'd pushed him too far, she saw immediately. His expression became shuttered, and he stood.

"I was going to turn Pascoe in then, and hang the consequences," he said coldly. "But that was the day your best friend ran off with your groom, if you'll recall. I made one last deal with Pascoe, Tammy. I made it for you."

He turned from her. There was just enough light to see him lift something from the temporary flooring on which he was standing. She saw him unscrew the top of the gas can.

She was to be the sixth firefighter to die in a fire at the Mitchell Towers, Tamara thought dully. She'd known that as soon as she'd found herself here. But watching her murderer prepare for the blaze that would take her life brought the full impact home.

Except she couldn't die.

She hadn't told him she'd loved him. He'd been right—the core of betrayal at the very center of her existence had prevented her from letting him in completely. But tonight she'd learned the truth and as terrible as that truth had been, it had set her free.

He was her heart's heart. He was the only man she would ever love. She needed to live so she could finally tell him.

Her back was against a steel reinforcement rod and by moving slightly it was possible to bring her bound hands to the sharp edge of the metal. Cautiously she began sawing at the cord around her wrists.

"I told Pascoe he'd crossed the line with the deaths of those firefighters." Jack glanced over at her, his face set. "I said the choice was up to him—he could either stay in Boston and have me blow the whistle on him or he could leave and never come back. If he chose the second I would keep my mouth shut, but only if he did a job for me.''

With care he tipped the can until a thin stream of liquid splashed out onto the flooring. Immediately the sharp smell of gasoline assailed her nostrils.

''Rick was already cheating on Claudia a couple of months after he dumped you. You were better off without him, punkin.'' If he realized how grotesque it was that he should be using the lifelong endearment at the same time as he was preparing her death he gave no sign. ''Pascoe assumed the woman in the car with Rick was his wife, not a girlfriend. He reported to me that our deal was complete.''

After everything he'd told her tonight, after everything she'd learned, for some reason this seemed the most hideous revelation of all, Tamara thought numbly. It had been murder-for-hire. In Jack Foley's twisted mind, it had been done to avenge *her*.

Reckless fury boiled up inside her.

''You're completely *insane*,'' she said tightly. ''Maybe once upon a time you were Jack Foley, but the minute you made that first deal with Curtiss and Pascoe you became the beast. I'm glad Aunt Kate died before she found out what you really were—and people *are* going to find out. Knopf for one suspects you. If McQueen hasn't already figured it out, he soon will.''

''Knopf's a fool and Stone McQueen created a man that never existed,'' Jack snapped. ''He rigged a second fire at the Mitchell Towers to resurrect the spectre of Robert Pascoe—the arsonist only he could battle, the arsonist the department needed him to fight. That's what they'll say. Who's going to believe him over the hero who once saved his life?''

"Nobody, Foley. So I guess I'll have to stop you now."

Tamara's heart leapt as a broad-shouldered figure emerged from the shadows at the far side of the structure, where earlier that evening she'd seen a set of jerry-rigged stairs rising from the lower stories to the top of the half-constructed building. Stone came toward them.

"You don't want to do this, Jack. You love her. Even you can't go through with something like this. Are you okay, honey?" he added in an uneven aside to her.

"He's already spread the gas, Stone," she said shakily. "I—I'm tied up here. I can't move."

"You realize it works out better this way for me, laddie, don't you? No—don't come any closer." Even as he spoke Foley tossed the can down and quickly drew something from his pocket. A flame flared immediately from the lighter in his hand.

"Think what you're doing, Jack." Stone froze where he was. "After all these years of loving Tam, caring for her, *protecting* her, you can't do this. You know you can't."

"That's right, McQueen." The wavering flame reflected the implacability on the older man's face. "I spent my life protecting my Tammy and in the end she turned away from me. In the end she turned to you. My little girl's made her choice, and this is the only one I'm left with."

"I knew this was where you'd arrange it, Foley," Stone said hoarsely. "When I realized you'd taken Tamara I knew you'd bring her here. I've lived with the memory of the Mitchell Towers tragedy, but my guilt must be nothing compared to yours. You went to the funerals, too, didn't you?"

His voice took on an edge. "Let's hold roll-call for

them one last time. Do you remember their names? Do you see them lined up in your dreams? Terry Cutshaw. Max Aiken. Larry—"

"I remember their names, McQueen!"

For the first time since he'd brought her here, Tamara saw a spasm of agony cross Jack's face. His hand trembled and the wavering flame dipped. She closed her eyes, cold fear washing over her.

"Dammit, I *worked* with Max. I knew Terry's father. Do you think I *wanted* them to die?"

"Larry Steinbeck," Stone said in a low tone. He took a step closer to Jack. "You were one of the few allowed in to see Monty Stewart before he died, weren't you? Is that when it finally sunk in what you'd become, Jack?"

"Stay where you are, McQueen," Foley said raggedly. "I used up the last of the rocket fuel for the rooming house, but there's enough gas around here to send us both to hell."

"Dear God." Behind her, Tamara felt the cords binding her hands sever and give way, but for a moment she couldn't move. "That's what you *want*. You don't intend to come out of this alive at all—you want this to look as if you died a *hero*."

"Donna Burke." His jaw clenched, McQueen ground out the last name. "They were the heroes, Foley. They went up against the beast. You embraced it."

"And no one's ever going to know, McQueen." Jack's tone was agonized. "I've had to live with what I became, but I'll be buried as a *firefighter*."

Even as the last word left his lips he tossed the lighter at the pool of gasoline a few feet away. Tamara saw the tiny flickering flame fly through the air and arc downward to the liquid dark patch spilled across the wooden floor.

With a shockingly abrupt whoosh the gas suddenly became a lake of flame, its azure rim racing outwards from the center with frightening speed. A wall of fire instantly sprang up between her and the two men, and through it Stone's gaze swiftly sought and found hers. With quick determination he advanced toward the fiery barrier.

"No!" Jack threw his bulky weight at McQueen. "This is how it ends!"

Taken off guard, Stone staggered sideways as the older man crashed into him. He turned to face Jack just in time to receive the full force of a blow that snapped his head back on his neck.

"For God's sake, Foley!" Regaining his balance, he glared at Jack, strong-arming his next punch so that it flew harmlessly wide. "Get the hell out of my way."

Again he turned to the fire. It had leapt to twice its height even in those few seconds, Tamara thought fearfully, struggling to unlash the cord binding her ankles together, and instead of being an easily definable barrier it had now grown to encompass almost a quarter of the fifth-storey area.

Her eyes widened. The fire was twenty or thirty feet away from the stairs, and encroaching fast. Within minutes their only means of escape would be cut off.

Tamara's attention flew back to Jack as he launched himself at McQueen once more, but this time McQueen was ready for him.

His fist smashed into Jack's jaw, knocking the stockier man completely off his feet. Tamara saw her uncle's bulky figure fall heavily to the floor, and remain there.

Without hesitation, McQueen strode through the wall of fire to her side.

"My wrists are bleeding," she said unevenly, looking

up at him as he kneeled in front of her. "My fingers keep slipping when I try to untie my feet."

"*Baby.*"

Instead of going to the knots at her ankles, his hands framed her face, strong fingers outspread against her hair. He was shaking, she realized as she saw his lashes fall briefly over his gaze.

"I got to your house and I knew he'd taken you. I could still smell whatever it was he used to knock you out," he said, opening his eyes. They were brilliant with pain. "I was so afraid I wouldn't get here in time, honey."

He took a shuddering breath and pulled her to him. She felt his mouth on hers briefly, and then he released her and reached into the front pocket of his khakis to retrieve a small penknife.

"Hold still."

With one easy sawing cut the cords parted. He stood, hauling her to her feet with him and catching her by the shoulders as she swayed against his chest.

"I'll carry you," he said promptly.

She shook her head. "I'm okay. Stone—the stairs."

"I know." Before she realized what he was about to do, he was stripping his sweatshirt over his head. A moment later he was tugging it over hers.

"Keep your arms inside and as much of your face covered as you can," he said tersely. She opened her mouth, and he forestalled her. "Don't argue, honey."

Before she could reply his arm was around her, hugging her to his body so tightly she was almost lifted off her feet as they began to run toward the flames. She felt the heat hit her like a blow as they reached the barrier of fire, and then they were flying through it and to the other side.

"Get to the stairs." In the wavering red light McQueen's expression was grim. "I can't leave him here to die."

"I'll help you carry him." She took a step toward Jack's crumpled body, but he shook his head.

"It'll be easier by myself."

She pressed her lips together, and then nodded. "Hurry, Stone."

They were going to make it, she thought as she sped to the stairs. Even if they couldn't get Jack all the way down to safety, the fire crew would be here soon enough to complete the rescue. She got to the first step and looked back.

McQueen, his head bent, was pulling his leather belt from the loops of his pants, obviously intent on using it as some kind of supportive sling in carrying Jack. His back was toward the man he'd disabled.

Except Jack was no longer lying there.

"Stone! Behind you!" The appalled scream tore from her throat.

Everything seemed to happen at once.

Even as Stone began to turn, Jack swung the two-by-four he was holding. It hit the back of Stone's skull with sickening force, and immediately his legs gave way under him. He fell heavily and lay there, unmoving.

Propelled by momentum, Jack's swing carried through, only arrested when the two-by-four crashed into the blazing base of one of the support beams rising from the floor. As he let the length of wood drop from his grip, the support beam, its base now little more than charcoal, gave way. It swayed once and then came crashing directly down onto Jack's spine.

Under the weight of the beam he staggered and fell across McQueen's legs. Through the hungry roar of the fire she heard the sound his head made as it hit the ground.

She knew he was dead even before she ran over and fell to her knees beside him.

The five-year-old child she'd once been had seen him for what he was, she thought remotely, feeling nothing but relief. And tonight her adult self had recovered the truth. Jack Foley was no one she knew. He was no one she could grieve over.

And she wasn't going to grieve over Stone McQueen, either, she thought grimly, because she wasn't going to let him die. She saw him stir slightly, and then his eyes opened and his clouded gaze met hers.

"Your legs are pinned, Stone," she said before he could speak. "They're probably not broken, because Jack came down on them first, but there's a beam lying across him. He—he's dead, Stone."

"I hear sirens," he rasped.

"We don't have time to wait for a crew. The floor's unstable and any second the stairs are going to be cut off completely," she replied, her voice edged. "The only jakey available right now is me, Stone. I'm going to get this thing off you."

"No."

With an effort McQueen lifted his head. "I screwed up just about every damn thing I ever did in my life, honey," he said softly. "The only thing I did right was to love you. I want you to go."

"I screwed up, too, McQueen," she said. Her vision blurred.

He was too big. He was too aggressive. He was a loose cannon. He loved her.

And she loved him—so much and so badly she knew

she wouldn't be able to survive if anything took him away from her again.

"I should have told you. I'm telling you now. I love you, Stone. And we're leaving here together."

She leaned toward him. Just for a moment she laid her fingers against his lips, and she felt him kiss them.

"That's for later," he whispered, his gaze on hers. In his eyes she saw a world of love and longing. "Just in case, Tam."

Just in case this all goes bad, Tamara thought fearfully. *Just in case this one last time the beast wins.*

She straightened her shoulders. Only feet away from her, it was watching her, towering above her, grinning redly at her as if it had been waiting for this moment all of her life, and knew that she had been waiting, too.

She looked into its face.

And saw nothing.

"It's just a *fire,*" she said huskily. "I'm a firefighter. I *hate* fire, dammit!"

She got to her feet and positioned herself above the beam, just clear of Foley's lifeless body. Bending her knees slightly and bracing herself, she gripped the beam with both hands. She took a deep breath. With a grunt of effort, she heaved.

The thing had to weigh hundreds of pounds, she thought, squeezing her eyes shut and feeling her muscles pop. Her thighs began to tremble with the strain and her knees felt as if they were about to give way. She could feel sweat beading on her forehead, and for a moment despair washed over her.

She wasn't strong enough, she thought wrenchingly. She wasn't going to be able to do this.

Through her lashes she saw him. His gaze met hers. He gave her a slow, incredibly sweet smile.

Calling upon a reserve of strength she hadn't known she had, Tamara gave a final, agonized heave, and felt the beam lift.

"Can't—can't hold it long," she gasped. "Can—can you make it, Stone?"

But already he was struggling free from under the weight of Foley's body, and as her muscles began to scream he staggered to his feet beside her.

"Let go, Tam."

She felt him take the full weight of the beam from her, and she stepped back, dizzy with relief. Swaying, she watched as he lowered the massive support to one side of the body. Then he had her arm and they were running toward the stairs.

Two seconds longer and they wouldn't have made it, Tamara thought faintly as together she and Stone began to make their awkward way to the ground. The fire was blazing throughout the fourth storey, but the third was just beginning to burn. She heard shouted voices coming from below, and she opened her stinging eyes completely to see the flashing lights of a fire engine.

Beside her McQueen halted. She turned to him and saw a corner of his mouth lift.

"Marry me, Tam?" His gaze held hers. "The white dress, the church, the whole freakin' nine yards? I love you so much, honey," he added softly.

Trust McQueen to pop the question in front of a whole damn fire crew, Tamara thought shakily as he pulled her to him and waited for her reply. She was aware of the uplifted faces and quick grins of the helmeted figures below, and when she rose to her tiptoes and drew his mouth down to hers she dimly heard whistling and cheering coming from the assembled crowd.

She touched her lips to his. She drew back, and saw those smoke gray eyes watching her.

"You're such a jerk, McQueen," she whispered, her eyes filling with tears of joy. "Of *course* I want the whole freakin' nine yards."

Epilogue

Stone had the bride backed into a corner of a storage room just off the reception hall's kitchen. His eyes were closed, his hands were on her breasts and he was kissing her.

And that was all he was going to get to do, he thought in frustration, lifting his mouth from Tamara's and feeling aching heat spread through his groin as he saw those parted, pink-velvet lips, those dazed and starry eyes meeting his. Hell, just down the corridor were a couple of hundred firefighters and their spouses, not to mention a seven-year-old flower girl who'd insisted on bringing her Great Dane puppy to the celebration. But Chandra, who'd helped arrange this wedding over the past six weeks, was looking after Petra, Stone thought. He and the bride could play hookey for another few minutes.

Immediate desire flamed hotly through him. Beneath the froth of white lace he could see a flash of red satin.

"Tell me who you're wearing that for, baby," he said hoarsely, pushing the white lace aside and running an unsteady finger along the provocatively low-cut red bra.

"I'm wearing it for the man who bought it for me," Tamara murmured. "I'm wearing the matching thong, too, McQueen. Hot enough for you, big guy?"

"Uh-huh," he said huskily, giving in to the heat and lowering his mouth to her breasts. Slowly he licked the hollow between them. "I'm an investigator again, though, honey," he muttered. "It's my job to do something about it when I'm called to a fire."

"You're not supposed to make it hotter, McQueen," Tamara gasped, her fingers sliding through his hair.

He was going to give his wife the same bad reputation he had, McQueen thought a few minutes later, trying to impose some control over himself. He would just have to wait until the honeymoon officially began in an hour or so.

They were spending it in her bedroom. Petra was sleeping over at Chandra's and leaving tomorrow for a weeklong camping trip with her and Hank and their little boy.

"I never made it with a married woman before," he said thoughtfully as he watched her straightening the lace on her dress.

"Then I guess you haven't made it with a pregnant married woman, either, McQueen," she said, tucking her arm through his and looking up at him. "Shall we get back to our guests?"

"Yes, honey," he said obediently, walking to the door with her. He started to open it, and stopped dead.

"What did you just say?" He stared stupidly at her.

"I said that after the leave of absence I took to get Petra settled in ends, I'm going on maternity leave," she said, her voice suddenly uneven and her eyes glowing with happiness. "You probably planned it that way." Her laugh was breathless.

"We're going to have a baby? I'm going to be a *father?*" At her tiny nod pure joy flooded through him.

He was going to be a father, he told himself incredulously. The woman he loved was even now carrying his child—*their* child, he thought, tightening his embrace around her and feeling the wetness behind his lashes.

He'd once hit rock bottom. It had been a long way back up.

But in the end he'd found his heart's heart, Stone McQueen thought as he bent his head and kissed his pregnant bride.

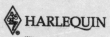

#697 HER HIDDEN TRUTH by Debra Webb
The Specialists
When CIA agent Katrina Moore's memory implant malfunctioned while she was under deep cover, her only hope for rescue lay with Vince Ferrelli. Only, Kat and Vince shared a tumultuous past, which threatened to sabotage their mission. Could Vince save Kat—and restore her memories—before it was too late?

#698 HEIR TO SECRET MEMORIES by Mallory Kane
Top Secret Babies
After he was brutally attacked and left for dead, Jay Wellcome lost all of his memories. His only recollection: the image of a nameless beauty. And though Jay never anticipated they'd come face-to-face, when Paige Reynolds claimed she needed him—honor demanded he offer his protection. Paige's daughter had been kidnapped and nothing would stop him from tracking a killer—especially when he learned her child was also his....

#699 THE ROOKIE by Julie Miller
The Taylor Clan
For the youngest member of the Taylor clan, Josh Taylor, an undercover assignment to smoke out drug dealers on a university campus could promote him to detective. Only, Josh never anticipated his overwhelming feelings for his pregnant professor Rachel Livesay. And when the single mother-to-be's life was threatened by a stalker named "Daddy," Josh's protective instincts took over. But would Rachel accept his protection...and his love?

#700 CONFESSIONS OF THE HEART by Amanda Stevens
Fully recovered from her heart transplant surgery, Anna Sebastian was determined to start a new life. But someone was determined to thwart her plans.... With her life in jeopardy, tough-as-nails cop Ben Porter was the only man she could trust. And now in a race against time, could Ben and Anna uncover the source of the danger before she lost her second chance?

Visit us at www.eHarlequin.com

HARLEQUIN®
INTRIGUE®

Opens the case files on:

Unwrap the mystery!

January 2003
THE SECRET SHE KEEPS
BY CASSIE MILES

February 2003
HEIR TO
SECRET MEMORIES
BY MALLORY KANE

March 2003
CLAIMING HIS FAMILY
BY ANN VOSS PETERSON

Follow the clues to your favorite retail outlet!

HARLEQUIN®
INTRIGUE®

Elevates breathtaking romantic suspense to a whole new level!

When all else fails, the most highly trained, covert agents are called in to "recover" the mission. This elite group is known as

THE SPECIALISTS

Nothing is too dangerous for them...
except falling in love.

DEBRA WEBB

does it again with an explosive new trilogy for Harlequin Intrigue. You'll recognize some of the names from her popular COLBY AGENCY series, but hang on to your hats this time out. Because THE SPECIALISTS are more dangerous, more daring...and more deadly than any agents you've ever seen!

UNDERCOVER WIFE
January

HER HIDDEN TRUTH
February

GUARDIAN OF THE NIGHT
March

Look for them wherever Harlequin books are sold!

HARLEQUIN®
Makes any time special ®

If you enjoyed what you just read,
then we've got an offer you can't resist!

Take 2 bestselling love stories FREE!
Plus get a FREE surprise gift!